John T.

# LA REFAUDIO

| Suffolk County Council | |
|---|---|
| 30127 08241353 0 | |
| Askews & Holts | Aug-2014 |
| AF | £7.99 |
| | |

John Trythall has been a teacher of French all his adult life, a head teacher, and a Principal of a college teaching English to foreign students.

To the France I love

Copyright © John Trythall

The right of John Trythall to be identified as author of this work has been asserted by him in accordance with section 77 and 78 of the Copyright, Designs and Patents Act 1988.

All rights reserved. No part of this publication may be reproduced, stored in a retrieval system, or transmitted in any form or by any means, electronic, mechanical, photocopying, recording, or otherwise, without the prior permission of the publishers.

Any person who commits any unauthorized act in relation to this publication may be liable to criminal prosecution and civil claims for damages.

A CIP catalogue record for this title is available from the British Library.

ISBN 978 1 84963 900 2

www.austinmacauley.com

First Published (2014)
Austin Macauley Publishers Ltd.
25 Canada Square
Canary Wharf
London
E14 5LB

Printed and bound in Great Britain

# Acknowledgments

Pam Cripps for her typing and support. Tony Diamond who read the book twice, checked it and offered useful advice. Peter Fox who has kindly checked the French. Mary, my wife, who has been a constant and kindly support. Vinh Tran at Austin Macauley who has been a courteous and patient support.

# Chapter 1

*No Going Back!*

Paul Treloar left Oxford in 1951. He had been there for five long, miserable, lonely terms. It was a tragic admission of failure!

To Paul it was a relief. Why?

He had failed Prelims three times, always in the same subject – French, L'Histoire de la Révolution Française, by de Tocqueville, a tedious, boring book – for Paul! The other three subjects he passed easily – Latin, The Venerable Bede, geographical history.

Why was French such a difficulty? He had been hard of hearing since the age of six, an ear infection after measles. He was infected in both ears! Then double mastoiditis, an operation which cured the infection, but left him with over sixty per cent hearing loss. In the higher registers there was a loss of as much as eighty per cent. He always remarked with a sigh that no woman could whisper sweet nothings in his ear.

His mother was dreadfully upset when he left Oxford. She was proud of her two children, one a former art student now working in London, the other at Oxford!

"Go back, there's a dear," she pleaded.

No way, Mother." Paul was quite decisive. "Besides I can't. I failed prelims for the third time."

"What are prelims, dear?" Mother asked.

Paul sighed. His mother was of a generation of women who had hardly touched university. Her greatest achievement was L.R.C.M. 'Licentiate of the Royal College of Music.' She was a pianist and an organist.

"It is our first exam after two terms. Afterwards we go on to our degree studies."

"The Provost said you could go back and have a fourth attempt," persisted Mother.

"Oh, he did, did he? Gracious of him!" There was a trace of bitterness in Paul's voice. Oxford was not the kindest of universities for handicapped students. Nobody seemed to make allowances for a hard of hearing student.

Paul sighed again.

"No way am I going back," Paul insisted. "I shall never pass in French. I've a complete blockage for the silly subject. I can stare at a page, and it's an utter blank to me."

"Please, dear, try!" Mother was persistent. She always called him 'dear', except when she was cross or upset with him. Then she reverted to his Christian name.

Paul hated being deaf. He accepted his handicap with fortitude, without complaint.

On the other hand he wanted to be just like everyone else. He had survived school relatively normally, apart from difficulties with French. But Oxford was a disaster. He was a social outcast, and an academic failure too in one subject. It was only in sport that he held his own, but even that was limited. He wore glasses. School had protected him, but at Oxford it was a different story.

Paul shook his head at his mother's persistence.

"Please, dear. Take this. It may help," Mother pleaded.

She passed over a cheque. Paul looked at it; it was for one hundred pounds, a lot of money in 1951. But Paul would not take it and passed it back. Now she refused to accept it. He put it on the coffee table between them. There was a momentary silence, an air of discomfort. Mother was used to getting her own way, even with open bribery.

"I'm sorry, Mother," he said regretfully.

Mother got up and made to leave the room. There was the beginning of tears in her eyes, a ploy she sometimes resorted to when not getting what she wanted.

"Your father was just as obstinate as you," she muttered, "and he paid the price!"

Paul felt suddenly contrite. He moved to comfort his mother. She was too quick; she slipped out. The door closed between them.

Paul's father was forty-two when the war began. He didn't have to join up. But he did! He was part of the Territorial Army. He was captured at Calais, a rearguard action which made Dunkirk possible. He won the Military Cross for bravery. He was killed while escaping.

It was not the first time Paul was called 'obstinate,' and certainly not the last.

Sadly he went up to his room. He packed his bag. Tomorrow he was going up to London to see his sister.

# Chapter 2

*Outspoken*

"So you've opted out," was his sister's greeting on the doorstep of her flat. "Mum's very upset."

"Sis, I had to," muttered Paul. His sister had the same outspoken manner as their father when alive.

"There's no 'had to' about it," she stated firmly. "You've let the side down, and that includes yourself."

"Oh, Sis!" Paul looked woebegone.

His sister, noting this, suddenly smiled. She became her usual friendly self.

"Come on in, little bro, and we'll have a chat," she said in a kindly tone.

Paul entered.

"Now, tell me more, no wait. We'll have a coffee first," she said.

Paul was always glad to see his sister. She had the same positive, cheerful nature as their father, as well as his outspokenness. Both Father and Daughter did not worry, unlike Mother and Paul.

He looked around while she bustled around over the coffee. The flat reflected her moods, from the over-tidy to the chaotic. He reckoned she was going through an orderly phase. This was confirmed when the coffee came. Normally served in old, chipped cups, this time there were light blue cups and saucers and little decorative mats to prevent marking the little side table.

The front hall gave onto a sparsely furnished sitting-room, with one corner curtained off to hide the kitchen. There were two bedrooms off the sitting room, one just large enough to take a double bed, the other so small, it could barely accommodate a two foot six bed, and not much else. The extraordinary thing was one could only reach the bathroom through the minute bedroom, a bad piece of planning which horrified Mother when she came to stay. It meant at night one couldn't go to the toilet when someone was sleeping in the small bedroom, or risk disturbing whoever it was there.

Mother bought Sis two china potties, an outmoded Victorian luxury, which Sis would have nothing to do with.

"Well, bro, tell me about Oxford, or its non-existence as far as you are concerned," she said cheerfully.

She settled down on a cushion in the big wicker chair, another Victorian relic. It creaked as she sat down. Paul looked at her admiringly. She was a lovely girl despite the very casual clothes she usually wore. Like many women of her time she still wore a fawn skirt. The trouser revolution by women, by replacing skirts with more masculine wear was still to come. Sis had long fair hair which reached down to her shoulders, and a pleasant face with eyes that twinkled in such a friendly way. She was quite tall, about five foot eight, with an attractive, shapely figure.

So Paul did as requested, and told her of his failure in French prelims; but he added a further dimension – his own loneliness and unhappiness at Oxford. He didn't like talking about his difficulties, but his sister, though outspoken, was someone he could talk to, and forget his inhibitions.

"Socially I'm not in their league," he admitted. "And my lousy hearing doesn't help. No girl will look at a man who wears a prominent deaf aid under his tie."

Sis nodded.

"I think you underestimate women," she said thoughtfully. "you're not a bad bloke, Paul, all things considered. You just lack confidence."

Paul said:

"I found it difficult to hear what people were saying, especially in party situations," he explained. "I pick up what I call fag ends," Paul explained, "namely bits of conversation. When I try to enter a conversation, I find I've misunderstood the whole story, and look stupid. I retire in embarrassment or confusion, especially when people laugh at my mistakes."

He smiled ruefully.

"I once took a girl to a Commemorative Ball," he said. "It was a dismal failure. I couldn't hear a word she said. After a while we hardly talked at all, and she drifted away to be with friends she knew, and invited me to follow. The ball was a dead loss after that as far as I was concerned; it was a waste of money as well."

"You've always been a quiet, shy sort of bloke," Sis agreed.

Paul sighed. His sister had always seemed to understand, even though she teased him unmercifully, as siblings would.

"What are you going to do now?" she enquired.

"I'm going to France," Paul said.

"What, France, where the froggies live?" She was almost laughing. "It's ridiculous. You hated French at school and at university, and now you want to go to France. It's ridiculous, unbelievable. Why?"

Trust a sister to be so outspoken! But somehow Paul didn't seem to mind. He could take being laughed at by his sister because he knew she cared!

"It's difficult to explain!" Paul pleaded.

"Try me!" Sis was relentless.

"Three reasons, I suppose," Paul said thoughtfully. "One is to improve my French, so I could pass that wretched Oxford examination. It would mean taking a pass degree, not an honours, because of the time lapse between matriculation and degree. It has to be within four years."

"Why?" asked Sis.

"You have to take honours within a certain period from matriculation. If I went back at a later date, I could never fulfil that requirement."

"What are the other two reasons?" Sis asked curiously.

"Well," said Paul hesitantly, "Dad, when he escaped from the Germans after Calais, wrote full of praise for the French who helped him. They never once asked for money. I'd like to get to know these kind people. At the moment they're just Frogs, at least that is what we called them at school. Mother did say Dad had been very critical of the French as soldiers.

But he certainly wasn't when he wrote his letter home before he died."

Sis nodded.

"I read his letter," she observed. "He certainly came to like the French."

"The third reason," admitted Paul hesitantly, "is that I want to be a writer."

"You want to write!" exclaimed Sis in surprise. "What brought this on?"

"I've always wanted to write, off and on," Paul said. "It's a great panacea for somebody with a hearing loss. You know also that Dad wrote film scripts, not very successfully."

Sis nodded.

"Mum told me once he wrote a film script, sent it to somebody for comment. The wretched man stole his script and presented it as his own. Mum was furious; she never liked the man."

"What did Dad do?" asked Paul.

"Oh, typical Dad. He just laughed and said he was flattered so well known a writer should choose to steal his work. As you know, there wasn't a trace of vindictiveness in Dad."

Sis was silent a moment in memory of her dad. There had been a close affinity between them. "But what's writing got to do with France?"

Sis still sounded incredulous.

"I've read Somerset Maugham and Hemingway," Paul tried to explain. "They both spoke highly of Paris and how it influenced their writings."

Sis sat back and sighed.

"You've never ceased to surprise me," she said. "I never thought you'd get to Oxford in the first place, but you did!"

"I cheated a bit," admitted Paul. "Well, not cheated....."

"How come?" Sis asked

"Well, I said – truthfully – I wanted to go into the Church, be a parson. They accepted me on that basis, I think, though they never really said so. But you knew how I felt at the time."

Sis nodded and smiled, her wicked smile.

"What happened to that saintly ambition?" she asked.

"Oxford killed it off, or the sinful world did," Paul admitted. "Somehow I lost the urge, I'm ashamed to say. I've not been to church for a while, or said my prayers."

"You were a bit of a sanctimonious bore," Sis observed. "But I put up with it. You were still that funny brother of mine."

She contemplated him seriously, that teasing smile gone.

"How are you going to manage in France?" she asked, "Financially I mean. You've never had much money to speak of."

"Oh, I'll get by," Paul said. "English tutor in a French family, a bit of bar work, perhaps."

"You'll be lucky," Sis said. She was always the practical one of the family. "France is teeming with good barmen; it's part of the culture. Besides, you're hopeless in French, and you'll have difficulty hearing the orders!"

Paul pondered a moment.

"Sis, I think I've got a possible opening," he said, "and I need your help."

"What, already?" she queried, meaning the opening rather than the help.

"Yes, but you won't, maybe, like it," Paul observed.

"Well, try me!" she said. "I've put up with your mad schemes over the years. Another one won't kill me!"

"I put an advert in two French newspapers, Le Monde and Le Figaro," explained Paul, "saying I wanted a post as tutor in a French family, and I've had a reply. A man thinks he can help. He wants to come to London to see me."

Paul hesitated.

"And ...?" prompted Sis.

"Well, can you put him up for a couple of nights?" ventured Paul, fearing the response.

Sis looked aghast, as he thought she would.

"What, me, put up a Frog, who uses a hole in the ground when he wants to go to the toilet," she exclaimed. "Not on your nelly, no, no!"

"Don't call him a Frog, Sis," Paul said hesitantly. "He wrote quite a nice letter. He's a human being just like us."

But Sis shuddered, with pretended horror.

"He'll rape me," she exclaimed, shuddering again.

"Nonsense, Sis! I'll be here." Paul tried to reassure her. "Otherwise I'll have to put him up in an hotel, and I can't really afford it."

Sis contemplated him for a moment and then smiled mischievously.

"Oh, all right," she said. "But I refuse to sleep alone in this flat with a Frog. You really must be here!"

Paul looked at her and then laughed.

"You might regret that," he said. "Remember the French are supposed to be very good lovers."

But Sis shuddered again. Paul still laughed.

"He's coming to see me, not you, Sis," he said. "I'll have to be here, defending your virtue."

"Thank God for that," muttered Sis, smiling.

# Chapter 3

*A Disconcerting Visit*

Paul went to Victoria Station to meet his future French hope. It was his only hope; no other man had replied to his advertisements. He had no idea as to the Frenchman's age, or his work, nor how he would recognise him, nor even about any possibility of a job in France. It all hung on a dismal thread.

They were each to carry a placard, with their name written large on it.

Sis was concerned at the lack of information.

"It may be a con, Paul," she warned. "Be careful and don't be too trusting, which is your weakness. He may be angling for a free visit to London."

"I'll be careful," laughed Paul, tending to be dismissive of his sister's concern.

The one thing Paul knew, the man was called M. Rémond.

The train from Dover was late. When it eventually came in, twenty minutes overdue, a man detached himself from the throng of emerging passengers and came up to Paul.

"Monsieur Treloar?" he asked, in a pronounced French accent.

Paul nodded and smiled. He said politely:

"M. Rémond, I am very pleased to see you."

Paul felt like laughing at the very unusual appearance of the Frenchman, but restrained himself. M. Rémond was, to an Englishman, an incongruous looking figure. He was a middle-aged man, bordering on the elderly, somewhat rotund, wearing a pinkish-grey suit, or so the colour seemed under the station lights. The general effect of pink was accentuated by a mauve shirt and a loud, mauve, striped tie. He had obviously taken great pains over his dress. He wore light brown shoes, not the more traditional English black shoes with a grey suit. He looked lumpish, unfit, in clothes that did not seem to suit him very well. His English was reasonable, but not his accent, strongly French. When he walked he seemed to waddle, in an unfit way.

He also gave forth a personal scent which was tempered by the wear and tear of travel.

"Have you had a good journey?" enquired Paul.

"The sea, bad!" M. Rémond replied, and he made rolling motions with his hands to indicate a rough sea.

Paul decided to take a taxi. He had originally planned on the bus. The age and possible frailty of his visitor had changed his mind.

At the flat Sis had an urge to giggle. She suppressed it, and greeted him with courtesy and care. Paul was grateful.

Supper was an anxious meal. Sis had prepared shepherd's pie. Paul had protested it was too simple a meal.

"Simple or not," stated Sis, "we're eating English!"

M. Rémond sat down. He showed his appreciation by asking for a second helping. What puzzled Paul was the copious amount of bread he ate. M. Rémond then attacked apple pie and custard, followed by cheese and biscuits, a plain cheddar.

"You are a good cook," he told Sis, wiping his mouth on a napkin.

M. Rémond did not speak much during the meal. It was an uncomfortable occasion. Afterwards he told Paul.

"I look for you a family. En ce moment I may have a family in mind, but I am not sure."

Paul was astonished. The man had come all this way just to tell him that! No certain offer or information!

"He's checking up on you," said Sis grinning, later when they were on their own. Then she added.

"He's a poof. He told me he was not married. He lives with his mother. Watch out, Paul." And Sis grinned mischievously once again.

The next day Paul showed M. Rémond around London, all the old, familiar sights, the Tower of London, Buckingham Palace, Westminster Abbey, and Trafalgar Square. They made very slow and tedious progress. M. Rémond waddled slowly in his walk and seemed very unfit. But Paul resisted the temptation to take a taxi. He just used his knowledge of bus routes.

"I come to London two times before War," he told Paul. "London now, not the same. Much damage." He then added wistfully, "I love London. It is a fine city, in spite of damage."

Paul was surprised a Frenchman should speak like this, in an emotional way, about a city.

"Did Paris suffer in the War?" asked Paul.

"Oui et non. The maladie – the suffering – was dans le coeur – in the heart – at being occupied. The Germans not understand the French, not like the English."

Paul nodded. He began to like this strange Frenchman who could talk about feelings, like the heart, le coeur. But Paul still could not understand why he came all this way to England – to tell him very little of work in France. Paul asked Sis about this later.

"Oh, he gets a free stay in London – at our expense!" she said airily. "But I suspect he's a lonely man. Be careful, Paul."

"Oh! Sis," ventured Paul reproachfully. "I think you are right in one sense; he is lonely. But I don't think he's a poof. He seems quite genuine. I think before the War he found genuine happiness in London. He told me he worked here for a time. He's a banker, now with the Bank of France. I feel he likes the English and appreciates what we did in the War, standing up to the Germans. He has a great admiration for Churchill."

But Sis, like Paul, could not quite make up her mind about M. Rémond, why he had come all this way, with no definite news of how he could help. It seemed such a waste of a journey. As a poof – if he was a poof – she didn't feel threatened by him, or that he was interested in women.

"He can't have much money to come to England in this way," she added.

"He's better off than we realise," Paul explained. "He tells me he has a vineyard south of the Seine – a small one, and a flat in Paris, and he works for a bank, soon to retire."

"My! ..." said Sis, somewhat astonished. "Does he give any indication of how he can help you?"

"None whatsoever. Just a promise to write," explained Paul. But Paul was already beginning to lose hope.

On that sombre note, M. Rémond went back to France the next day! Though he did give Sis a bunch of flowers, Sis still said.

"Forget him, Paul. Nothing will come of it."

# Chapter 4

*France. Here I Come!*

But it did!

M. Rémond did not let him down! A telephone call came five days after M. Rémond's departure.

"I find family for you near Montauban," he said.

Paul was elated. Sis, ever practical, looked up Montauban on a French map.

It was in the south of France near Toulouse, very central.

Paul was disappointed. His dream of living in Paris was shattered!

"It's a start!" Sis pointed out. "You'll be in France, learning the language, get to know the people. An opportunity in Paris may come later."

With that, Paul had to be content.

There were also instructions from M. Rémond. Paul was to take the Southampton – Le Havre boat on Friday night. M. Rémond would meet him when the boat came in early Saturday morning. Further details then.

As the boat left Southampton harbour on that Friday, Paul murmured to himself.

"France, here I come."

He felt somewhat apprehensive, even homesick. He had never really seen much of life beyond boarding school and university. He was on his own now.

"Poor little deaf boy," his sister commented. She was more on his side than Mother, who tended to wash her hands of his crazy ideas, or what she knew of them. Paul was not so open with her as he was with Sis.

Sis offered to lend him some money, or rather she didn't lend it, but in typical Sis manner, put forty pounds in a white envelope.

"Take this, Paul," she said. "You may need it in your madcap schemes."

When Paul protested, she argued firmly.

"Paul, now stop it. I am the only one in the family who earns a decent wage. Mother is on a pension, and you've just come down from university where you lived on a grant, which I imagine you have spent."

Paul protested again. "Please, Sis, you've been very kind, but I really don't want any money. I've saved most of what I earned last summer on the cross-channel boats. They paid very well. It should get me to France, and cover any expenses until I start work."

But Sis still insisted.

"No, Paul, I think you're walking on eggshells, going to France, and relying on somebody you don't know. I still don't trust that man. Keep the money as a safeguard and if you don't use it, perhaps you could give it back sometime."

And then she added-

"It's silly of me to say it, but I do love you, Paul. I think you've had a raw deal in life, losing Dad and with your hearing disability. We've stood by each other very well over the years, and we need to carry on, face whatever life throws at us. But don't get entangled with any French girls; they don't shave under their arms! They can't be trusted!"

Paul didn't know what to say. The support from his sister was unbelievable. Near to tears he drew her to him, gave her a huge hug and a kiss on the cheek. He murmured

"Thank you, Sis!"

As Paul stood on the deck, watching the lights of the coast of England slowly disappear in the distance, he felt tears come to his eyes.

He hoped that life would work out. But he had perhaps been very stupid in his insistence of going to France.

He suddenly heard a greeting behind him.

"Why, Paul, what are you doing here?"

"Maggie! I might almost ask the same of you!" he answered.

It was 'scatty' Maggie, a contemporary Oxford undergraduate. She was unusually barmy, hence the nickname of 'scatty', but intelligently so. She was one of the few girls who owned a car, which she kept hidden away up at Headington. There was a rule that no undergraduate could keep a car, a rule rarely enforced and even more rarely heeded. Few students could afford to own a car in 1951.

But Maggie could! She was better endowed financially than most.

Her scatty reputation came because she drove without shoes. In fact the more often she could discard her shoes the happier she felt. She would even take them off in lectures and tutorials, and then not find them. Everyone would scurry around looking for them, making a joke of it by hiding them still further away. Paul got to know her first because, after a lecture, he had found one of her lost, discarded shoes. She was charmingly grateful. It reminded Paul of his mother. She used to take her shoes off in the cinema.

They would get kicked around by people passing along the row and accidentally knocking them all over the place. They were sometimes difficult to find.

Maggie was scatty in other ways – often forgetful, an ignorer of rules, essays rarely in on time.

But Paul liked her. In staid, conventional Oxford, full of ex-servicemen, she was a bright star that shone in a drab, impoverished world recovering from war.

They smiled at each other on the strange background of a boat, miles away from Oxford spires.

"You first," said Maggie.

"I've left Oxford," admitted Paul. "It was a tragedy coming."

"What, left Oxford – never! Why?" Maggie cried.

"I failed prelims again," Paul confessed.

"Oh! French, I suppose?" Maggie said, knowing of his problem.

Maggie was also aware of his difficulty in hearing. In fact Maggie was a girl who had ready sympathy. She was one of the few girls who accepted a shy young man wearing a hearing aid, and would not ignore him! Paul was grateful. He would have liked to know her more, even take her to a college ball, but Maggie was a popular girl. He rarely got a look in.

"Blow French!" said Maggie dismissively, "I suppose it's too late now, but what I would have done is spent the vacations in France, immersed myself in French, and come back with more confidence."

"Takes money," said Paul, thoughtfully.

"Oh!" remarked Maggie, realising she had made a mistake. Rich girls did not always realise the problems of the not so rich.

"But what are you going to France for, if you dislike French so much?" asked Maggie.

So Paul explained his reasons. Maggie's reaction was much like Sis' – full of the illogicality of his actions.

"The trouble with you, Paul," Maggie said perceptively, "is that you don't explain yourself very well. Then, when you do, everybody is taken by surprise."

"I'm told lack of communication is one of the failings of being hard of hearing," Paul admitted.

"You can say that again," said Maggie. "I never knew you very well; you were part of the background of Oxford life, but you never had very much to say for yourself. But I thought you a nice, gentle bloke, which is saying something in comparison with the usual Oxford male undergrads."

They were silent for a moment. Then Paul hesitantly said, aware of his lack of money,

"Shall we go below and I'll buy you a drink?"

Maggie shook her head.

"No, there's such a fug below, and it often makes me feel sick," she confessed. "Let's find a couple of deck chairs and sit out on deck. It's not too cold, and it's a lovely night."

Which they did.

To Paul that night was heavenly! He was on deck, sitting next to a young, attractive, intelligent girl, and he was actually talking to her.

She had a distinctive voice. Paul remembered she sang in a choir. She was always rushing off to a rehearsal! He always found girls with good singing voices had good articulation.

He had her to himself for a whole night. They didn't touch; they just talked, mostly about Oxford. It made Paul a little sad that he was no longer part of that world. He vowed one day to go back, even though it would mean a poor degree!

They eventually drifted off to sleep. It was an early May evening, not particularly warm, though they were well wrapped up having managed to procure a blanket from a kindly steward, which they shared.

Paul marvelled. You had to say goodbye to Oxford in order to spend a night with an Oxford girl, however innocent the night.

Eventually they woke as the ship juddered, while manoeuvring into Le Havre harbour. Maggie got up, somewhat frazzled, and announced she was going to risk the fug and have a tidy up.

Paul never saw her again. Somehow, in the chaos of going ashore, he lost her. He wanted to write to her. He knew her college but curiously not her surname. All he had was a pleasant memory.

M. Rémond greeted him once he had passed through the formalities.

"You 'ave a good – 'ow do you say – voyage?" he asked.

Paul noted the dropped 'h' – 'ave rather than have. It was a continual French problem – 'h' and 'th'!

Paul looked wistfully around for Maggie, but no sign of her. He felt saddened he was to lose someone who had been kind to him. It was the story of his life. He hoped perhaps to see her in Paris.

"You 'ave breakfast?" M. Rémond asked, breaking into Paul's thoughts.

Paul shook his head.

"I give you breakfast," he promised. "But first we must leave Le Havre. It's very crowded here."

Paul had his first surprise. M. Rémond led him to a car, which was only a little bigger than a playground bumper car, just two seats in the front and a space at the back for a boot, barely big enough for Paul's suitcase. It had small, strongly built wheels with the usual inflatable tyres. The whole machine looked a toy, a miniature of a normal car. The streets of Le Havre were cobbled; the car bumped happily over the stones. The port and the town looked a little woebegone as if not yet recovered from the ravages of war. Some of the buildings were damaged by bombing.

Once they had left the port, the countryside was beautiful, lush and green and wooded, just like southern England.

They stopped at a bar or auberge or estaminet – Paul did not know the French term – and went into a small dark room where M. Rémond and a rather sluttish girl had a long conversation. Eventually what was produced was a bowl consisting of two fried eggs and two slices of ham swimming in hot fat. Paul thought the ham was a substitute for bacon. According to M. Rémond bacon was non-existent in France.

Paul managed the ham and eggs, but he found the fat rather off-putting, and left it as much as he could.

M. Rémond suggested he dipped the bread in the fat but Paul was not keen and resisted. M. Rémond just had hot, milky coffee. He seemed very fond of dipping, because his bread went straight into the coffee, but Paul was not so keen when his coffee came. The coffee itself was warming, sweet and satisfying.

At the estaminet for the first time Paul experienced a French toilet, a smelly hole in the ground, the contraption his sister had disliked.

M. Rémond's country house, when they got to it, was a long, rambling building on only one floor. It seemed a bit of a shambles outside, but warm and comfortable inside. The windows had green shutters, which Paul was to find usual in France. The shutters were mainly a protection from the sun. An old lady came out to greet them. She was dressed in black, which was another feature – black. Paul found black dress common in France with the elderly. It gave the impression so many women outlived their husbands. Black was a sign of mourning, M.Rémond explained.

Paul took her to be a domestic. When he and M. Rémond sat down to lunch she served them, but did not eat with them.

At supper Paul, thinking of his mother's complaint that since the war domestics were hard to come by, remarked-
"You are lucky to have a domestic".
M. Rémond looked up,
"Non, non, she is not a domestic; she is ma mère, my mother."
"Your mother?" Paul couldn't help exclaiming. M. Rémond nodded.
"I do apologise."
This was muttered in embarrassment. The incident was over, but Paul couldn't help feeling astonished that a man could treat his mother like a domestic. Such an impression!

In the afternoon they went to look at the vineyard, which was obviously M. Rémond's pride and joy. It was a beautiful sight! Enclosed within a stone wall, rows and rows of vines stretched from end to end with military precision. The vines were attached to wires and, being early May, had hardly begun their growth.

Paul wandered down the rows while M. Rémond chatted with an old, gnarled man who obviously looked after the vines.

Paul was impressed. He was beginning also to be more fascinated with M. Rémond, despite the fact that he treated his mother as a domestic.

The Frenchman no longer appeared as the strangely dressed, effeminate, lumpish figure in London. In France M. Rémond wore country clothes, a grey shirt unbuttoned at the neck, a pair of blue trousers held up by braces, and an old brownish cardigan which partially obscured the braces. He looked more of a real man, and Paul felt that Sis wouldn't giggle at him now.

In the evening after supper, M. Rémond talked of Paul's new family.

"The Father is M. Koenitz. He 'as five sons. He and 'is wife regret not 'aving a daughter. I met him through the Bank. He comes up to Paris from time to time on business. He owns a farming estate near a small village, about twenty kilometres from Montauban on the river Aveyron – the village that is, not Montauban."

"Je suis sure you will be very 'appy là-bas," continued M. Rémond. "He is like a squire in the district. I know not his wife, but am assured she will be 'appy to see you. The boys are lively and need organising."

"How old are the boys?" asked Paul.

"Je ne sais pas – I know not," and M. Rémond shrugged his shoulders, a French gesture Paul was having to get used to.

"And how much will I be paid?" asked Paul.

Again a dismissive shrug from the Frenchman.

"We go to Paris demain soir -tomorrow evening, Sunday," M. Rémond explained. "You will 'ave three days in Paris, and then you go by train to Montauban. Est-ce que ça vous plaît? – does that please you?"

Paul nodded and expressed his gratitude. He slept peacefully that night in a large wooden bed.

The next day, in early evening, they set off for Paris in the tiny car, which managed a fairly good speed over the straight roads of France. One incident upset Paul during the journey.

Paul found M. Rémond a reckless driver. Eventually, he concluded that most French drivers had a death wish. He didn't know why, perhaps it was some sort of reaction after the war to prove their manhood. France had succumbed quickly to the German invasion. The French inability to resist the enemy seemed to prey on their minds, and showed in their reluctance to talk about it.

That evening M. Rémond drove at the maximum speed the little car could reach, which was may not be as fast as a normal car, but it seemed to be faster than any car in England.

Paul eventually fell asleep, tired after all his new experiences.

Suddenly he was woken by a thud and a yelp from a dog. But M. Rémond did not stop.

"Please stop," begged Paul, "you must have hit a dog."

But M. Rémond made a joke about too many stray dogs in France. One less wouldn't matter. Paul felt like crying. He had left behind the spaniel he loved at home. He suddenly felt very upset, very alone in a strange country, with a strange man who could happily run over a dog, and who treated his mother like a servant. He could see why his sister had instinctively distrusted the man.

The journey to Paris took about two hours or more. They went to a small flat in which dwelt another elderly lady in black, and a small, yappy dog, the type of dog Paul always called 'Rags'. There was more hair than body.

M. Rémond left him there, and explained that he had to go to work the next day. Paul could explore Paris on foot. He gave him a map and said he would collect him in the evening for dinner.

# Chapter 5

*Paris at Last!*

Paul enjoyed his day in Paris by himself. The next day he made his way down to the Seine. Like the Thames in London, the Seine was a stately, glistening attraction on a sunny May morning. The air in Paris seemed cleaner, brighter, more invigorating than in London. Certainly Paul felt he could walk miles in such a pleasant atmosphere. No wonder people fell in love with Paris, and wished to go back as often as they could.

He walked the length of the Seine from a point near the Eiffel Tower as far as Notre Dame, then back again on the other side, marvelling at the booksellers showing their wares on the river parapets. Occasionally he would sit down and contemplate the bustle of a big city. He stopped to have a coffee at a cafe whose tables were spread out in the sun on the wide pavement along the boulevard. The whole of Paris – or the part he was in – seemed more open than London. The traffic was not so congested, but faster and accompanied by much blowing of horns. To catch the buses there was a different way of queuing for the passengers. At the bus stop one took a ticket which displayed a number.

When the bus arrived numbers would be called and one entered on the back platform when one's number came up. Some people cheated by picking up discarded earlier numbers on the pavement. The French had little idea of queuing. It was more of an undignified squabble when the bus arrived.

He found something to eat for lunch by buying a small baguette, and some sliced beef from a delicatessen.

He got back to the flat about four. He and his new landlady exchanged smiles; the dog yapped behind the safety of his mistress' black skirt. Paul lay down and had a rest after all his walking.

M. Rémond came for him at seven, wearing a dark grey city suit, one he should have worn in London.

Paul was to have dinner in a restaurant, the best in Paris, according to M. Rémond.

To Paul the restaurant was a disappointment. It was through a shop, which sold little cream cakes in rows on shelves. The entry was not propitious, or not one Paul would expect in England.

The restaurant itself was a long, low darkened room with a row of tables along each side, and a gangway for the waiters down the middle. Each table was covered by a white paper – ye gods, paper! – tablecloth.

On each table was the bare necessity of a knife and fork, a paper napkin, and a wine glass.

The table setting was so sparse! M. Remond sensed Paul's reaction.

"Ha, en Angleterre, vous savez, you put importance on layout, on appearance, En France c'est ce qu'on mange – it's what one eats that is important."

Paul did not like the disparagement of English customs. He was so used to English superior attitudes over French ways. But the food was in fact excellent. They started with a pate, on thin slices of toast, followed by a steak cooked beautifully, pink on the underside. This was followed by vegetables and delicately creamed potato. Then came the cheese, a Camembert with a creamy centre, followed by fruit, a choice of an apple or orange. Paul would have preferred apple pie rather than a plain apple. One then took a walk into the shop area and savoured a couple of small, creamy cakes. M. Rémond would put a whole cake straight into his mouth and gobble it down. It was no wonder he was overweight! Paul remembered that the food at his own home had been plainer and much less abundant. Perhaps that was the influence of his own mother; she ruled the roost, as cook!

Apart from the poor presentation in France, there were other matters that surprised Paul. The first was the sheer abundance and quality of the food. England in 1951 was still struggling. It seemed that France had endured four years of

German occupation, to come out better than the victor across the Channel. There seemed an unfairness about the situation, but Paul did not say so.

Paul never knew how much the meal cost and didn't like to ask. He thought in England it would have cost a bomb!

An extraordinary practice to his English eyes was the use of the same plate and knife and fork for pate, meat, vegetables, and cheese. It was only when it came to the fruit that the plate was changed. With each course the plate and the knife and fork were wiped down with bread. Not a spot of gravy or food was left. The consumption of bread was copious. Paul thought his fussy mother would have called it 'disgusting'!

The drinking of wine was just as impressive; it seemed to Paul there was a different wine with each course. He just couldn't cope, and kept having to put a hand over his glass. At Oxford he had drunk beer, but in small quantities, usually a lemonade shandy. M. Rémond seemed surprised at his abstemiousness. Paul was just not accustomed to wine.

As the restaurant was not far from the flat, Paul walked home by himself.

Taking the Seine as his bearing, he was quite confident of getting back. M. Rémond left him and waddled back to his flat, wherever it was.

Paul passed a girl struggling with a suitcase. He gallantly offered to carry it for her. The offer was said in English. Paul was still not confident of his school French. He was surprised the reply came in English – good English, though with the usual French accent.

"That would be very kind," she said. Paul could sense her smile in the dark. The case was not heavy. While they walked they chatted – in English.

"You speak very good English," Paul remarked.

She laughed.

"I live in England during the War," she explained. "My Father was in the Free French Army. I even went to an English school, a public school, all girls. I did not like it very much; I longed to be in France. I was homesick."

They chatted further. Her destination was not very far. Paul felt she must be about the same age, though it was hard to be certain in the dark streets where the lighting was poor. He too had been at school in the War which gave some indication. Though he could see little of her, she seemed pretty and very feminine, letting out an occasional delightful giggle.

Eventually he asked:

"I'd love to see you again, but the day after tomorrow I go to Montauban. Could I have your address? I hope to come back to Paris eventually."

He was amazed at his forwardness, the shy Englishman who had rarely come across a girl at Oxford. He wondered whether he was being over-presumptuous. But the girl giggled and said it would be nice to see him again, and muttered something about being able to practise her English.

When they parted, she wrote on a piece of paper her name and telephone number.

Paul kissed her on the cheek and she gave another giggle. Paul loved, at that moment, feminine giggles. His world had not featured many giggles, apart from his sister's, but she was not normally a giggler.

He returned to his flat, a pleasantly happy man; even the yappy dog got a pat. Then he went to bed, and soon fell asleep.

He awoke later, and was horribly sick all over the bed. He struggled to the bathroom, and was sick on the way, all over the carpet. In the bathroom he was sick once more, but this time fortunately in the toilet pan. His landlady must have heard him. She came out with the dog who promptly started to lap up what was on the carpet.

The landlady hastily picked it up and shut it out of the way in the kitchen. She grunted at the mess, and then rang M. Rémond. The rich French meal had been too much for Paul's war-deprived stomach.

M. Rémond was furious!

"Pourquoi, why could not you get up?" he said, seeing the mess upon the bed.

Paul tried to explain he awoke, and was sick before he could move. He had never been so violently sick before. But that did not appease M. Rémond.

"You better now?" he asked.

Paul nodded. His stomach felt relieved now it was all over.

"Bring your case," M. Rémond snapped. "We go to a 'otel."

Paul dressed, and finished repacking his case. He didn't know what to do with his messy pyjamas, but Madame muttered something, and took them from him. Paul had a spare pair.

The hotel was small and not very welcoming so late at night. But Paul had a clean bed, with a stricture to keep it that way from M. Rémond. There seemed to be a very unsympathetic side to this Frenchman. Paul felt he could not help what had happened. It was the same attitude as when the dog was run over on their way to Paris – a complete male indifference and annoyance!

"I meet you the day after tomorrow in the evening to catch overnight train to Montauban," he explained. "C'est mercredi soir, Wednesday evening, n'est-ce pas? You have two days to explore Paris."

Paul thanked him and apologised for the inconvenience he had caused. M. Rémond shrugged his shoulders and left abruptly, still seemingly displeased. Paul sighed and for the second time that night made for bed. He felt sorry their relationship had ended in this way! But he was beginning to feel a sense of dislike for this Frenchman, wholly illogical on Paul's part. As ever in their young life together his sister was right in her judgement of character. Paul tended to feel the best of everyone, not so his sister!

The next day Paul, feeling a little jaded, was standing in the entrance hall to the hotel, studying some leaflets in English about Paris, when he heard a voice behind him saying,

"You must be English, reading that stuff!"

He turned round. He was to meet yet another girl! Three since leaving Oxford! It was unbelievable! There she stood, pretty, smiling, good figure, a brunette, wearing a blue skirt, a pale blue blouse, and a grey cardigan. She looked immensely attractive.

Paul admitted he was English. He told her his name.

"I'm Betsy Orbets," she told him. "It's nice to meet an Englishman. I've been too long in Paris, seeing only Frenchmen."

They exchanged information. She had been six months in Paris, studying French at the Sorbonne. Her money was running out since she had taken the exam – 'Diplôme du cours de Langue Française'. She would return to England. She had the same fascination for France as Paul, but it was wearing thin. He judged she was homesick.

They felt rather silly standing in the narrow hall of the hotel, chatting away in English.

"Let's go for a coffee," suggested Paul.

They went. There were so many bars in Paris, so many places just to sit and natter. The talk in France was more important than the drink. It was what Paul had read about Paris, and he loved the thought of such an opportunity.

Over coffee Paul told Betsy about the family he was going to work for.

"Be careful," said Betsy. "French children can be very difficult. I tried helping a family and had to give it up. I had two girls and a boy. You have five – five – boys where you are going. I wish you luck!"

Paul told her he was going to explore Paris for the second day. He also told her about blotting his copybook over the French dinner.

"You've got to remember," Betsy told him, "the first French priority is food. Honestly, nothing else matters. They eat well, but I don't think their hygiene is all that good. They never wash their hands! Did you know French dark chocolate is much better for you than our milk chocolate?"

"I don't like their dark chocolate," stated Paul.

"You've been warned!"

Eventually Betsy offered to give him a guided tour of Paris.

"But it must be on foot," she stated. "I have very little money."

Paul gladly accepted. She took him to the Louvre and they spent a good hour looking at the paintings and other exhibits. Then they went to the Cathedral of Notre Dame. Paul noted she crossed herself with holy water on entering, and she genuflected to the altar.

"Are you a Catholic?" Paul asked.

"Why, yes." she said and smiled. "It's one of the joys of France, living in a Catholic country."

Paul almost grimaced, but remembered his manners just in time. He had been brought up in an Anglican school, and history had shown Catholics had been a thorn in the flesh for the English.

"Were you brought up a Catholic, or are you a convert?" he dared to ask. He hadn't really met any Catholics before.

"I was born a Catholic, brought up as a Catholic, it's in me, part of me. You'll excuse me." she told him.

"There's nothing to excuse," Paul said smiling.

But Paul watched in wonder as this pleasant, attractive girl knelt down to pray, and then crossed herself once again.

She smiled at Paul's face of wonderment.

"We don't bite, you know," she said, still smiling. "I suppose you must be one of those Englishmen who regard Catholics as an abomination."

"No, no," said Paul hastily, "I haven't really met any Catholics before."

"You haven't lived," teased Betsy. "We're only human beings; we just believe the true church is the Catholic one."

Paul went 'um' rather doubtfully – and rudely – but he couldn't help liking this forthright girl. It seemed to him, since the War, girls had grown up a great deal, much more mature and confident. Or perhaps, in his isolation, he had never really known girls. It was a lesson he still had to learn – or was learning!

He smiled at her.

"It's wonderful being in Paris," he said. "So many writers have spoken warmly of it. I envy you, having spent so long here."

She smiled and whispered as they were in church,

"It has its ups and downs, like life, I suppose. I found the French very insular. They accept you up to a point; beyond that you were on your own, a different breed. I found French men rather arrogant, rather intrusive. They felt a solitary English girl fair game. I had to be wary."

Paul marvelled that this girl, probably about the same age as himself, should have the courage to come to Paris alone.

She leant closer to him to talk quietly; he had already explained he had a hearing handicap. He thrilled at her closeness, her smell, not so exciting as Maggie's, but delightful all the same. He knew he mustn't touch her, but longed to do so.

They went next to the Boulevard St. Michel where they had a latish lunch, Paul paying. It was incredibly cheap, just a piece of meat, creamed potato and salad, followed by fruit, (no cheese).

It was all Paul wanted. His stomach had settled, but he was cautious.

"They call this road the 'Boule Miche'," Betsy explained. "It leads to the Sorbonne; it's noted for students, artists and writers, mostly young."

Paul was thrilled he was in the heart of Bohemian Paris!

The Sorbonne buildings did not impress Paul. Compared with the beauty of Oxford, it failed to strike a chord of delight. He mentioned it to Betsy.

She jokingly replied,

"Ha, it's not outward appearances that matters; it's the contents within. It's rather like eating in France. The appearance of the table doesn't matter; it's the quality of the food that's important. The Sorbonne has a very high academic record, renowned throughout Europe! She smiled impishly at Paul.

He felt himself rebuffed for his Oxford priggishness!

Afterwards they went on to Montmartre. The beauty of the white Basilica Paul thought spectacular, perched on a hill overlooking Paris.

As time was getting on, they took the Metro back to their hotel district. Betsy had a carnet of tickets, a sort of pre-paid voucher.

"You bought me lunch," said Betsy. "I'll treat you to the Métro. Not a fair exchange, but it's the least I can do."

She was a very smiling, teasing person. Paul felt himself a little too serious and boorish beside her. 'Stuffy' would probably be the right term. She reminded him of his sister.

But, as with Maggie and the French girl, he found she was only a fleeting companion. When he expressed a hope that they could spend the evening doing something, or even tomorrow, she replied sorrowfully,

"I'm sorry Paul. This evening I'm going to a village near Paris, and spending the next couple of days with friends. As you are going to Montauban tomorrow evening, I'm afraid it's the last we shall see of each other."

Paul was crest fallen – the story of his life, or at least of Paris!

She gave him her name and address in England. They said goodbye, but no teeny-weeny kiss. Paul was never to see her again.

Before leaving for Montauban he gave her an envelope with all the small French change he had. It was only the small change; he kept the big notes. He hoped it would help her in her last few days in Paris.

Paul's homesickness or depression returned. He had fallen out with M. Rémond. As far as girls were concerned, they had come to nothing, and he had a dreary twenty-four hours or so before catching the train to Montauban.

# Chapter 6

*La Refaudio, Here I Come!*

The next day Paul met M. Rémond after ten at the Gare Austerlitz. M. Rémond was still rather distant, as if he had not forgiven Paul for the waste of a good meal, and the consequent expensive mess that had ensued.

However, he did pay Paul's train fare to Montauban. Paul protested.

"You've done so much for me. You even paid my hotel bill. I went to pay this afternoon, and found you had paid in advance."

M. Rémond shrugged his shoulders as if to say 'it was nothing'.

They argued, but M. Rémond was adamant. Paul never knew why he was so kind to him, an Englishman. He sensed it was something to do with the War. He wished he knew the story, if there was a story. But it might all have been Paul's wild imagining. Maybe M. Rémond was just a kind, lonely man, much hurt by life, and Paul had been a disappointment!

Before he left M. Rémond gave Paul a parcel containing his washed and ironed pyjamas. Paul was very touched by this gesture, certainly the work of the landlady.

The overnight train journey, troisième classe, was one of the most uncomfortable Paul had ever experienced. He noticed the French passengers all brought a rug or a 'coussin' (cushion). He soon knew why! The seats were hard, wooden and slatted; sleep was impossible. His bottom found it easier in a standing position, which was just not possible, except to go for a walk along the train.

Again, the French passengers all brought food and drink. There was no buffet car!

The worst agony, sitting opposite, was a comfortable, overweight mother and her whining daughter, possibly aged six. They had all that was necessary, and, my, was he envious! To make matters worse the child whimpered and grizzled for what seemed the whole night long. Paul sat uncomfortably, salivating, watching cold chicken, hard boiled eggs, mineral water, disappearing down an ungrateful, spoilt throat. Then cheese and brioche and fruit followed. None was offered to Paul, and he must have looked pretty longingly at everything – as well as having nothing – obviously!

The night was cold and dismal, and he could hear the rain pouring down outside. Continual drops ran down the carriage windows. It was not a good portent for the beginning of his new venture in France!

In the early hours of the morning – Paul was too frazzled to note the exact time – the train arrived at Montauban. The station was clean, very green, lined by trees and bushes. It had one strange feature. The platform was almost at ground level. The step down was quite difficult, especially with a large suitcase. Paul found it easier to climb down first, and then reach up for his bag and drag it out. For a tired man it was quite an effort. The rain had eased a little, but there was still a dreary wetness.

No sign of M. Koenitz. Paul made his way to the entrance hall where he found a bench and waited. The other passengers who had alighted with him soon disappeared. They were met by friends or relatives amid much kissing and cries of welcome. The only two people left were station staff in their peaked caps and blue uniform.

It was half an hour before M. Koenitz turned up. No greeting, no words of welcome from the little man. He was nervous, agitated, tense.

"Vous, M. Treloar?" he asked sharply.

Paul nodded.

"M. Koenitz," the Frenchman vouchsafed sharply by way of introduction.

"Come!" he then barked at Paul.

Paul came, or rather followed!

He went with M. Koenitz onto the forecourt where a solitary black car was parked. The car was almost as peculiar as its master. The headlights were behind the mesh of the grill. Paul wondered whether this position obscured the headlights at night. It was also a car that had its engine at the back. This Paul discovered to his consternation, when he tried to put his case in the back boot, only to find it was filled by an oily motor. M. Koenitz whisked the case impatiently away and tried to put it in the front boot. But that proved impossible as it was filled with children's clothing, little bootees, oil and petrol cans, and a mixture of tools. Angrily M. Koenitz threw it on the back seat of the car. No gentle treatment with property not his own!

M. Koenitz looked like a jockey, with a jockey's slightness of frame. He wore jodhpurs and light riding boots. His chest was covered by a safari shirt, with breast pockets on either side. He had no hat, but his head was covered by a thick crop of short dark brown hair. His manner was abrupt, irritable, impatient.

Paul wasn't certain whether he liked him. Feeling tired, he was suddenly overcome with miserable loneliness. With it came the thought as to whether he was doing the right thing! As Sis had said, he lacked confidence.

If M. Rémond en route to Paris was a reckless driver, M. Koenitz was a maniac. Paul felt like screaming out,

"For God's sake, slow down!"

His mother, in her back seat driver manner, would have protested vehemently. Fortunately there was not much traffic about at that early hour.

Paul's initial impression of Montauban was of a dark and gloomy town. The overhanging trees that lined the road added to that impression. There were no street lights, or if there were, they were turned off.

M. Koenitz veered off the road, and slammed to a halt between two trees.

"Town 'ouse," he announced curtly. Like M. Rémond he had difficulty with English 'h', like all Frenchmen in fact.

The town 'ouse was a grey, solid, concrete building, maybe two flats. There were two main entrances. The lower entrance was in the front; the upper entrance was up a flight of concrete steps to the left of the building.

M. Koenitz, in his usual abrupt manner, left the car, slammed the car door, and made for the left hand steps. He said nothing to Paul, who didn't know what to do. Should he follow or not?

M. Koenitz solved the problem by waving for him impatiently at the top of the steps.

The inside of the flat was, like the town, dark and gloomy, but it was mainly due to the shutters, all firmly closed. The only light was a single bulb in the middle of the room.

While M. Koenitz padded around, Paul sat on a chair. Eventually Paul's new employer went to a desk in the corner. He took out a white envelope, and extracted a photo. He beckoned to Paul to come over. He opened one of the shutters to let in more light. By then the light outside was becoming clearer.

The photo was of six children ranging from the biggest boy on the left to a baby on the right. The baby picture seemed to have been superimposed on the photo of the boys. One could see the join; the colouring also was different.

"My cheeldren," announced M. Koenitz.

Paul was surprised. M. Rémond had distinctly stated five boys; there was no mention of a baby!

M. Koenitz started to introduce them in a mixture of English and French.

"A gauche, Jean-Pierre, dix ans." His gaze lingered on that of Jean-Pierre – with a lingering glance of affection. He continued,

"François, huit ans, a boy quelquefois – sometimes – very difficult. Marc – six ans – Régis – quatre ans, et le petit Nano – Emmanuel – deux ans."

He stopped.

"Who is the baby?" asked Paul.

"Ma fille – Christine – the daughter of my mistress." He hesitated, uncertain whether to continue.

"Ma femme n'a que les garçons – my wife has only boys. My mistress – a girl. I wish they live together – my wife and mistress – in the same house. My wife no want."

Paul's heart sank. What sort of family was he going to be involved with? He imagined a wife made weary by endless childbearing, aged by a husband who had deserted her because she could only produce boys. Paul had heard, through some medical article, that the sex of a child was down to the father, not the wife. Whether it was true or not he was uncertain. But obviously M. Koenitz blamed his wife for the situation.

'Typical male!' his sister would have said, sarcastically.

Paul felt he was entering a family full of discord, and he felt despondent. He wished he had known about the situation, but he imagined even M. Remond would not have been aware of the unhappiness.

M. Koenitz put the photo away. He said abruptly,
"Come!"

But he spoke no more of his family.

The car sped along another few miles. They came to a river, fast moving and swollen by the recent rains.

"Aveyron," said M. Koenitz, indicating the river.

The car swept across the bridge, and through a shabby village of faded cream-painted houses. As yet nobody was stirring.

They turned left through the village. Paul noted a church on the right, with a small bell tower perched on its roof. The road merged into a country lane that ran parallel to the river that Paul could just see across the fields. On the right was a hill overlooking the village and fields. A short distance and Paul noticed a large, modern house perched on a plateau, cut out of the hill. M. Koenitz pointed,

"My 'ouse," he said. "La Refaudio – The Refuge."

It was a beautiful house, with a lovely view over the river valley. A track led up to the plateau, but it was so muddy the car just skidded to a halt, its wheels turning uselessly, splaying out mud.

With a sharp turn of the door, M. Koenitz got out of the car.

"Merde!" he expostulated. Paul had heard the word before, and had learnt it meant "shit."

Paul realised why the Frenchman was wearing riding boots; they coped with the mud which was deep in places. Again, Paul didn't know whether to follow; there had been no indication. Eventually, however, M. Koenitz waved to him impatiently from some garage doors. Paul felt his shoes were not suitable for such mud. But he found it easier trudging up the side where the ground was firmer.

The house seemed built on three floors. The ground floor was the garage, the 'cave' (cellar), and some primitive living quarters. In the far corner of the garage were concrete steps. Paul followed M. Koenitz to emerge into the main quarters of the house, the entrance hall – highly polished floor, small, scattered carpets or rugs. M. Koenitz tramped straight across to a further staircase that presumably led up to the bedrooms on the next floor. A trail of mud followed him, to which he was indifferent.

Paul stood irresolutely by the entrance door; his whole training told him he must remove his muddy shoes; this he did.

An attractive woman, probably in her late thirties or early forties, appeared at the door on the left, which Paul later learnt was the entry to the kitchen. She looked at the muddy footprints and called out crossly,

"Ecoute, Jacques."

Then she saw Paul, made a tcch of disgust, and disappeared, returning with some newspaper to put the shoes on. No greeting, no smile of welcome! It was much as at the station. Paul felt very unwelcome in his new home.

A girl appeared with a dustpan, brush and a cloth. An apron covered her brown skirt and pullover. She began to clear up the mud.

M. Koenitz reappeared down the stairs, minus boots; he introduced the attractive woman, who had appeared behind the girl.

"Ma femme – my wife. She no speak English," M. Koenitz explained in a rather offhand way.

Paul looked with interest at the woman. She was no slouch, no burdened wife oppressed by frequent child bearing. She had kept her figure, by some miracle. She was dressed in a slim, patterned tweed skirt and the familiar English twin set of jumper and cardigan. She looked a lovely woman.

But still no smile!

Paul felt as if he wasn't wanted, disconcerting for a young man who had come a long way to live with this family and, hopefully, to work for them.

"Come," was the familiar call from M. Koenitz, almost as if Paul was a dog, accustomed to sharp commands.

Paul followed him meekly through a door on the right. It led into a spacious sitting-room. The room was like an English sitting-room. It had wooden fireside chairs, around a well-lit fire. Though it was May, the morning had a certain chill, especially with the recent rain. The fireside chairs had soft, reddish brown cushions. There were two long windows, and, glory be, no shutters, though with curtains matching the brown of the fireside chairs. On the side opposite the door was a baby grand piano. Paul indicated it and said,

"Do you play?"

M. Koenitz shook his head. "It is the piano of my wife. She is singer, opera singer," he explained. "She sing to you."

Paul noted this piece of information with interest. The wife was no longer an over-burdened hausfrau, but a woman of talent! This was more promising.

"You like breakfast?" asked M. Koenitz.

The words were like manna to food-deprived Paul.

"Yes, Ple-e-ase," he said gratefully, and with enthusiastic emphasis.

M. Koenitz went out. Paul continued his perusal of the room. He was particularly attracted by the piano. His mother played and sang – beautifully, or so he always thought. He managed to turn the pages for her.

Near the far window overlooking the valley was a dining table, with chairs for eight, and a bowl of flowers in the middle.

The whole room was clean, welcoming, and very reassuring to a tired and anxious Paul. There was an obvious care for the house.

Paul sat down in one of the fireside chairs, and stretched out his hands to the fire. He felt very tired. The girl who had cleaned up the muddy footprints, came in with a tray on which was a bowl of milky coffee, a chunk of bread from a baguette, some butter and, heavens be praised, some jam. As always the coffee was milky and sweet, but Paul enjoyed it. When finished, he put the tray down on a little table, and sat back. He thought he heard slightly raised voices, mostly M. Koenitz' gruffer sounds.

After a moment, M. Koenitz came in.

"Je vous laisse – I leave you," he said. No indication of how long, or where he was going. He left the room with his usual abruptness. Paul sank back in the chair and soon fell asleep, deep in the land of nod. For a while he was untroubled by the poor reception he had received.

# Chapter 7

*An Italian Chance of Scenery*

Paul was woken delightfully by young giggles alongside his chair. He opened his eyes and saw two smiling, small boys, looking at him with curiosity, as if he had come from another planet. When they saw he was awake, they gave a little squeal, and rushed off shouting "Maman, Maman!"

Eventually Maman came in, the attractive lady whom Paul had seen in the hall. She still remained cold and unsmiling. She said.

"Vous avez bien dormi?" But Paul did not understand. She put her head on her two hands and repeated the question. Paul nodded, at last understanding.

"Les enfants veulent se promener. Vous voulez y aller?"

Paul understood the word 'promener', and nodded. He got up and followed her and the two little boys down to the cave. On their way Paul noticed his case in the hall.

Once below Madame seemed to remember.

"Ha, vous ne savez pas les noms," she said.

She indicated the elder of the two boys,

"Régis," and asked Paul to repeat it by a movement of her hands.

"Régis," said Paul and smiled.

Paul cottoned on, and said again "Régis".

She repeated the same procedure with "Nano".

Paul remembered he was two and Régis four.

The boys put on little booties and she procured from somewhere boots for Paul. They were a little tight, but he managed.

Then Régis took one hand, and Nano the other, with words presumably of advice from Maman. They led him out of the garage, and down a path the opposite side of the road to the house. Paul now trudged down the muddy track on the opposite side to that earlier to reach the road. They went along the road away from the village until they came to a footpath leading down to the left to a group of farm buildings.

They walked down. A woman appeared at the door of what seemed the main building.

"Ha, mes petits," she cried. The boys rushed to her, and were smothered with hugs and kisses. The boys cackled with glee. The woman then turned politely to Paul. Régis said something. The woman stuck out a hand said politely,

"Monsieur."

They shook hands and she smiled. It was a better greeting than Paul received at the big house, La Refaudio, where the atmosphere did not seem very happy.

The woman invited them into a room, the kitchen, which seemed the main living room of the house. The boys sat down with alacrity at the large table that dominated the room. They seemed to expect something, and soon their expectations came. A plate of biscuits was put on the table, glasses and some red drink, which the woman called grenadine. Paul was also invited to sit down, and a small liqueur glass was put in front of him. Into it was poured some liqueur, the sight of which made the boys giggle again. They were great gigglers, those two, and very excited. Paul imagined they were delightfully mischievous.

The lady waved a hand in front of her mouth to indicate the liqueur was hot, and it burnt the tongue.

"Très fort, très fort," she kept repeating.

Then a stocky man entered. To Paul's delight he spoke a little English, but with a strange accent that was certainly not French. He tended to make two or more syllables out of words, especially verbs. For instance "come" was pronounced "come-a" and "speak" was "speak-a". He kissed and hugged the two boys – more giggles! Both he and his wife presumably, were obviously fond of children in a demonstrative way.

The man was dressed in old clothes, ragged blue trousers, kept up by braces either side of his barrel chest. His face was rough and reddened by the sun. He saw the liqueur his wife had given Paul.

"Très fort – very hot-a," he said, and wagged his hand in front of his tongue, as if to cool it.

His wife gave her husband a small glass of the same liqueur. He promptly tossed it back in one go, uttered a loud "ha-a", and then beamed with satisfaction. This prompted another giggle from the children.

"Bon! Bon! Good-a," he said, thoroughly pleased.

Paul was a little more circumspect. He took a little sip, but even that made him gasp.

"The drink-a is-a made here," the man said.

"You mean it is home-made?" ventured Paul.

"Oui, oui, yes, yes," said the man. "I regret-a my wife no speak-a English but my brudder, he come-a soon. He speak-a very well the English. He spent-a nearly four years in England as prisoner-of-war."

Just as he said this, the door to the rest of the building opened, and a man emerged, followed by three girls.

"My brudder," said barrel chest proudly, having difficulty with English 'th', making it sound like a 'd'.

Paul studied the new entrants with interest. The 'brudder' seemed younger than his sibling, a little taller, and not so powerfully built. Paul marvelled at the two older girls. They looked very pretty, dressed in coloured skirts and white blouses. They were obviously twins; one could hardly tell them apart. They must be in their late teens.

The third girl, younger, about twelve, was more of a tomboy. She wore a scruffy pair of trousers as if she had just been working on the farm, and a thin bluish jumper that had various stains and marks on it. She looked a scruff, but it didn't seem to worry her. She looked a particularly robust type of character.

The elder brother hastened to introduce his sibling, and the three girls.

"My brudder – he take-a his nieces into Montauban for shopping. They are les belles filles – beautiful girls, n'est-ce pas?"

There was an immediate cry from the youngest girl, saying she was not beautiful – jamais! – never!

To which her father gently admonished her.

"Ah, Simone, un jour – one day you regret-a what you say."

Not all of this Paul cottoned on to, except the name 'Simone'.

"What are the other girls called?" he asked.

"This one is Stéphanie and the other is Loretta and you find-a not which is which!"

The father suddenly laughed.

"Madame up there," he indicated La Refaudio, "has-a only boys. I have-a only girls. One day I marry Madame and she 'as-a girls, and M. Koenitz marry-a my wife and 'ave-a only boys."

He gave a chortle at his witticism but nobody else laughed. The younger brother came forward, to the rescue.

"My name is Raymond," he said.

They shook hands.

"I speak-a English better than my brudder," he said, smiling. "For more than three years I Italian prisoner-of-war in England. I am in Somerset."

"You are Italian?" Paul queried.

"We are all Italian," he said, and he stretched out his hand embracing the whole family.

"But, how come you are in France?" asked Paul.

"Ha, it is a long-a story. Before war we do not like Mussolini. We escape from him to France."

"But how come you retain Italian nationality?" persisted Paul, though politely.

"We 'ope-a one day to go back to Italy. But maybe now it is-a too late. We are-a settled here," the younger brother explained.

"I tell-a you a funny story," he continued, and he smiled. "When Italian mother is how do you say – 'enceinte'?" He indicated a rounded tummy.

"Pregnant?" hazarded Paul, who thought he had heard the French word before. He was a little suspicious of somebody who started off a story with the epithet 'funny'. It was invariably not funny, just strange or peculiar.

"Ha, yes, pregnant. When she is pregnant, she go to Italy to 'ave-a child. The child is registered in Italy, therefore, Italian. Then she travel back-a to France with baby."

Paul was interested. He thought it explained the different, more melodious accent when speaking French. He remembered also the Italian love of children, that was evident in this very happy family, and the exuberant way they greeted Régis and Nano.

"What is the family name?" Paul asked.

"Salvetti. Nous sommes tous – we are all – les Salvettis." The younger brother said, grinning widely.

"You like-a it chez La Refaudio?" asked the father.

"I do not know," hesitated Paul. "I only arrived this morning."

"Madame Koenitz, very beautiful woman. But life is-a si triste, so sad," explained the father.

They know, Paul thought, of the tragedy in the family. It made Paul rather sad, and uncertain about his own future.

The younger brother began to usher the girls out.

"We go-a," he said. "We spend much money, and Simone never stop eating."

He smiled at Simone who pulled a face.

After they had left, Régis, who had eaten his fill of biscuits, announced he wanted to go down to the river. The father announced immediately.

"Non, il est trop dangereux. The river is too dangerous."

Then Paul saw this strange obstinacy which was characteristic of all the Koenitz children. That is, they made a scene until they got their way. Régis won. Paul stood by, disconcerted. He presumed the children were his responsibility. If somebody said the river was dangerous, then no trip to the river! But a compromise was reached. Father Salvetti would come as well. Paul felt relieved; M. Salvetti would know the river better than anyone.

So they walked beside the field to the river, Paul holding the hand of Nano, Régis the hand of M. Salvetti.

The river was indeed in full flood, swift and dangerous, bearing debris from higher up. The water was not quite up to the top of the containing banks, but it was near enough. It was awesome in its power and speed.

"Il y a deux ans – two years ago – the river flow-a into the fields," remarked M. Salvetti. "Even into the village. Bad, bad, très mauvais."

The boys began to move along to the bridge, Paul and M. Salvetti in anxious attendance.

"They play-a on the bridge," remarked M. Salvetti, "a game-a with little sticks."

At the bridge began hilarious fun, mingled with anxiety by the two adults. The boys would count 1-2-3, then throw a stick in the river by an arch. They would then rush to the other side, anxious to see over the parapet, to find out which stick came first. Fortunately there was no traffic. Paul and M. Salvetti would lift their charges so they could see more easily. Eventually tiring of the game, they made their way back to La Refaudio through the village. Paul thought it rather a long, roundabout route, but the boys seemed accustomed to walking. Only Nano had a piggy back on M. Salvetti's broad shoulders.

It had been a happy morning for Paul, something to restore his spirits after a frosty reception at La Refaudio.

But there was an unnerving, 'épouvantable' trial to come.

# Chapter 8

*An 'Epouvantable' Trial!*

The next part of the day proved quiet for Paul. He had lunch with Madame and the two boys. As a meal it was much the same as Paul had already experienced – eating off the same plate, plenty of bread consumption. Wine with water as a staple drink. But the wine was different from chez M. Rémond. It was a rough, coarse, red wine. The surprising thing, the boys also drank the red wine, including two year old Nano, but always watered down. It became a pink, watery refreshment.

After lunch, Paul had another nap by the fire, always a welcome warmth! The children played upstairs in their bedroom. Surprisingly they had very few toys, and most of them seemed broken. Paul had bought them two small Dinky cars that they greatly appreciated. They sprawled over the carpet, pushing the cars around and making car-related noises. Madame smiled her thanks, but looked rather dubious. Paul didn't know why until later.

This peace of the afternoon was shattered by the arrival back from school of the three older boys. They created hell, mostly ignored Paul, and pestered Madame and Anne-Marie, the domestic, for food and drink. By far the worst was François, the second eldest, only eight years old. His idea was to annoy the others, particularly the oldest, Jean-Pierre. François' shouts and cries were piercing. "Epouvantable," Madame would say, hands to ears, a word which Paul interpreted as something like 'dreadful.' She uttered often cries of "tais-toi", an appeal for quiet, which the boys mostly ignored. The one boy who really wanted to be quiet was Jean-Pierre, who had a small room in the cave. But François would give him no peace. Eventually Jean-Pierre would lose patience, and would shout at François. He was also bigger and stronger, and would hit out. François would burst into tears, and seek consolation from his Mother. She wisely expressed sympathy for Jean-Pierre. When François had recovered sufficiently, he went upstairs to make life difficult for his younger brothers, including Marc. It was then Paul realised why so many toys were broken. François seized on the two Dinky cars. He trod deliberately on one, and kicked the other into a corner. Régis rescued it, but François promptly snatched it from him and threw it out of the window. All this happened so quickly, and Paul was so astonished, he barely had time to interfere.

It was Régis' turn to go crying down to his Mother. But when she came up it was largely ineffective. Eventually François did agree to go, but with Marc, and look for the discarded car. Paul felt it was largely an excuse to get out of the house. Which it was!

They had a messy time playing in the mud and no Dinky car was found! Paul found it the next day lodged against a tree.

When supper came that evening it was most 'épouvantable'. Paul had never come across anything like it. It began with bread throwing. They had obviously done it before. They rolled the bread into little pellets, and chucked it at each other. Madame would continually make cries of "Arrête," or "écoute" or "tais-toi" but to no effect. The worst culprit was obviously François. He enjoyed the whole messy occasion, chased round the table, and shoved things down people's backs, particularly Nano, who finally dissolved into tears. He sought comfort from his distressed mother. She was really upset by everything, particularly when Jean-Pierre, in a sudden burst of anger, chased Francois round the table. Jean-Pierre was the only one who could stand up to François. But Jean-Pierre had such a quiet, retiring, equitable nature, it took a lot to get him started.

Paul felt sorry for Madame. She was like Jean-Pierre. She needed someone, a husband perhaps, who could exert authority! When François grabbed Paul to seek shelter from Jean-Pierre, Paul felt he'd had enough. He quietly got up, seized François with an unrelenting grip by the arm, and led him protesting, out of the room. He took him upstairs to his bedroom, sat him on the bed, and made him stay there. His difficulty was to explain himself. He kept saying "non", shaking a finger, and pretending to throw something. He dragged out a memory of school French – 'arretez' – stop, and then making the action of throwing things.

Eventually, Anne-Marie came up. She was a pleasant girl, or really a woman of 28, as Paul discovered later. But Paul still would not let François leave the bedroom. Anne-Marie talked to François quietly. He seemed to calm down. Anne-Marie, mostly by signs, conveyed to Paul François would eat in the 'cuisine' – kitchen – with her. To this Paul agreed thankfully and returned to the dining-room. All was quiet and sensible. Madame smiled her thanks. It would be dangerous to say Paul had no more trouble. There were other times he had to take François out of the room, but as time went on he managed to explain better to François why he must behave.

Over the days things quietened down. The weather improved and the children were able to play outside.

After supper that first evening, Madame put the youngest to bed, Anne-Marie washed up, and things were much more peaceful.

After a while, and a period of wandering around seeing what happened with the children, Paul retired to the sitting room to write a letter to his sister. He felt closer to his sister, who had always supported and encouraged him, except at the beginning. Mother had resented his 'swanning off' to France – her words. He told his sister about the relationship between the French husband and wife, about the difficulty with the children, and the happy visit to the Salvetti farm. He expressed concern about the future.

While writing the letter, Madame appeared, sat down at the piano, and began to play. This was obviously her relaxation. Then to his surprise she began to sing. She had a lovely, clear voice. Paul could understand M. Koenitz's description of her as an opera singer. She reminded him of his mother who also played and sang. It made him feel he had let his mother down badly, and he began to regret his behaviour.

"Poor Mother," he concluded.

But it was wonderful to hear Madame play and sing. She was entirely a different woman, confident, expressive. She caressed the piano as if it was her special child. At first she played softly and quietly. But then she began to play with more vigour and expression, her lovely body moving with the music. She had a repertoire of songs she seemed to know by heart. After a while she resorted to sheet music, and Paul moved over to turn the pages for her, as he had done for his mother.

When she finished, Paul began to muster his little store of school French.

"Vous jouez been," he said. 'You play beautifully' he meant to say. He wanted to say also she was beautiful, but he thought he'd better not.

Madame smiled at him, the first real smile he had had from her. She was relaxed, not the nervous, unhappy woman he had experienced earlier.

She indicated she was going upstairs and made motions to Paul of turning out the lights. She left Paul with much to think about. She was the cultivated, beautiful, Parisian woman, or lady, he had read about.

# Chapter 9

*Settling in, hopefully!*

The next two weeks passed much as the first day. Walk in the morning with Nano and Regis. Sometimes Madame came with them. One morning Madame said,
"Nous allons à l'église."
So off they went to the church. It was only a short distance along the lane towards the village.
Madame was a sturdy walker. Like her sons she enjoyed a walk. Nano's little legs had difficulty keeping up, but Paul was quite happy to give him a ride on his shoulders.
At the church Madame and the boys genuflected and crossed themselves with holy water. The church had a quiet spirituality which Paul appreciated. He sat contentedly while Madame busied herself dusting and arranging things. There were two other women there, one sweeping the floor, the other arranging the flowers. A priest came in and talked with the women. Madame introduced him to Paul, and they shook hands. He was a quiet man and didn't stay very long.

On leaving he said something about an important occasion, 'en quinze jours', a fortnight, which Paul later learnt was the First Communion, roughly equivalent to confirmation in the Anglican church. But in France the children were younger.
Another morning they visited one of the three farms on the Koenitz estate. Paul didn't understand the administrative details, but it was obvious that M. Koenitz was an absentee landlord.
The farm buildings of the third farm were between the village and the river bridge. The place was less tidy than the Salvetti farm.
The father was a grim, austere man. Whenever Paul saw him, he was clad in a boiler suit. Though he and his wife were

again Italian, they had none of the Italian cheerfulness, nor seemingly any outward love for children. There were no biscuits and drink for Regis and Nano, nor even liqueur for Paul and Madame.

They had one teenage daughter called Julie, a sultry girl, who hardly smiled while they were in the house. But she came with the children to the bridge, and joyously joined in with them, throwing sticks in the river, which had calmed down somewhat. It made the suspense more exciting waiting to see which stick came through first. She also gladly helped Paul to lift the children to see over the parapet.

She intrigued Paul because she had large, tremulous breasts with no containing support. They wobbled delightfully when she ran. Paul also noticed, like most French women, she did not shave under the armpits.

The game exhausted, she went with them back to La Refaudio, where Madame gave them all biscuits and drink, though no strong liqueur!

The day of the First Communion arrived. During the fortnight that led up to it, there were several changes for Paul. His French improved remarkably and quickly. All his school French came flooding back. He had learnt French as a dead language, like Latin. Because of his hearing loss, he had failed to learn it as a living language. But now he could, and did! He had learnt the irregular verbs by rote, but now they had a living application. He improved so much, he began to have useful but hesitant conversations with Madame. She in turn began to unfreeze, particularly as he proved his worth in dealing with her sons. Francois improved in behaviour, though there still arose moments when Paul had to drag him yelling up to the bedroom. To Paul, François was still a little eight year-old boy, 'un petit enfant,' not exactly spoilt but unhinged, difficult. Paul thought he had some of the madness of his father.

The weather improved. The days became hot and dry and beautiful. It wasn't only the days that became beautiful. Madame blossomed! She not only had physical beauty, but dress sense and poise. Paul had often heard of the loveliness of

Parisian women, but he had never encountered the reality. They were said to be far superior to English women, particularly in dress sense. Paul rather doubted their superiority. He felt English women had a certain homeliness and decency that far surpassed anything French.

But Madame was really something. She not only had natural beauty and poise, but a richness of talent and intelligence. Her piano playing, which she tried to practise each evening after the children had gone to bed, was far superior to his mother's. He didn't mean to belittle his mother, but she at times lacked confidence. This musical uncertainty did not apply to Madame.

M. Koenitz came back the day before Jean-Pierre's First Communion. In a strange way he affected the whole atmosphere. The children seemed to become inhibited as if they were uncertain how he expected them to behave. Given M. Koenitz's uncertain behaviour of character, this was understandable.

He seemed uncommonly fond of Jean-Pierre, but as he was the central character on Sunday, this was to be expected. However, Francois seemed to be seething at this favour. Paul took him aside and tried to talk to him kindly. He wasn't noticeably successful, but for some reason Francois seemed to keep a lid on his temper, which was gratifying. The visitors helped. Most of them brought presents for all five children.

Sunday morning Madame took charge of Jean-Pierre, and put him into a dark suit, white shirt and dark bow tie. Madame found it difficult to tie the bow tie. Paul stepped in. With his experience of Oxford formal dress, it was a problem soon solved.

When they got to the church, Paul found the girls were all in white dresses, in contrast to the boys in dark suits. Jean-Pierre's suit was much too tight. It fitted him badly. It made the boy look stodgy and awkward and very self-conscious. Paul felt sorry for him. He was understandably the most sensible of the Koenitz boys. But, because of the occasion, Jean-Pierre was more than usually quiet and withdrawn.

The service itself was tedious and maybe too long for children as young as ten. The presiding bishop's talk, if it was a bishop, seemed directed at one stage to the adults, at another to the children.

The surprising thing to Paul was the separation of the sexes, women and girls to the left, men and boys to the right. He had never come across this arrangement before. It meant Paul had to sit with M. Koenitz and the boys, while Madame and Anne-Marie graced the other side. M. Koenitz was restless and inattentive. The service didn't seem to mean much to him. It was only his interest and pride in his eldest son that kept him attentive.

After the service, there was a feeling of excitement and relief, especially among the children. At La Refaudio, trestle tables were put out, covered with white cloths (not paper) and eventually with a whole range of food, chicken, ham, salads and inevitably wine. But not the rough red wine – a nicer, sweeter white wine, whose name began with the letter 'M', but Paul could never cotton on to the name.

The relatives, even friends, were mostly M. Koenitz's, and Paul was not impressed. The Koenitz family were northern industrialists, or so Madame explained. 'Industrial' in English was much the same word in French, except for a slight spelling difference, and, of course, the change of accent.

It was curious that none of Madame's family and friends came. There was either a rift, or they didn't much like M. Koenitz.

The northern industrialists ignored Paul. Either they didn't like the English, or Paul, in their eyes, was a mere menial. He rather resented their attitude, but there was nothing he could do, except remain in the background. But he felt further resentment because their regard for Madame, the hostess, left much to be desired by way of courtesy. He couldn't imagine why this was; there must have been some upset in the past. What was apparent, Madame seemed to dislike them in her turn.

"They're filthy rich," said Madame using a word for filthy which Paul had not heard before. He had, even more strongly, the feeling she did not care much for her husband's family. He could only think they blamed her for her husband's disloyal behaviour.

Certainly they may have been justified in thinking Paul a mere 'menial'. Paul did what he could, but most of the work in setting out and serving the refreshments was done by the Salvettis (husband (braces hidden) the wife, the twins in their attractive skirts, the brother, an even better-dressed Simone. All worked hard, adding a certain cheerfulness to proceedings. They even produced a smile from the normally reticent Jean-Pierre.

One of the Koenitz men, a larger version of husband Koenitz, came up to Paul and said in English, Paul felt rather rudely:

"When go you back to England?" he asked.

"I don't know," Paul replied. "It depends on Madame."

The man grunted and then walked away, leaving Paul feeling he shouldn't be there.

When they left, M. Koenitz also made to go, but his wife spoke a few angry words to him. As far as Paul could make out, it was about the car – among other things. Paul knew the car was a bone of contention. If M. Koenitz took the car, it left Madame stranded in a remote village several kilometres from Montauban. She relied on the ever-generous M. Salvetti for transport when necessary. In true Italian love for an attractive woman, M. Salvetti was happy to oblige. But Madame felt hesitant about taking advantage of his kindly nature.

Paul never knew how she managed to change the mind of her selfish husband. But she did!

The next day she went to the station with M. Salvetti and collected the car from the station forecourt. The car had been left there overnight by M. Koenitz.

But the whole episode seemed to upset Madame. For the whole week she was quiet, did not play the piano or sing. She found consolation in her two youngest children, and would spend much time with them.

Paul found himself almost redundant until the three eldest boys came back from school, tired, moody, hungry, demanding. It was then, as the evenings lengthened into June, he began to teach them English games, the sort he enjoyed as a boy. The most enjoyable was 'kick the can'. There was a part of the plateau to the left of the house where there were trees and shrubs. It was ideal for 'hide and seek', 'kick the can', and a game with tennis balls that Madame supplied. Sometimes in the evening after dinner they stayed indoors; they played 'old maid', 'rummy', 'racing patience', and 'Newmarket' which they preferred. All these games Paul taught them in hesitant French. They were delighted in using French coins for Newmarket. Because France was suffering inflation, constant changes of Government, one thousand francs were equal to one pound Sterling. There were plenty of valueless coins available.

Madame, despite her depression, was glad of the more controlled activity of the children. Sometimes Anne-Marie joined in. There were constant attempts to make her 'la vieille' (the old maid).

But it was difficult at times. Nano was obviously too young. He and Paul made one joint player, sitting on Paul's lap. Jean-Pierre often wouldn't play, preferring to read a book in his little room in the cave.

François was often disruptive. The best two players were Marc and surprisingly, Régis. The latter was quick and intelligent, like his mother, and proved no slouch.

On the whole there was no culture of playing games such as in England. Frequently Paul had to give up the game, particularly when François had a tantrum. But they always seemed to want to come back to a game the following evening.

The next weekend M. Koenitz came back, rather surprisingly, because nobody seemed to expect him, not least Madame.

As with François his very presence seemed to create a tense atmosphere. Madame withdrew into herself. Paul wondered how a man could so openly leave the arms of his mistress and expect a welcome from his wife. Paul felt, if he had been a woman, he would have been disgusted, nay furious. But Madame seemed just to withdraw into herself. Of the children, only Jean-Pierre seemed remotely pleased to see him. It was obvious he was the apple of his father's eye. This made François even more disruptive. It created a quandary for Paul; he didn't want to discipline the boy in front of the father. It was his job, not Paul's. Yet François' behaviour seemed worse than ever. Madame at dinner retired with a 'mal à la tête'.

M. Koenitz did nothing, just grinning as if nothing was wrong. Eventually Paul lost patience. François deliberately knocked over a jug of water. When Anne-Marie came to clear up the mess, he deliberately got in her way, pulled her apron strings, and threw her mopping-up sponge at Jean-Pierre. Paul got up, seized François by the arm and led him out, not noticing the baleful look M. Koenitz gave him. François really kicked and screamed, and it was some time before Paul quietened down. This time no Anne-Marie came to help Paul. It was as if the whole household was afraid to move when M. Koenitz was home.

In the end Paul managed to persuade François to go down to the kitchen to finish his supper. There Anne-Marie received them quite happily and François settled down. Paul also stayed to eat his supper. He couldn't face the dining-room without Madame, away with her headache.

Later in the evening, after the children had gone to bed, M. Koenitz spoke to Paul.

"I believe children should do as they like – comme ils veulent. No adult should restrain them," M. Koenitz explained.

Paul stood astonished. All his life he had been corrected when he did wrong, both at school and at home.

He wanted to say that children, like dogs, should be trained, but he couldn't say it in French convincingly. The matter was left, but Paul felt that M. Koenitz must have had an unhappy childhood.

Paul went to bed, considerably disturbed. His sympathy lay whole-heartedly with Madame. She was an intelligent, lovely woman and had given her husband five healthy boys. Such loyalty, loveliness, and intelligence deserved a greater loyalty from the husband. Madame was a woman any man would be proud to marry. Paul had gathered having a mistress was a part of French culture, but it hardly seemed to be fair on the wife. But Paul's concern was more with the sanity of M. Koenitz. That a man should wish both wife and mistress to live together seemed an impossible situation. It was not Madame's fault she had only boys.

Paul understood, rightly or wrongly, that the sex of a child lay with the father's genes. Then the way M.Koenitz neglected his estate, left his wife with no car, and seemingly little money, it was all a mystery to Paul's staid, Protestant mind.

But further shock was to come, which left Paul gasping. No wonder in the War the French were regarded as unreliable.

# Chapter 10

*The Unfortunate Surprise*

Sunday dawned bright and clear. M. Koenitz wanted a picnic for five people. They were going to a motor-bike rally. The trouble was only three boys could go. The car seated five. The other two were M. Koenitz – of course – and Paul. Of the three boys M. Koenitz wanted Jean-Pierre, Marc and Régis. Immediately there were reactions from François.

"Why not me?" yelled an aggrieved little boy.

"Because you cannot behave when we go out," stated M. Koenitz. There was obviously some incident in the past. In a way M. Koenitz was asserting a discipline in which he did not believe.

'Gosh!' thought Paul, 'the man does punish, but subtly!'

Madame entered the fray.

"François must go," she said. "Régis is too young."

This prompted a protest from Régis.

The argument waged to and fro. Paul even offered to give up his place, but M. Koenitz said "No".

Eventually they set off with what seemed the most sensible solution – the three eldest to the rally, the two little ones with Madame. She placated her charges by saying she would take them out in the car but during the week. And then she added rather pointedly, 'if she had the car.' M. Koenitz chose to ignore that remark.

The rally itself Paul felt rather tedious. He had never been particularly interested in motor-bikes. His love was for most team games with a ball, like cricket.

They sat on a knoll enjoying the sun. The motor-bikes went off on a given circuit, splaying mud and grass everywhere. With much snarling of vicious little motors, they would disappear over the brow of a hill, and then come racing back about ten to fifteen minutes later. They would race by to the cheers of the spectators, and then disappear again over the same brow, leaving tracks in the field from the cut up grass. The circuit was repeated five times. The amusement was a lone cyclist, who would appear gingerly, well behind the rest, and pretend to accelerate in front of the spectators. They cheered and jeered, and he waved a hesitant arm, creating a wobble. He nearly came off (much laughing!). After the fifth circuit, hot and tired, they stopped for lunch.

Picnic lunch, as always in France, was lengthy and protracted, at least by English standards. It was a good two hours before the race started again. During the lull, the French drank wine, ate and chatted, and tinkered with their motor-bikes. One rider seemed to be a woman, but Paul couldn't be sure. She (or he) wore a waistcoat under her jacket, much reinforced by stays and immensely tight.

Paul waited for her to take it off, but she didn't. Her breasts, if she had any, must have been squashed tight under that rigid waistcoat. Was it to protect her spine in an accident?

Paul noticed M. Koenitz also looking at the problematic, waist-coated girl. Paul realised that he was in fact rather a dirty, middle-aged man. But then wasn't he, Paul, the same, though not middle-aged?

When they had eaten, they went for a walk, all five of them. The countryside was beautiful, too beautiful to be spoilt by noisy motor-bikes. The ground was really churned up along the route the race had covered.

Paul wondered for a moment about Madame. Funny he only called her 'Madame', but she still was a very remote figure, obviously suffering. She hadn't sung or played the piano for a few days, preferring usually in the evenings to play with Régis and Nano, who were both kind and affectionate little boys.

Their older brothers had lost much of that affectionate nature. Paul wished he could do more to bring a smile to that attractive, sad face of Madame. It seemed that she was alone.

She often talked of her family who lived in Paris, but never came to visit.

During the subsequent biking there was little of interest, until a man fell off. It was quite a dramatic fall. A gasp emanated from the crowd. It wasn't a large crowd, but it could make enough noise. The bike skidded as it tried to move left. But the rear wheel went uncontrollably askew. The bike lost balance and went down. Both man and bike went into a spin before coming to a halt. The bikes behind managed to avoid him. The rider lay still. Men rushed forward to help. Soon the injured man stirred but was in obvious pain. A stretcher was brought from a lorry which was acting as a medical centre, with a red cross painted on its side. An announcer said the rider was all right, perhaps a possible fracture to the leg. He was being taken to the hospital.

After that bit of ghoulish interest, the riders did one more circuit. The winner was duly announced, and then the sparse crowd began to wend its way home.

The surprise came at the car. Jean-Pierre took the driver's seat, which was pushed forward as far as possible to allow his young legs to reach the pedals. They had obviously done this before. Maybe it was why M. Koenitz was reluctant to take François, who sat at the back, jealousy written all over his pinched face, looking as if he would speak out angrily at any moment. Paul had guessed right; he was jealous of the attention his elder brother received – justifiably so, Paul began to feel.

Jean-Pierre drove at a snail's pace, his father at this side giving quiet instruction. Paul couldn't tell whether the boy was nervous or not. Paul wondered what the French law was in regard to the age of drivers. Paul knew in England it would not be tolerated – a ten year-old boy driving a car, a machine that could kill. Ye Gods, it didn't bear thinking about – a child driving a car that even adults had difficulty in controlling!

They got home all right, though Paul sitting at the back with François and Marc was relieved. More and more Paul was convinced M. Koenitz was mad. Paul's mother would have said he had 'a screw loose.' Or were other French children driving cars?

But worse was to come.

When they arrived at the house, Madame came out. She saw Jean-Pierre at the wheel and was furious. It led to further argument, quiet-voiced by Madame, loud-voiced by M. Koenitz. Paul took the boys upstairs to shelter them from the dispute. But they could still hear a male raised voice. Inevitably M. Koenitz saw fit to slam out of the house, and Madame dissolved into tears. They didn't see her at supper, Anne-Marie providing the service the children needed.

Finally, after what seemed a bizarre and upsetting day, Paul could settle in the sitting-room and write to his sister. The events at La Refaudio made him think about his own home and mother. It couldn't have been easy for her, to lose a husband, a soldier killed in war, to have to bring up two children with very little financial support. With Madame it was far worse. She had five children and a disloyal, crazy and unsupportive husband.

Madame came quietly into the sitting-room, later in the evening. She had changed, no longer the elegant lady, but now a rather tired and sad hausfrau. She wore an apron, the sort that is like a coat and buttons down the front. She bore a basket which turned out to be a work basket, and a small pile of children's clothing which needed mending. No music tonight again, Paul thought, disappointed. No word was passed between Madame and Paul.

Her sadness was such that he had a sudden desire to comfort her, but didn't know how. The silence of the evening seemed interminable. Paul had one great asset now, possibly two. He was learning French so fast that, after a relatively short time, he found he could more readily understand, and more easily express himself. Moreover, his hearing had improved. The doctor had always said a warm, dry climate would do him good, and it was certainly the case now the rainy spell had passed. But the improvement in his hearing was a bit of a misnomer. The French, if they felt he did not understand, tended to raise their voices, or shout. That helped Paul. His lack of hearing was mistaken for lack of understanding.

He found he could do without his hearing aid, which was always an encumbrance. It was a relief to feel normal again.

Madame had a good clear voice – always an asset with a singer – and she had good, clear diction. It meant they could have conversations without too much difficulty. A dictionary came in useful. To express it in this book one can only write in English and leave out the tortuous struggle for understanding.

Finally Paul plucked up courage. He couldn't bear her unhappy face. He felt she was nervous and close to tears, hiding her misery in feverish work on the clothing on her lap.

"Madame, I am very, very sorry," he said in French, meaning every word.

She looked puzzled and began to withdraw into herself.

"Why?" she finally asked.

"I know about your husband," he said softly.

Madame looked at him almost coldly. She seemed to resent any interference in her private life, especially by a stranger who was not even French.

"What do you know?" she asked icily, not even raising her head from her sewing.

"That your husband has a mistress in Paris, and a baby daughter by her," explained Paul quietly. "I regret very much the sad situation for you. I don't know why, but he told me everything on my arrival in Montauban. He seemed very proud of himself as if it was a normal situation in France."

Madame seemed annoyed as if the situation was private between herself and her husband.

"I not talk about it," she said coldly, almost as if she wanted to say it's none of his business.

"But you are so unhappy. Is there nothing you can do? Or can I help?" Paul said.

There were two things that amazed him. One was that he had never come across such a situation in England; he felt he was floundering in unknown territory.

The other matter that made things worse was his difficulty in expressing himself in French. Yet he was pleased at the progress he had made. Not only was the French he had learnt at school coming back, but he was now reading French books with the help of his dictionary. He was also conversing every day in French with the children, or with adults like Anne-Marie and Madame.

But Madame concentrated on her mending, ignoring Paul, almost as if the subject was closed.

Paul felt himself excluded, as if he had been impertinent in raising such a subject. He was only an employee in the household. But Paul persisted, wisely or not, he did not know. He had a certain English reticence about personal matters, which didn't help. But things seemed to get worse when he saw Madame hastily brush away tears.

He changed the subject.

"I'm also very sorry," he said sadly, "that Jean-Pierre drove the car. I thought it a mad and dangerous situation, but I could do nothing to stop it. I thought you were upset when you saw what had happened."

But he had gone too far. Madame pursed her lips, quietly took up her sewing and left the room, saying nothing.

Paul cursed. His offer of sympathy had fallen flat. He sighed. He felt genuinely sorry for Madame, but there was nothing he could do. It was a situation that left him rather piggy-in-the-middle, and he couldn't see his employment lasting for long. He would have to go back to Paris. They would perhaps ask him to go. But he loved the children and his work with them, despite the difficulties Francois presented. It would break his heart to leave. For once in his short, handicapped life, he felt needed, even useful.

But Madame came back after half an hour, minus her overall, looking her more elegant self. She had washed her face. There were no sign of tears, except perhaps a certain redness about the eyes. He sprang up, relieved, tried to take her hand, which she withdrew. He mumbled his apologies awkwardly. But she cut him short.

"I too am sorry you are mixed up with a family problem," she said gently. "It is a pity for you, a problem you have probably not come across before."

But Paul shook his head. "No, Madame, it is a pity for you," he said emphatically, "not for me. This affects your whole life, not mine."

She in turn shook her head, and said,

"No, Paul, I am only sorry you are here, while my husband and I quarrel so badly. But there is nothing I can do. It's so hopeless ... so hopeless!"

Her voice trailed away.

"Can you not divorce him?" asked Paul.

At present, in England, the divorce rate was low. But Paul knew it existed.

"Never!" said Madame, almost vehemently, and then repeated it. "Never!"

"But why?" protested Paul.

"I am Catholic. Marriage is a sacrament; it is for life, for better or for worse," explained Madame. "The Catholic Church does not recognise divorce."

Paul didn't agree; nor could he believe such a situation could arise. But he couldn't help admiring such fortitude in Madame. But what could he do? There was nothing! She was trapped in a situation that seemed unsupportable, by her unbending faith.

Madame got up.

"I play for you at the piano," she said. "It soothes me."

And there the matter closed. But Paul went to bed later, very upset! He didn't like the situation where Madame was so disturbed. He thought her husband was mad to treat her so badly. She was a beautiful, intelligent woman. How could anyone want to leave her!

It made Paul feel more angry than he had felt for a long time!

# Chapter 11

*Warm Evenings*

Warm, peaceful evenings ensued after M. Koenitz' abrupt departure; they lasted through June, July, and into August. It meant the loss of piano playing and singing, but in a strange way they were quite delightful. For Paul, they were heaven, never to be repeated, never to be forgotten. In England such evenings did not exist, especially during the War. Nor was there such wonderful weather.

The day after her husband's departure, Madame said,

"We sit on the balcony."

She brought out two deck chairs, lined them with rugs, and placed them on the balcony in front of the main entrance door. This was really the top of the stone steps which led up to the first floor. There was just room enough for two deck chairs.

They could see the whole valley over the palisade, and the view of the river Aveyron itself. To the left were the distant village and church. It all looked so peaceful and calm in the evening light.

But the later hours were so enchanting; it was never completely dark. There was always light in the sky. It was rarely a cloudy evening, unless a thunderstorm was brewing. The evenings were rarely silent. The noise of crickets, the conversation of the Salvettis below, the occasional barking of a dog, all combined to produce a magic that was almost heavenly. In that magic Paul and Madame sat, and talked always in French, however difficult it was for Paul.

"Why you come to France?" asked Madame one pleasant evening.

So, not for the first time, Paul told her his reasons.

"You want to write, why, it's so magnificent!" she exclaimed. "That is what you do in the evenings?"

Paul nodded.

"That and letter writing, and my diary," He explained.

"Your diary?" she exclaimed. "I write a diary, but mine is always very morbid, very sad. The world will never see it. It is for me only."

For a moment they were quiet, drinking in the loveliness of the night.

"There's one pity about this pleasant evening sitting outside!" remarked Paul, thoughtfully.

"What?" asked Madame, lying back dreamily.

"You won't be playing and singing," he explained. "I loved your musical soirees in the sitting-room. They've stopped now while we enjoy these lovely evenings."

"Oh!" said Madame, "Well, if you are a good boy and behave yourself, I might just give a little tinkle on the piano before we go to bed."

She smiled at him mischievously.

"That'd be marvellous," he exclaimed sincerely.

Madame suddenly sat up.

"There's one thing I forgot which might make all this perfect," she said smiling.

"What?" asked Paul, puzzled.

"A glass of wine," she said. There's a nice bottle left over from the supper this evening. It's in the kitchen."

Paul rose to fetch it. It sounded a marvellous idea. But she forestalled him. She bustled off to get it, plus two glasses.

"This is heavenly," exclaimed Paul when the wine arrived. "You'd never get an evening like this in England."

"Mmm," uttered Madame languidly, seeming to agree.

Again silence.

"What brought this on, this love of music, the performing?" asked Paul, genuinely interested.

So Madame told him. As usual it had all begun at school, where she had shown much talent in singing. Also, over the years, she had taken piano lessons. Then at eighteen, she had been accepted by the Paris School of Opera.

"Did you enjoy your time at school, and then Paris?" asked Paul, genuinely interested. He had never before met any woman as talented as Madame, and with a career based on her singing.

"Oh, it was wonderful!" she exclaimed, "Some of the happiest years of my life."

Madame's eyes lit up at the memory, though in the gathering darkness it was difficult to see her clearly.

"What happened afterwards?" Paul asked.

Madame hesitated, as if reluctant to talk further. Paul didn't press her. He was hesitant to intrude on the personal life. He didn't know how far he could go with a woman so much older than himself. Finally Madame said,

"My husband, Jacques, came into my life."

"He bowled you over," Paul joked, trying to put into French a cricketing term.

"I don't understand," admitted Madame.

Paul tried to explain, but cricketing vocabulary was beyond his recently acquired French capacity.

"You fell in love with your husband," he finally concluded.

"Ye-e-s," said Madame slowly.

She thought a moment.

"I do not like to talk about my husband," she said, hesitantly. "We married when I was just twenty-three; they were very happy days. His parents bought us this estate. We built this house. Things went very well at first, but then gradually it all changed. Now I know not what to do, and I find life somewhat miserable."

Madame sighed. What Paul could see of her face, it was tinged with unhappiness. But she gave a shake of her shoulders, and repeated an earlier remark.

"But I wish not to talk about my husband. It is disloyal for a wife."

Paul marvelled at this woman. It was a new situation for him to be in, so close to a family that was rapidly disintegrating. His own Mum and Dad had disagreed, and Mum expressed disappointment over some things. But they remained together. It was never a question of break-up. They were happy together in reality.

"Oh, it's such a beautiful evening!" Madame continued. "Let us talk about something else. What about you, Paul? Have you had a girl you love? What about your mother? How does she manage, alone in the world?"

So Paul had to digress to his own life and family. He'd much rather talk about Madame. Paul told her he had never really had a girl-friend. Except for his sister he had little experience of women.

He tried to explain about his hearing, and consequently his loss of confidence with women.

"I don't believe you," she teased. "You, a good-looking young man – no girl! It's truly incredible – unbelievable!"

"Well, whether you believe me or not, it's a fact!" emphasised Paul. He'd always had difficulty explaining himself, except perhaps to his sister. The problem was even worse in French!

He was pleased to see Madame had suddenly turned to teasing mode. It made the evening seem much better, much more pleasant, in accord with the beauty of the evening.

Suddenly Madame became serious again.

"Paul, we – no I – have a problem. We are to have a visit from one of the Koenitz family," she explained.

"Why is that a problem?" he asked.

She tried to explain hesitantly.

"I wrote to them telling them of the difficulty I was having with Jacques, how he was absent most of the time. How he was not fulfilling his duty both to the estate and to the family, and how he rarely gave me money, or not enough."

"But why is the visit a problem?" ventured Paul. "Surely if somebody is coming down, they want to help."

"Yes, but it is a young priest; he is too unworldly to understand," she explained. She then added a little helplessly. "I say things are wrong, but they don't seem to believe me."

"Oh?" said Paul, not really understanding. He was so young, Madame couldn't help thinking, like the young priest coming. Her world seemed to close around her. She was alone, nobody to help! It made her feel very depressed, which she fought against.

Paul felt that he too was young, and yet he understood.

"Wait till you see the priest," explained Madame mysteriously. She was obviously very uncertain about his coming.

And with that Paul had really nothing further to say. But he felt it was a strange situation. Could the Koenitz family not send a better representative? After all the blame lay on their side.

Madame got up.

"I play you some music," she said. "In return you tell me tomorrow about your writing. I am interested. Have you something I can read? But no, it will be in English. I know some German and Italian, but not English."

Paul went to bed that night, both pleased and perturbed. He was pleased because at last he had established some relationship with Madame. She was no longer the ice maiden, cool and aloof. She had shown a very human side to her personality.

Distressed, yes - understandably so, but she was fun as well when she teased him, and showed she could laugh too. Then there had been the marvellous evening about them, warm, beautiful, soothing. It had been such a balm, something which he realised for the umpteenth time he had never experienced in England. And then to find he could actually converse with Madame, that his French and his hearing were good enough? Admittedly their conversation was not fluent, interrupted by explanations, references to the dictionary, and some hand signs. But their communication could only improve and get better as the days went by. The prospect to Paul seemed wonderful.

Paul sighed and soon fell asleep, his last waking thought that there was a niche for him to fill here. There was no fear of returning suddenly to England, or so it seemed!

But there was the priest coming! Paul had no experience of Catholic priests. They seemed an unknown quantity in England.

When the priest arrived two days later, he completely ignored Paul, almost as if Paul wasn't, or shouldn't be there. Paul felt like crying out,

"I'm here. I exist! I'm here! I'm a human being like you!"

But Paul didn't dare. There was not even the traditional French shaking of hands. Paul wondered if M. Koenitz had said something against him. But surely not? He was the man who had introduced him into the family. It was all very baffling.

The priest was undoubtedly young. Paul had heard it took several years to train a priest. The strange thing was that the priest ignored Madame almost as much as he ignored Paul. He spent all the time available with the children, which for Paul was a relief. But he felt a twinge of jealousy. They enjoyed spending most of their time with their young uncle. He spoilt them naturally, and seemed to have money to indulge them. They went on several trips to Montauban in his car.

Paul reckoned the priest must be about 27. Like Paul the priest re-lived his boyhood with the children, playing the games he had enjoyed as a boy. He also, like Paul, withdrew François when he had a tantrum, and spoke with him at some length. He had a better influence over the boy than Paul.

Paul wondered why the wretched man had come. It was certainly not to give Madame support and help, just to spy out the land, Paul supposed, but was not convinced. There was an indifference to Madame that made Paul wonder what M. Koenitz had said to his family. He lacked the loyalty of his wife!

"Why has he come?" Paul whispered to Madame.

She shrugged her shoulders and whispered back,

"I do not trust the Koenitz family," was all she had to say. Paul felt there must have been some incident in the past to hurt Madame. Perhaps they had wished for a better wife for their son than an opera singer in the chorus, however beautiful and talented.

The priest had unknowingly cemented the relationship between Paul and Madame, though it was something he never realised. In the evenings he would go to his room, presumably to pray and do his offices. It meant Madame and Paul could continue their chats on the balcony, and could commune with nightly nature. Paul told the story of his one Commemorative Ball, if only to illustrate his shyness and difficulty with women. He also explained one of his short stories, one about a young man who was not a soldier. It was one of Paul's favourites.

"What is a Commemorative Ball?" asked Madame.

"It is a dance all night, from 10 in the evening until 6 in the morning," Paul explained. "Then we go punting on the river and have a picnic breakfast with champagne or wine. It was in theory a fabulous occasion, but much depended on the girl you took. I was unlucky, but it was probably my fault."

"What is punting?" asked Madame, because Paul could not find the French for 'punting' in his dictionary.

"It is like boating in Venice, with a long pole," Paul explained. "I loved it. You didn't have to talk while punting, and your lady friend just lay languorously on the cushions in the punt."

"Oh," said Madame, "and you managed to dance eight hours?"

"Well, no," Paul said. "We had supper. There was entertainment, and fireworks, and several places to sit out."

"Sounds wonderful," said Madame. "I love dancing. And what happened to the girl, your partner?"

"Oh, I never saw her again," Paul admitted. "She was a blind date, not a very happy one. But it was probably my fault," he repeated.

"Eh! Blind date? What is that?" she asked.

Paul laughed.

"It's when you take out a girl without knowing anything about her, a stranger if you like," he explained. "Though I did see her in lectures. We were both studying history. She attracted me because she was very lovely. But sadly I don't think she thought much of me wearing a clumsy deaf aid."

"My, why a stranger?" asked Madame, in a teasing tone. "Did you not know any girls?"

"No," admitted Paul, shyly.

"Oh, you poor thing!" Madame continued to tease. "But you enjoy dancing. That's surely a way to get to know girls?"

"Immensely!" said Paul in reference to the enjoyment of dancing. "But I'm not sure it helps with getting to know girls. I never knew what to say to them, and I couldn't hear what they said because of the noise of the music."

"I too like dancing," said Madame with a smile. "Perhaps one day we will have the chance to dance. You like that, n'est-ce pas?"

"But not while we have the priest here," pointed out Paul. "I can't see him approving."

"Oh, don't worry about him," said Madame with a trace of dislike. "He goes the day after tomorrow."

"Thank goodness for that," said Paul, breathing a slight sigh of relief. "Has he done anything to help you?"

"Well, yes and no," said Madame. "He's mostly been a communicator for the Koenitz family. They have arranged for the children and me never to be short of money. They are also putting pressure on my husband to come back. They have stopped any financial support he may have from them, until we are back to normal, which is a step in the right direction. But I can't see how he will revise the situation with the mistress and the baby daughter. I'd love to have the baby here but not the mistress."

Madame sighed sorrowfully.

"Good for them!" said Paul, thinking of the Koenitz family support.

"Well, yes," agreed Madame. "But it's all about money, not a word of sympathy or comfort. It makes me feel their minds run only on money, never on the kind practicalities of life. It makes me feel they don't like me very much. Even our young friend, the priest, has never said he would pray for me."

Paul nodded in understanding. The more he saw of the visiting priest the more convinced he was like a man with a screw loose somewhere. He didn't know what it was, but the man's obsessive pre-occupation with the children seemed to go beyond the normal love of an uncle. Paul shook his head; he was no psychologist. Perhaps too there was the same mental failing in the priest as in the husband.

One bombshell Madame did introduce. It appeared the priest wanted Paul out of the house. When asked why, he wouldn't say.

"And do you?" Paul asked.

"Eh?" Madame looked puzzled.

"Want me out of the house?" explained Paul with a touch of anxiety.

"Never!" Madame said with emphasis.

Paul was relieved.

He went to bed that night quite happy, but sad for Madame. She seemed committed to life on her own, no support from her husband, and with the care of five children to boot. Boys like François weren't easy! The others were just boys, one or two, like Régis, full of comforting childish love.

# Chapter 12

*Oh, For a Dance!*

Mysteriously the car came back two days after the priest left. A message came through. It was at the station.

"It wasn't my husband telephoning," explained Madame. "It was some woman; I hate to think it was 'she'!"

Paul laughed.

"Probably," Paul agreed. "But at least we have the car back. How on earth did you manage?"

"Oh, it was our friend, the priest," said Madame smiling. "I happened to mention the difficulties we had without it."

"So he did some good!" Paul ventured to say.

Madame nodded and smiled.

"I have a surprise for you," she said, looking mysterious.

"Oh what is it?" asked Paul. "I like surprises."

But Madame went all mysterious and feminine again.

"It's a surprise," she maintained. "All will be revealed at the weekend."

So Paul had to be satisfied – at least for the moment. He marvelled quietly to himself at the new relationship he had with Madame, since the priest had come and gone. It was a relationship difficult to describe, but they were talking as friends, even as equals despite their difference in age. He felt relieved that things had improved so happily. It gave him confidence he would be able to stay at La Refaudio, that lovely refuge!

When Saturday came, there was the usual argument of the five boys, which two to leave behind. But when Régis and Nano heard the alternative was spending a day with the Salvettis, they jumped at the chance. There was no further argument!

They set out with the usual picnic, a baguette, ham, cheese and dark chocolate. It never varied. The children had grenadine, and there was a bottle of white wine for Madame and Paul.

"There is a cafe where we go," explained Madame. "We will be able to have coffee."

Much excitement among the children; they knew where they were going. But Madame had asked them not to tell Paul. They loved the secrecy.

Madame called it a "plage", a beach. Paul was puzzled by this. In England a beach would be by the sea. But to get to a beach (sea) from Montauban would be quite an impossibly long drive, impossible there and back in one day.

It took over one hour to arrive at their destination.

"There it is, the beach," proclaimed Madame. Paul looked around. There was an area of land that led down to a languidly flowing river. The river was on a bend, but one could not see around the bend; there were masking trees. About fifty yards ahead, on raised ground, was the cafe Madame had mentioned. In the centre of the area was a platform, rather like a boxing ring, but bigger.

"There is your wish," said Madame, indicating the so-called boxing ring, or platform. But nobody was on it.

"What's it for?" asked Paul, still not understanding.

"Something you said you enjoyed," Madame said, with a teasing look on her face.

Paul could not make out what the platform was there for.

"It's for dancing," explained Madame, "and I am going to have the first dance with you. But perhaps we will wait until others are dancing."

"Oh!" said Paul, still a little confused. But light was slowly coming, as he remembered relating the dancing at Oxford. He also saw a large speaker, fixed to a tall pole, which may explain where the music could come from.

"But there's nobody dancing," he pointed out.

"It's early yet," Madame said with a smile. "Wait and see."

With that Paul had to be content. But he was excited by the thought of dancing. Except at the Oxford Commemorative Ball, he had never come across the idea of open air dancing during the day, and on a so-called beach by a river.

The river, in its curve, left behind a sandy, muddy area on which children played. It might conceivably be called a beach, but it had none of the golden quality of sand on a sea beach. People, mostly women, were sunbathing in deck chairs or on rugs, in various stages of attire. The boys stripping off into costumes or shorts went whooping down to the beach. Madame took two deck chairs out of the car, the same deck chairs they used on the balcony. Madame didn't divest like many of the sunbathers. She wore a cream coloured summer skirt, no stockings, and a patterned, coloured, pretty blouse. She did have a cardigan when driving, but that was left in the car.

Her legs were shapely as she lifted the skirt above her knees to catch the sun. She was as beautiful as was the day. Poor Paul was so attracted by her! He was wearing just shorts and a short sleeved summer shirt which he kept loose, not confined by a belt, flapping in what little breeze there was. He was concerned at how hot the weather was getting. He had never experienced anything like it, and had not brought enough summer clothes, to his chagrin.

Madame closed her eyes in repose. She looked so relaxed, and even more lovely than at La Refaudio. She needed a day's break in a pleasant setting, after all the traumas her husband had caused. It was the first time Paul had seen her really relaxed.

Paul got up and wandered down to the beach to see if the boys were all right. But they were happy. They had teamed up with two other boys and were playing kick-about football. Paul felt an urge to join them. But he changed his mind. They were so young and seemed happy without him.

"You wish to play?" Marc asked; he was always the most considerate of the five boys.

But Paul shook his head and smiled. He paddled for the moment in the water, and then went back to Madame. She was still sleeping. He felt disinclined to disturb her. He was pleased she was resting.

He took out a book in French, the short stories of Maupassant, which he had read in English at Oxford. The French was becoming easier to understand, the longer he spent in France. He was delighted with his progress.

The boys came back after a while. They were getting hungry. They woke their mother and began to whine for food, at least François did. Madame began to dish out the picnic. She went to fetch drinks for the boys, while Paul opened the bottle of wine. As she came back, dance music started on the speaker, not blaringly loud, but soothingly quiet.

Then began for Paul what was a stupendous and unforgettable day. The wine, the sun, and a rested, lovely Madame, all contributed, Madame especially. He had tried to work out how old she was. He knew now that she had married at 23. Given the age of the children, she must now be about mid-thirties, with the bonuses of being lovely, musically talented, and intelligent. Her beauty was more than skin deep. She had preserved well. It was as if child-bearing and life had enhanced her into a mature and lovely woman. Paul could not get over the fact that she stuck to an unreliable and unfaithful husband. There was goodness there and real loyalty, not just show!

When they finished lunch, Madame packed away the remains of the picnic, and then announced,

"Come, Paul, we dance." She almost commanded him!

She took his hand and led him to the platform. There were already two couples dancing, one woman in a bathing costume, her partner in shorts and bare-chested.

Paul felt embarrassed. Such an exhibition of naked sexuality frightened him. At the Oxford Commemorative Ball, the women wore long dresses and the men were in dinner jackets, some with cummerbunds. Even at the dancing classes he had attended, everyone was properly dressed. But here they were almost naked!

Madame moved onto the platform. She smiled invitingly at Paul as he followed, and began to sway to the music. Then she moved closely into his arms. Paul was surprised and concerned. He had never danced with anyone so close before, nor so attractive. Usually there had been a few inches between them. It was an agreeable sensation, but it worried him. She was after all his employer, married, much older, something like 14 years. It was a sensation of closeness he had not experienced before, and he didn't know what to do. What was worse, Madame was a far better dancer than he was, or could ever be.

Here was a lovely woman moving up against him in appreciation of the music. He was lost. Above all she had very thin summer clothing on. Paul was trapped. All he could do was to give himself up to the pleasure of the moment. And it was a real joy! One such as he had never experienced before. How could he describe this moment of holding a lovely woman for the first time when young? It was a sensation that would live in his memory for many years to come! Because of his shyness and faulty hearing, he was a comparative innocent.

Madame herself seemed not to notice his concern. The music seemed to hold her to the exclusion of everything else. Paul thought that it must have been as an opera singer that she had learned to dance. Certainly she followed the rhythm of the music better than he did.

After a few moments of dancing, and such exquisite moments they were, Madame slowly withdrew from Paul's arms, smiled quietly at him, and then indicated one side of the platform. There stood the three boys, grinning hugely all over their impish faces.

"Maman's dancing," cried the exuberant François. Paul thought they had gone down to the beach, but there they were, laughing away. They had probably never seen Maman dancing before. It was a new side to their mother's character.

Madame smiled at them.

"You are naughty boys," she said. "Now run along. You've had your fun. If you are good, I'll buy you a cake."

This was a reference to the fact that the cafe sold little, delectable, cream cakes. They ran off, laughing, to the plage. Madame took Paul's hand.

"Come on, let's dance. You have good rhythm," she said smiling.

Paul could not believe she was telling the truth about his so-called rhythm, but he didn't query it. He melted more willingly into her arms.

A still tentative Paul tried, this time, to attempt one or two little steps which he had learnt in dancing classes, and Madame responded. They began to move together even better than before. After a while, Madame spoke in a weary tone.

"Oof! I must rest. I'm too old." And she smiled at Paul and led him back to the deck chairs.

Once settled, she said to Paul.

"Thank you Paul. I enjoyed that. I've not danced for ages."

"I enjoyed that too," said Paul sincerely. "But didn't you dance with your husband?"

"No never," and Madame looked sad. "He never liked to dance. He thought it was for women, not men."

Paul reflected a moment.

"Why can't you divorce him?" he asked. "He's treated you very badly." He spoke somewhat tentatively. "You're a lovely woman. A man will surely want you. I'm sure you could soon find another man, and he will love you."

"Not with five children!" responded Madame immediately. "They'll be around for years to come. Nano is only two."

"But you don't love your husband," pointed out Paul. "Besides you have lovely children. Any man would be glad to take them on."

"I do love Jacques. I did," said Madame quietly, confirming her love for her husband. "He was great fun when we first met. Then when the children came he began to drift away, lose interest in me, and them, except perhaps for Jean-Pierre."

Madame reflected a moment.

"We've been over this before, Paul," she said. "The marriage vows I made are for always. I cannot break them. Besides there are times when I feel sorry for him. He's lost. He doesn't know what he is doing, either to himself or to others."

Madame was silent for a moment. Then suddenly she smiled.

"You know, Paul," she said, "There is a man in Montauban who wants to marry me."

"And what did you say?" asked Paul.

"A very firm 'No'," she said, "but he's a nice man, very kind, like you, my little Paul."

"Don't call me 'little'," pleaded Paul. "I'm a grown man."

"Oh, but I do, I must," stated Madame smiling. "You have given me a few precious moments of pleasure, and I am grateful. You've also made me feel young again."

"But you really are young, Madame," responded Paul. "You are only in your thirties, so I believe. That's young to me. And, what's more you look young and beautiful, despite having five children. It's a miracle. You must be very fit."

"Flatterer, you!" exclaimed Madame, looking pleased. "But you have to feel young, and I haven't felt it for a while, until now. As for my fitness, opera training demanded it. I've tried to keep it up."

After a few moments, Paul went down to see if the children were all right. Madame gave him money for those delicious cakes, which the children guzzled down happily.

Then it was time to go. The drive back was the usual happy one, with tuneful singing in the car. They begged Paul to teach them an English song – which he did.

Rather ambitiously he chose "Jerusalem" which was his school song, sung with gusto at the beginning and end of term. But it was a little too ambitious, so he changed to "Ten Green Bottles a-hanging on the Wall," which they enjoyed much more. They also tried to teach Paul a French song – 'Frère Jacques'. Paul did not let on he knew it already. But the whole sing-song was thoroughly enjoyable, especially when Madame joined in with her lovely voice. They had an unforgettable day.

When, after dinner, and with the children in bed, Madame and Paul sat on the balcony, Paul confessed.

"It's been a wonderful day!"

Madame smiled.

"I'm glad," she said. "I too have had a memorable time."

When finally they went up to bed, Madame came into his arms and for one memorable moment they kissed. It was only a peck, but to Paul it was a wonderful experience.

Madame sighed.

"The end of a wonderful day, even François behaved," she observed with a sense of relief.

# Chapter 13

*Holidays at Last!*

The end of June brought the end of the school term. Madame and Paul were faced with almost three months of holiday with all five boys, such were the long holidays in French schools.

"It is terrible sometimes," Madame said. "One doesn't know what to do with them at different moments all day."

Paul grunted. The prospect rather frightened him too. In a small village, there was little entertainment for children. Madame for financial reasons was reluctant to drive into Montauban. Her husband, or more precisely now the Koenitz family, provided enough money for bare necessities, but little else. The only asset was the marvellous weather. It meant the children spent the days out of doors, except for meals. Sometimes at lunch they had picnics by the river, but there were no sandy 'plages' in the area.

"What did they used to do?" Paul asked.

Madame shrugged.

"Well, they often went down to the river. Both Jean-Pierre and François learnt to swim. Sometimes I took them down, or Anne-Marie on one or two occasions per week. The Salvetti twins at the farm looked after them at times, and even swam with them. I used to pay them a little. That was when Jacques was around, and more money was available. But now ...."

Her voice trailed away in sad hopelessness.

"And M. Koenitz?" asked Paul. "What did he do?"

"Hardly anything," Madame admitted. "He was often away; I could not rely on him. He would leave them and wander off, or come back to the house. There was no reliable supervision. I think he contacted you because of my constant complaining."

"Why did he not help more with the children?" asked Paul hesitantly.

"Oh, I don't know," said Madame hopelessly. "He had his vague moments. He also believed children should be brought up without too much adult interference. It was one of his strange ideas."

"Uhm," muttered Paul. "He said much the same to me. Children should be free of adult discipline. He didn't like the way I dealt with François. Why do you think he thought that?"

"He was reacting against his own childhood," Madame explained. "He had a severe, oppressive upbringing. His parents were strong disciplinarians. He didn't like it at all, and left home early. He was only reunited with his parents when he married me."

Paul nodded.

"He told me that children shouldn't be disciplined," Paul agreed. "Forgive me saying so, Madame, but I couldn't help thinking he was a bit funny in the head. Much of his behaviour was somewhat odd, I felt."

Madame was pensive.

"It's made life difficult," she said. "Anyway, let's change the subject. What about you, Paul? What plans have you for the future? I mean after the summer."

"I think I'll have to follow my sister's advice, find a job, and write in my spare time," explained Paul. "I don't see how I can live in Paris without money."

"What job?" asked Madame.

"I would like to be a teacher if I returned to England," Paul explained. "Prep schools in England take on unqualified teachers. I was happy at school. I'd like to give back some of that happiness. But the real reason is that teachers have long holidays, during which I can write and travel a bit."

"But is teaching wise?" queried Madame. "You said you had difficulty hearing in some situations. I would have thought it was the last employment you ought to take up."

Paul smiled ruefully.

"That's what my mother said when she consulted the doctor," said Paul. "But I'll manage. I'm confident. My hearing has improved while I've been in France."

He failed to realise that the English would not accept his lack of hearing as lack of understanding of what they were saying, as people did in France.

One aspect of this conversation intrigued him. He was talking with Madame in a way he had never talked with anybody before, except perhaps his sister. It marked a new stage in their friendship, if he dared call it that. The dancing at the river beach had made him aware of her attractions as a woman, but now she was a 'confidante' as well, somebody to whom he could open his heart. But it seemed she could be the same with him, even mentioning the problems with her husband, something she had been reluctant to do. It was a fascinating position to be in; it carried its own responsibility and honour, and he was touched.

Even with his own mother he had never succeeded in so personal a relationship. It was the kind of companionship he craved in his heart. His hearing had mitigated against such a situation.

The next day he went down to the river with all five boys, plus a picnic. Madame came down to make certain they were all right. She soon went back. The river now flowed quietly, and at a much shallower depth. The banks were now quite high out of the water. Access to the river was either by jumping straight in, as Jean-Pierre and François did, or by a small gully. The two elder boys would come out via the gully, the banks were too steep. Paul eventually joined them in the water, and found it very refreshing and cool. The other three younger children played on the grass bank. Occasionally the Salvetti twins and Simone joined them, and Julie, the girl from the other farm. It made for a wonderful time. Madame teased Paul, saying he had four girls to give him delight, and they were so young and attractive.

"They're nice," Paul admitted. But in fact they were a great help with the Koenitz children. They were able to play with them, and even teach Marc to swim. He gained in confidence in the water; it was mainly due to one of the Salvetti twins; Paul was never certain of the name.

He couldn't tell them apart, except that one was left-handed, and the other right. Otherwise they dressed alike, and did their hair in the same way.

These trips down to the river were the cause of the first misunderstanding or upset between Paul and Madame, not that they ever had many upsets.

Madame had begun to tease him that he was not as emotional as the French, but calm, unflustered in his relationships, even phlegmatic! She also coined the phrase 'platonic' to describe their special relationship. It was an expression she had picked up from M. Salvetti, who said they were a platonic couple. It was indeed a platonic friendship! Madame seemed happy with this. But with Paul it was a contrast between the respect towards a woman who was older and his employer, and his feeling towards a very lovely and gifted woman. The two didn't match!

One day the boys were playing by the river as usual, or in the river. The three eldest were in the water. Marc miraculously was beginning to swim a few hesitant strokes in doggy paddle fashion. Nano and Régis were playing on the bank, which was fairly high above the level of the river, now the waters had subsided.

Paul could not understand the fascination the two little boys had in the grass and the earth. Nano was perilously near to the edge, but he seemed quite safe until François came out of the water and up onto the bank. In a curious, incomprehensive, stupid act he gave Nano a little nudge and sent him tumbling into the water. Paul, who witnessed the whole scene, gave a cry and jumped in after Nano.

He landed just beside Nano, grabbed him and hauled him above the level of the water. He had to make his way along the edge of the bank until he came to a less steep part. Then he managed to hand him up to Jean-Pierre, the ever-reliable, quiet, eldest boy.

When he managed to haul himself out of the river, he lost his English calm, and went for François, giving him a huge smack on the behind. He had never before felt so angry.

"Tu es vraiment bête," Paul yelled angrily. "How stupid you are!" He turned François round and gave him another wallop on the behind, really hard.

"Allez-y!" Paul cried. "Go straight back to the house." And when François hesitated, he yelled at him, "Allez-y! Go! Go! Poor Nano might have drowned!"

François went off, not altogether a pleasant look on his face. This worried Paul, that so young a boy should have so little realisation between right and wrong, or of the danger he could cause to somebody as young as Nano! Not for the first time, he wondered about Francois' mental stability, just as he had the same worry about the father. Was there something mentally wrong about both of them?

Paul turned to Nano who was crying, more from shock than injury. Paul could only guess that during those very few seconds Nano had been in the water, he had unconsciously held his breath, or perhaps he, Paul, had grabbed him before he went under. But after a while, Nano seemed none the worse for his immersion. Paul was very relieved. Of all the boys, he had established the best relationship with Nano in recent weeks. Nano had taken to sleeping in Paul's room, waking him in the morning with such a cheerful, lovely smile.

After that episode, the three unaffected boys, especially Jean-Pierre, seemed to regard Paul with some awe, amounting almost to hero-worship. Paul withdrew into English understatement, not wishing to claim any renown for what he had done.

Paul's shorts and shirt dried quickly on him in the hot sun. When he got back to the house he made the mistake of putting on a nonchalant air, merely informing Madame Nano had fallen in the river, not mentioning his anger with François. The latter had in the meantime blubbed that Paul had hit him, not explaining why. Madame being French was furious, firstly because of Paul's seemingly uncaring attitude at Nano's fall in the river and, secondly, not even referring to his hitting of François.

Fortunately for Paul, Jean-Pierre, Marc and Régis soon filled Madame in as to what had really happened. That evening, sitting out on the balcony, Paul finally found out what had been said, and why Madame had been a little cold toward him for a while.

"J'étais bien fachée avec vous," Madame admitted. "I was very angry with you."

"I'm very sorry," said Paul. He had been somewhat astonished at Madame's first reaction. It was the first time for a long time that Madame's attitude had changed towards him.

"Eh bien, first of all you showed little feeling about Nano falling in the river," said Madame, somewhat accusingly.

"Oh," said Paul, beginning to understand. He should not have been so calm about everything. The French would have been much more excited, gabbling away with much emotion.

"But.....," he started to protest, and then he stopped. How could he explain that a public school Englishman tried to play things down, that one just didn't show emotion or too much pride. In fact he had shown emotion in his sudden anger with François, but Madame had not seen that.

"I rang my friend in Montauban," Madame said. "He explained your strange, quiet nature."

Madame stopped for a moment, then continued.

"He knows the English well. He was exiled in England for four years during the war. You began to make sense after talking to him. He spoke of English reserve, not blowing your own trumpet. But, j'étais furieuse your indifference to Nano falling in the water."

"I was actually quite upset," admitted Paul, "which was probably why I was so angry with François."

"Hm," uttered Madame, "Jean-Pierre told me everything." There was silence for a moment between them.

"I'm sorry," said Paul, feeling a little miserable that he had been so misunderstood. It would seem that in future he would have to cry and wail and act passionately if a similar situation arose! But how could he? It was not in his nature.

Madame touched his hand gently.

"No problem, Paul," she said kindly. "You did well. You were very brave."

"There is no brave about it," stated Paul. "I could swim; Nano couldn't."

For a moment Paul couldn't help thinking about bravery. His father had been awarded the Military Cross for bravery. That had been real bravery, risking his own life. Paul hadn't done the same, jumping in the river. His own life was not at stake, only Nano's.

"But there is a problem, a real problem, with François," said Paul. "I don't think he realised the danger he had caused. There almost seems an evil streak in him. You must talk to him, Madame. I can't."

"I don't think I can either," admitted Madame. "He doesn't seem to listen to me, does the same thing again the very next day. I find him the most difficult of all my children, and the most difficult to understand. And, even worse, he doesn't seem to respond to affection."

Paul was silent a moment. Then he said.

"Try Anne-Marie. Get her to talk to him. There seems to be a little rapport between them."

Madame agreed, nodding.

# Chapter 14

*Trying Moments!*

M. Koenitz came back towards the end of July. It was decidedly a fraught and not very happy occasion. Paul didn't know what had happened, but the man seemed not to like him at all. Whether Madame had said something – or the priest more possibly was a complete mystery to Paul. Though abrupt in speech and manner, M. Koenitz had not hitherto shown any active resentment of Paul's presence at La Refaudio before. It would have been illogical if he had. After all he had introduced Paul to help Madame with the children, and this Paul had done. Perhaps Paul was too successful, certainly more successful than the father should have been, or even could have been!

On the first morning of his arrival back, Paul and M. Koenitz met on the stairs, the landing halfway up. Madame was also present. Paul had taken to smoking a pipe, which he felt, went with his phlegmatic, calm image.

M. Koenitz demanded abruptly,
"When you go home?"
Paul gave his usual answer.
"That depends on Madame!"

Whether M. Koenitz regarded this as a rather cheeky answer, Paul never knew; it was certainly not meant to be. M. Koenitz' hand suddenly shot out, knocking the pipe clean from Paul's mouth. If Paul had not withdrawn his head quickly, he would have been hit. Madame gave a little gasp of horror. After a moment of surprise, Paul bent down to retrieve his pipe, which had ended up in a corner of the landing. Paul did not feel he wanted to indulge in any physical confrontation with a man who was older, smaller, and probably not as fit as he was. But as Paul bent down to retrieve his pipe, M. Koenitz aimed a kick at his behind and Paul went staggering. As with

François, Paul lost his temper. His fist came up from a low position and went slap into Koenitz's face. The man pitched back and nearly fell. He clutched a bleeding nose. Madame was horrified and went to fetch a towel.

M. Koenitz shouted something at Paul, impossible to understand, and then he stomped on upstairs to his bedroom, followed by Madame with the towel. He and Madame had separate bedrooms – understandably! Paul went to his bedroom, and sat down on his own bed, feeling thoroughly miserable. Then reluctantly he got up, got out his suitcase and started to pack. After a few minutes Madame appeared, and stood surprised.

"What are you doing?" she cried, worry in her voice.

"Packing," said Paul tersely. "I can't possibly stay."

But Madame's reaction was quick. She took his case firmly took out the clothes, and said almost as an order.

"No you don't. You stay. My husband asked for it. It was not your fault." And then she added hesitantly and sincerely. "I need you. Both the children and I need you."

But Paul protested.

"I hit your husband. What else can I do, but go? It was wrong, what I did."

And for once he gave a Gallic shrug.

"You are not to blame," she said. "He tried to hit and kick you. Stay, please, Paul, I beg of you."

Paul looked so woebegone, Madame did the one thing that would change Paul's mind. She went up to Paul, took him in her arms, and gave him a long kiss. When they parted, she said impishly,

"Now you know how much I need you."

Paul was taken aback, but he made no further attempt at packing.

The rest of the day passed apprehensively for Paul and for Madame. Paul was afraid that M. Koenitz might come down and could become violent towards Madame. She whispered to Paul to take the children out in the afternoon. He demurred, saying he was anxious about her.

"I'll be all right," she whispered.

But M. Koenitz did not come down even for lunch. Paul asked Madame.

"Has he ever hit you?"

But she evaded the question, not answering. He rather assumed from her evasion that her husband might have hit her, which worried him even more.

That evening M. Koenitz was like a prowling lion. He was all about the house, but Paul could hardly make out what he was doing. Except for Jean-Pierre he ignored the children as they went to bed, which, to Paul, seemed rather a pity. Children were at their most loveable at bedtime, especially children as young as Madame's.

Suddenly there came a cry, and then a scream, from the 'cave', the cellar.

Madame dashed down, followed closely by Paul, and Anne-Marie. There they found Jean-Pierre held firmly by the arm by M. Koenitz. Jean-Pierre was shouting.

"Je ne veux pas, je ne veux pas," amidst sobs and struggles to release his arm from a tight grip. Seeing his wife, then Paul and finally Anne-Marie arrive, M. Koenitz let go of Jean-Pierre's arm. The boy rushed towards his 'Maman' who enfolded him in her arms. He blurted out his story. His father wanted to take him to Paris, to be with his mistress, and Jean-Pierre was scared. His father was acting so strangely. Jean-Pierre wanted to stay at La Refaudio. Seeing the game was up M. Koenitz let out an exclamation of disgust, and stomped out. A moment later they heard the car rev up furiously, and shoot off.

It was the last they were to see of the car, and of the husband!

Later that evening, Paul and Madame sat as usual on the balcony. Paul tried to console Madame, but not very convincingly.

"Why does your husband behave so strangely?" he couldn't help asking.

But Madame shook her head. "I just don't know," she said sorrowfully, and then added more plaintively, "I just don't know. I wish I knew. I wish I knew. He's always been difficult, but never like today!"

"Was he a problem when you first met?" asked Paul.

"Eh bien. – non. Well no. When we first met he was marvellous, swept me off my feet, so to speak," said Madame. "It was his family that were strange. The father was remote, very strict, kept himself very much to himself. His mother went slowly demented, each year getting increasingly worse. I could never make her out. In the end she went into a nursing home. I never saw her again. My fear is that Jacques will become like her, impossible to talk to, almost impossible to live with."

Madame looked as if she was going to cry.

Paul took her in his arms, and held her quietly. It was the least he could do.

Finally Madame stirred and said with courage.

"This won't do, Paul. Let's have a glass of wine and drown our sorrows. Ça te plait? – That pleases you?" she said, trying to smile.

It was the first time she had ever used the tutoyer form with Paul, the 'tu' instead of the more customary 'vous'. In a way it was a compliment and Paul was flattered. The second person singular was used only "en famille", or with loved ones. He felt his relationship with Madame had moved one step forward.

The next few days were aimless and full of suspense. They had to content themselves with local pleasures, namely the river and the Salvettis. Meanwhile Paul was beginning to worry about his future. He had done very little writing at La Refaudio. Certainly his work there looking after the children had no career. Though he was beginning to love Madame, he likewise began to see no future in their relationship. She, with her Catholic convictions, would never marry him. Besides he had no money to support her, or her five children.

His thoughts turned to teaching. He talked to Madame about it.

"I shall be sad if you go, Paul," she said. "But I knew sometime you would have to go. But we'd miss you. You've been a wonderful support at a difficult time. I thought at first you would go much earlier. You so obviously wanted to be in Paris."

She hesitated a moment.

"But you, as a teacher, I just don't know," she continued. "I can't imagine it."

"Why not?" asked Paul smiling.

"Well, you say you have a hearing handicap," stated Madame. "I don't know it, or I haven't noticed it. If you have, then teaching ought to be your very last option."

She pondered a moment, wondering whether she should go on.

"You're too nice a person to be a teacher, Paul," she said in a kindly tone. "Most teachers in France are nasty, assertive men, happy to wield power over the young. It's just not for you."

Paul laughed and said jokingly,

"You obviously don't know me, Madame. I can be quite nasty when I want."

But Madame demurred, saying,

"I do know you, Paul. You are one of the kindest men I've ever met. And I'm sincere; I mean it."

For a moment they were silent. Then Paul uttered a quiet "thank you."

He was full of gratitude to this kind lady, who had done so much to restore his confidence and self-esteem since leaving Oxford. He began to tell Madame of his plans.

"I wrote to my sister and asked her to send me copies of The Times Educational Supplement – which she has done. In one was an advertisement for a general teacher in a prep school in Somerset."

"What is a prep school?" asked Madame.

"Boys between the ages of eight to thirteen, preparing for entry into a public school," explained Paul.

Madame nearly asked what was a public school, but didn't. Paul didn't feel he could explain the complexities of English private education, , in his limited French.

"Anyway," he continued, "The headmaster of this school in Somerset is coming to France in August. He wondered if he could call in about lunch time and interview me then. If acceptable I could start on September fifteenth. It would be marvellous to get the job. The money is poor, but it's a start."

Madame pondered a moment.

"The difficulty is in August we go to Lourdes," she explained. "If he can come early in August before the tenth, that would be fine."

So it was agreed and a visit arranged for the seventh.

Meanwhile Paul had pricked up his ears at the mention of Lourdes. He had been fascinated at Oxford by Lourdes and its miraculous cures, and the story of St. Bernadette. It would be a wonderful part of France to visit.

"Am I allowed to go to Lourdes?" he asked hesitantly. "I'm not a Catholic."

Madame smiled rather mischievously.

"Oh, no," she said teasingly. "You stay and look after the children. I shall just disappear. You will have Anne-Marie to help you. Won't that be nice for you? You can sit on the balcony and practise your French. I shan't mind what else you get up to."

Paul's face fell. Madame laughed and said.

"Of course, you MUST come, silly boy," she said laughing. "The trip's arranged with you in mind. I won't go without you!"

Paul breathed a sigh of relief.

"You are a wicked lady," he said smiling, "to tease me as you do. But, seriously, what about the children? Who is going to look after them," he asked. "I'll stay if it helps."

"Well," Madame began to explain. "Jean-Pierre will come with us. I don't want to risk him being kidnapped by his father. Anne-Marie is coming as a reward for two years helping me.

And you of course, Paul, my reliable helper. The rest of the children go to the Salvettis. They know François, and can usually cope with him. Besides, he's been behaving much better since you smacked him, and Anne-Marie had a talk with him."

Paul felt he was really looking forward to this visit. It seemed also to be a gift from Madame to him and Anne-Marie, for which he was really grateful.

Madame seemed to appreciate what he had been doing, looking after the children, and the love he showed for the little Nano.

But in the meantime there was this headmaster's visit to cope with. Paul wasn't looking forward to it. He couldn't understand how any man would want to employ him, unqualified and hard of hearing. He would have to tell him that even in France he didn't wear his hearing aid.

# Chapter 15

*A Job! A Career!*

Paul was not impressed with the headmaster when he came, nor with his wife! And Madame shared his feelings.

The head was a largish man, probably in his fifties. He looked unfit and had none of the relaxed, good humour of the average Englishman. There was something rather grim and unrelenting about him, as if he would be a difficult man to cross. He also seemed more like a businessman than a teacher. The future didn't look promising.

His wife was a formidable woman, as large, if not larger than her husband. Big-breasted, she bore down on one like a tank, sweeping all before her. She was a real battle-axe. Madame had a French word to describe her, but Paul could never find out what it meant. It seemed to be part of French 'argot' or slang.

"They do not impress me," Madame said. "They will rule by fear over the little ones. It will not be a happy school. I advise you not to accept."

But Paul felt that it might be a start. He could always move on to another school if Madame's predictions were right!

The salary was infinitesimally small – forty pounds for the term, just over three pounds per week, but the board and lodging were free!

It was something, however tenuous, for the future, so he accepted. He promised he would arrive at the school on the fourteenth of September, the day before term started.

"What are your plans for the future?" Mr. Choley, the headmaster, asked him. "You have no qualification or experience."

So Paul told him of his wish to go back to Oxford, re-take prelims in French, for which he now felt strangely confident. Madame had been a good teacher; French was now alive and vibrant as a language. If he managed to get a degree, however poor, he would then go on to the post-graduate Diploma of Education. He would then be a fully qualified teacher.

"You'll be beyond me," Mr Choley remarked. "Few prep schools can pay Burnham."

Burnham was the recognised salary scale for qualified teachers, way, way beyond the pittance Mr Choley was offering.

Mrs Choley interrupted.

"So, you would not consider our school as a long-term prospect?" she asked.

There was a glint in her eyes, a glint Paul would get to know well in their future relationship. Paul evaded the issue.

"Please." he begged, "Let me try to find out first whether I like teaching. Then we can consider future plans."

So on this rather tenuous ground they parted company, shaking hands on the understanding that Paul would be there for the autumn term. There was no signed contract. The whole situation seemed very dubious, and Madame wondered how a school could be searching for a teacher when term began only a month or so later.

Paul was impressed with Madame. She made it clear to Paul she disliked the Choleys. But to them she showed an affability beyond comparison. The only problem was that she praised Paul to the skies saying how good he was with the children, and mentioning how he had rescued Nano from the river. As a testimonial it was probably too fulsome for English ears. Paul began to realise how beautiful and kind Madame really and truly was.

He saw Mr Choley eyeing her with middle-aged lasciviousness. Mrs Choley noticed too, and that angry glint was in her eyes. Madame was aware of the interest, and characteristically found it rather amusing.

'You'd better watch out,' Paul thought to himself, 'when you are alone with the beauteous Madame. Make eyes at Madame and your life won't be worth living.' Somehow he didn't think the headmaster would get away lightly with his battle-axe wife.

Then Paul thought, perhaps rather wrongly, that Mr Choley must be sex-starved. He couldn't imagine him making love to Mrs Choley. The situation would be too gross.

Anyway, the Choleys left after lunch for their tour south. They were full of dubious, gracious smiles. When they had left Madame muttered to Paul.

"Ne vas pas, Paul – Don't go. You'll never be happy. You'll leave after a few months."

But Paul shook his head. Madame was probably right, but Paul felt he had little choice. This was a good post to get, obtained while he was not in England, and without any experience or qualification. He had to take whatever crumbs came up, however stale!

"You are obstinate, pig-headed," Madame accused him, not for the first time.

"Pig-headed or not," Paul said. "I've no choice, unless I stay with you."

"That I would love," Madame murmured.

Paul looked at her thoughtfully and asked,

"Madame, could I mention two things to you?"

Madame nodded with her usual kindly smile.

"Well," said Paul hesitantly, "Is there another name I can call you, other than Madame? It sounds so formal. I've known you now for nearly three months, and am beginning to like and admire you very much."

Madame thought a moment, then said,

"My Christian name is Marguerite. I should be happy if you used that name. But I feel it's more appropriate if you continue to call me 'Madame' in front of the children, my husband and anyone else, or they might get the wrong idea."

Paul nodded thoughtfully.

"That would be wonderful," he said. "Marguerite is a lovely name. Margaret in English."

"Thank you," said Marguerite simply. "What was the other matter you wanted to mention?"

"It's more difficult," admitted Paul, "but I haven't been paid for all the time I have been here. I'm really rather short of money, especially if we are going to Lourdes."

"Oh, good heavens!" uttered Marguerite. "You poor boy! I'm very sorry. Jacques never said anything to me about money arrangements, and I've been so short of money myself."

Paul sighed. He didn't like being called a boy, for one thing. But he recognised it was her form of endearment in fun. He'd also heard it said that rich people had difficulty in recognising that other people had needs. He didn't blame Marguerite, but the Koenitz family seemed to be very tight-fisted. Perhaps that was why they were rich?

"I don't know what to do," said Marguerite. "I'll write to the Koenitz family and let you know."

Paul smiled weakly his thanks, but wasn't very hopeful. His only relief was that he still had the money in his suitcase which his sister had given him. He must hang onto that to get back to England.

Nothing was said further about money for the time being.

One extraordinary development, which pleased and amazed Paul, was that Madame would come down in the evening having changed into attractive clothing. Usually she continued to wear what she had worn during the day. But now it was different. After the children were in bed, she would change and come down looking fresh and attractive. It was normally just a crisp white blouse, and a cardigan in case the evening was chilly, and a blue or green cotton skirt, or sometimes a dress which showed off her figure.

She also put on a little make up and fragrant perfume.

Paul liked it and said so.

"My, Marguerite, you look a treat!"

She looked gratified, and smiled happily.

Now, too, their goodnights were a kiss and a hug. It took all Paul's will, not to take things further. It was all he could do not to fondle those lovely breasts.

Madame still teased him about being platonic. But Paul was very inexperienced as regards women. One thing he noticed was that Madame always slept with Regis in her room. Whether it was an intentional safeguard Paul never knew.

# Chapter 16

*Lourdes!*

Now the ordeal of the Choleys was over, thoughts turned quickly to the forthcoming visit to Lourdes. It was more than they could hope for, but everything went very peacefully for the departure. Jean-Pierre heaved a sigh of relief that he was safe from his father. He had found the recent experience rather traumatic. He was a very quiet, introverted boy. The other boys were only too glad to be going to the Salvettis. Even François showed no jealousy of his elder brother.

The journey to Lourdes was by train, so hopelessly overcrowded it was impossible to find a seat. It was a long and tedious journey, hot and stuffy and smelly, of which the less said the better. At Lourdes in the early evening they had to walk to find their hotel. Fortunately it was not far, and at that time of the day it was cooler.

Then the fun began.

"I only have one room," announced the lady proprietor. "But it has four beds."

"One room," echoed Madame. "Yes, we are four! We booked for two rooms! We have two unrelated people, an Englishman and a girl who helps me at home."

The lady shrugged her shoulders, with apparent French indifference.

"There are four beds. I have a 'paravent' – a screen," she said.

Madame and Anne-Marie started giggling. Paul remained puzzled; he couldn't hear or understand what was being said. Jean-Pierre remained as usual silent and calm.

Eventually Madame agreed to the screen. They went up to their room to deposit their bags.

"I am sorry, Paul, truly sorry," Madame said. "The four of us have to sleep in this one room. You and Jean-Pierre sleep this side of the screen, the door side of the room. Lourdes itself is packed to the brim in August."

She indicated the screen, already in place. "Anne-Marie and I will sleep the other side near the window. Do you mind?" Then she repeated her explanation. "There are many people in Lourdes. It is crowded, peak season in August."

She thought a moment, and then she added mischievously, "You must behave, be a true gentleman."

Paul said and added with a grin,

"I'll do my best. Jean-Pierre and I will try not to peep."

Madame then said, again a mischievous smile on her lips.

"There is one other problem. The hotel is not the best. There is only one toilet, one hole in the ground, as you so rudely term it!"

"Good Lord," said Paul aghast, not knowing really what to say.

"If we have – er – a problem during the night there is a pot which I will place here," said Madame with a giggle.

She put a tin pot near to the screen, between the two sides.

Paul smiled to himself. That tin pot would make quite a noise should anyone use it. He looked at Jean-Pierre. They both laughed. The serious Jean-Pierre had a sense of humour.

"I'm sorry, Paul," Madame said, "but I could only afford the cheapest of accommodation."

Paul was surprised, but secretly admiring, that so beautiful and refined a lady should be prepared to slum it just to get to Lourdes! The town must be a really special place! Madame suddenly appeared to Paul as a distinctly human and down to earth person. Paul imagined his own mother being horrified at the primitive conditions in the hotel, but Madame didn't turn a hair. In that respect she was very much like his sister.

"Now we go out," said Madame. "Find something to eat."

They were a happy group. Somehow the problems of the hotel had put them into a cheerful mood. Madame linked arms with Paul, Anne-Marie with Jean-Pierre. They almost danced down the street with joy.

To Paul it was a wonderful moment! The evening air was so balmy and warm, Madame's presence so near him, all combined to make an unforgettable moment in life. Madame seemed to feel it as much as he did. Just for a brief second, she appeared to clutch his arm so tightly that he winced. Paul remembered a sad comment of her existence, which Madame had made.

"I have to take life, all the worries, all the unhappiness, and just savour the little daily joys. Nano's smiling face, Regis' little quirks, the sound of the church bells, all really mean something."

Paul felt this was one of her moments, as it was his. They found a small cafe serving reasonably priced meals. It reminded Paul of the cafe in Paris which had made him so sick. The tables had white paper tablecloths; the entrance was through a shop – a boulangerie. But despite the poor portrayal, it did not affect the food which was excellent – when it came. The restaurant was so crowded, so noisy, so chaotic that the waiters had a job keeping up with the service.

Eventually Madame chose just a first course. When they had eaten it they went. But on the way out Madame brought some provisions from the boulangerie, saying,

"Demain – tomorrow – we must take a picnic. It will be easier."

So, tired, they left the cafe. It had one important asset – it had a toilet, which they all used – just in case!

Outside, Madame said,

"Now for the Stations of the Cross."

She explained to Paul it was Christ's journey to his eventual death. At each station they would stop and pray. They joined the huge procession, were given a lighted candle, and wended their way up the hill. Periodically they stopped, and prayers were said through a loud hailer. It could be heard throughout the town. It was a wonderful spectacle. The procession, lit by candles as darkness fell, must have stretched over a mile, there was such a mass of people.

"It's beautiful!" Paul whispered to Madame. She smiled in agreement, but her lips still moved, as if in prayer. Paul was rendered quiet. He found himself saying a prayer for his sister, for his mother, even for close friends and relatives. Even more important, for Madame herself and her little family.

The whole crowded atmosphere at Lourdes deeply moved him. It seemed to take more than an hour before the procession reached its conclusion. Paul found it somewhat tedious towards the end, understanding very little, but to Catholics like Madame and Anne-Marie it obviously meant something. Finally Madame ceased praying, smiled at Paul, and said,

"Back to the hotel. But first we must find a toilet."

Her method was simple. She went back to the cafe where they had had supper, walked quietly through the busy restaurant, straight up to the toilet. Nobody challenged them, nobody questioned their presence. It was quickly in and out. To salve her conscience a little, Madame made a small purchase of four rolls in the shop. They laughed a lot at this little episode, and entered the hotel in a happy mood.

"Goodnight, boys," Madame said "Dormez bien – sleep well – and, er, no peeping!"

Paul laughed. He went to bed, but was disturbed by the thought of Madame so near. He wondered how her body must be in a nightdress. Then he shook his head. It came under the classification of impure thought, and it wasn't how young men should behave, or so he believed.

The next day they all rose, did a perfunctory wash in the basin. Then the boys left, leaving the girls to their longer personal attention. Paul and Jean-Pierre went to join the wait for the toilet, another primitive hole in the ground. The queue was long and slow. When the two boys left, Madame and Anne-Marie had joined the back of the queue.

"They'll be a quarter of an hour or more. Let's get a breath of fresh air, Jean-Pierre," Paul suggested.

Outside, it was cool, and a breeze seemed to come down from the Pyrenees Mountains to the south. Even though it was early, there seemed to be plenty of people about, and even a few wheelchairs.

When they returned, they went into breakfast, the usual milky coffee, a piece of baguette with butter, but no jam, which Paul looked forward to, being English.

After breakfast, Madame said,

"We'll explore the town for an hour or more, drink the water, say our prayers, and then go for a walk up the river valley towards the mountains. It's a lovely walk. I have done it before."

During that day, Paul made two mistakes, and came to a surprising decision.

The walk around the town was moving. They came to a hospital where many of the ill were being treated, including some invalids in wheelchairs. Everybody was very quiet, though there were a large number of people there.

Madame gave Paul a cup of water to drink.

"Drink this, Paul," she said. "And pray your hearing may be restored." then she smiled. "That is your wish, isn't it?"

Paul nodded. He drank the water, which seemed no different from any water, perhaps a slightly stronger taste. But it was fresh and cool.

After that visit, they took a walk to the river. At the end where the path gave out they sat and partook of the picnic Madame had bought.

The walk up the river valley was beautiful, but arduous. The ground was rocky and hard, and the uphill climb was constant and tiring. It was so hot! Madame had hired a donkey, and on the way up Anne-Marie and Jean-Pierre shared it. Each time it was offered to Madame, she declined it. When finally they felt they had gone far enough, they turned back, and Paul had a go on the donkey. This was Paul's first mistake, or rather he was the victim of an obstinate donkey.

Until now, the animal had been slow and placid. But once turned back down the trail, he put on an extra turn of speed, and forged rapidly ahead of the others. There was nothing Paul could do about it. He tried to slow it down but without success. It did stop on a bend, or Paul managed to make it pause. But it would not wait for the others. Even worse, despite all Paul's cajoling, it wouldn't even turn back! It was intent only on one thing, getting back to the bottom of the gorge.

Paul now knew how obstinate a donkey could be! So he gave up, and mounted the beast, which plodded gratefully home.

At the bottom Paul waited for the others. When they arrived, Madame said with a trace of sarcasm,

"Thank you for bringing the donkey back."

Paul wanted to explain that in a battle of wills with the donkey he had lost. But somehow he couldn't get the words out. He was mortified. He had felt he had lost face with Madame. He had been selfish. He was even more concerned because she looked tired and drawn.

Madame then announced she was going to a service with Annie-Marie and her son. She said it almost as if she didn't expect Paul to come.

So he wandered off, bought four little cakes (one each) and found a quiet spot by the river where he could rest and contemplate. The trouble was that the cakes started to melt in the hot sun. Instead of waiting for the others, he began to eat them. They were so delicious, and he was hungry. However, when Madame after church proposed coffee and cakes, he had to admit that he had already eaten four.

The look from a tired lady was rather scathing! But she made no comment.

Paul's moments of quiet contemplation had led him to the thought he wanted to find out more about the Catholic Church. He was greatly impressed by many factors, not least by the strength and support it gave Madame in her moment of trial. He knew the church taught her marriage was for life, and for life it remained, for better or for worse, the worse being her husband's infidelity. She was strong; she certainly would never have eaten four cakes! Then there was the piety, the belief, both here in Lourdes and back at the little village church close to La Refaudio. The faith of the village was alive and vibrant, far stronger than anything he had come across in England. He wanted to partake in that faith, know more about it, share it, the Catholic faith, love it. But his greatest admiration was for Madame.

Despite everything she remained cheerful and loyal. He was deeply touched! He admired her. He suddenly realised he loved her. You can't live in the same house as a lovely woman and not love her, he thought. He'd talked for hours with her, those wonderful evenings on the balcony. Never before, in his lonely young life, had he had such a relationship, deep, warming and interesting. And then the music was an additional joy. He had never been so touched by her singing. It was unforgettable!

He suddenly realised how lonely he would be to leave Madame! How devastated he would be! It was a love that haunted him, grew in depth, and he couldn't get over it.

The next day they returned to La Refaudio. They were certainly tired, and somewhat put out by poor toilet facilities, with limited opportunities to wash, or even to eat. They were glad to get back to civilisation again, as represented by the lovely house of La Refaudio. It had been an unforgettable, spiritual experience, especially for Paul. But he needed a less hectic time to sort out his growing interest in Catholicism, and even more his deepening love for Madame. His concern was that this was mixed up with his interest in the Catholic Church. One influenced the other. If Madame had not been there would he have been so captivated by the Catholic Church?

He felt he wanted to be a true convert to Catholicism. One influence had to be separated from the other, or it would not be a true conversion.

He decided to talk to Madame about Catholicism. The opportunity came the day after their return from Lourdes. They were once again on the balcony. After the heat of the day, the cool of the evening was welcome and refreshing. All day Paul and the boys had worn nothing but a pair of shorts, and had spent most of the day in the cool of the river. They had been joined by Anne-Marie in a shapeless bathing costume. But Madame had remained in the shade of the house.

That evening, both Madame and Paul felt completely relaxed. Paul felt it was time to pose his question, a question that began to cause Paul an inner turbulence.

"Marguerite," he asked, "how could I learn more about the Catholic faith?"

"What's brought this on all of a sudden?" Madame asked, smiling.

Paul went a little vague. He didn't want to be too personal in his remarks.

"Oh, I don't know," he said vaguely. "I've much admired the piety of the Catholic Church in France. The little village church is full on Sunday. In England church attendance has fallen off since the War. Church seems to mean something in this country, and I am very impressed."

"I'm glad!" said Madame. "I'd like to help, but I don't know whether I am the right person."

Paul wanted to demur. He had thought all along that her faith had given her a certain strength in very difficult times. But he avoided again being so personal.

"I wondered if I could talk with the priest at the village church," Paul asked. "He seemed kind and understanding, though very quiet."

"No," said Madame. "I know a better man, in Montauban. The only trouble is we haven't the car. I can't take you to him but he's a wonderful man, very spiritual. He may come to you."

"If he came here, it would be very good." ventured Paul.

It may not be possible," Madame replied thoughtfully. "He's a very busy man, much loved and much in demand."

"Well, can we start with the local priest" asked Paul, "and perhaps fit in the occasional visit to Montauban with the help of M. Salvetti? I'm keen to start."

"Mmm," went Madame. "I'll have a word with Father Patrice. He lives just by the church. But, Paul, why this keenness?" Marguerite queried. "You've never before expressed an interest in our faith. I'm intrigued."

But Paul remained quiet.

All he would say was, "Your faith has grown on me, particularly after the visit to Lourdes. It seems to give you such strength. I would like to know more."

"Is there anything I've done? Have I helped at all?" asked Madame. "After all, you've been with us some three and a half months now."

Paul wilted under this direct interest. He decided to speak.

"Yes, Marguerite, you have helped, more than you realise perhaps. I feel your beliefs have given you strength at a very difficult time, a stressful time. But I admire you so very much, how you have stood up to your problems, remained positive and even loyal to your husband, a loyalty I don't think he deserves."

Madame was silent for a moment. Finally she heaved a sigh, and said quietly,

"You've helped, Paul," she stated. "You've been kind and helpful and understanding and above all, you've done wonders with the children. The summer has gone far better than I'd ever expected. Can I call you a gift from heaven, an answer to prayer?"

Paul didn't know what to say. With typical English understatement he said,

"I've tried to do my bit, but you've done a lot for me. You've restored my confidence after my failure at Oxford, and for that I am immensely grateful."

They sat quietly, then smiled at each other after so much mutual congratulation. Finally, Paul came back to the theme with which they had started.

"Can you arrange for me then to see Father Patrice?" he asked.

Madame nodded, and there the subject ended, at least for the moment!

No mention of love, though it was a very real factor for Paul. It was strange that the disparity of age did not enter into the equation! No, he thought, one could really love an older woman, impossible though it may seem!

## Chapter 17

*Priestly Encounters*

Conversation, or instruction, began with le Pere Patrice three days later in the early evening before dinner. It was not entirely a good time for Paul. He came back to La Refaudio from looking after the children by the river. He washed and changed, and then, supperless, went down to the Presbytery.

Father Patrice was a quiet, kindly man with something of the austerity of his profession. He spoke no English. They had to converse in French, which by now was no problem for Paul.

"I understand from Mme. Koenitz you are considering entering the Catholic Church," he said, smiling kindly at Paul.

"Well, not exactly," countered Paul. "I am impressed by your church and would like to know a little more about it first."

"What exactly would you like to know?" asked the priest.

"Well, in what way does it differ from the Anglican Church, the Church of England?" Paul stated.

Father Patrice was quiet for a moment, and then he began to run through some of the historical and religious differences, most of which Paul knew, having studied history at Oxford.

"We recognise the Pope as the Head of the Church, the direct descendant of St. Peter by the laying on of hands. The head of the Anglican Church is the King, or the elected Archbishop of Canterbury."

Paul nodded in agreement. Father Patrice went on in a way that almost sent Paul to sleep. Finally Paul asked a crucial question.

"Why do you not accept divorce?" he said.

"Marriage is a Holy Sacrament," said the priest, "therefore unchangeable; marriage is for life."

"Therefore," challenged Paul, "if the marriage breaks down, even to mutual hatred, or disloyalty, no love left, man

"Pas de problème – no problem. M. Salvetti, comme toujours – as always – is too kind!"

So Paul waited with anticipation. Madame spoke so highly of this man! He wondered if any man could be so remarkable!

The day arrived. It wasn't M. Salvetti who took Paul but his talkative brother.

"You go-a to talk with Le Père Franchaud. He is-a a very good man, very friendly!" the brother explained.

Paul nodded.

"That's what I've heard," he agreed.

"You become-a Catholic?" asked the brother.

There was no end to the lively curiosity of the Italians!

"Madame Koenitz is-a very good Catholic! Verra nice woman!" stated the brother simply.

The Italian probing continued unabated, always with an innocent smile!

Paul nodded in agreement, but said nothing.

When they arrived, Le Père Franchaud had the customary elderly housekeeper who greeted them at the door.

"I'll be back-a in an hour or so," said the Italian.

Paul was led into a darkened room where sat Le Pere. A single lamp on his desk lit up the face of Paul's host. It was an older face than Father Patrice's, with a crop of white hair and a welcoming countenance. He was the first priest Paul had met with a twinkle in his eye, giving hope of a certain sense of humour. Their conversation was in French. Like Father Patrice, he had no knowledge of English. He appeared so kindly, Paul almost instantly warmed to the man.

"Ah, the young Englishman interested in Catholicism! An unusual situation! Why is this so?" was the priest's greeting with a smile.

Paul decided to throw caution to the winds and tell only the truth, or as near the truth as he could. Perhaps that was the problem with Father Patrice. They hedged around the truth.

"I love – I admire – a Catholic girl, a French girl," admitted Paul tentatively.

"And you wish to marry her?" asked the priest.

"Yes, – er – but I can't," admitted Paul.

and wife still have to remain together. It's an impossible situation!"

"Yes," said the priest.

Paul sighed.

"That I cannot accept!" he stated. "One has to continue in a loveless marriage which has no meaning. It's a ridiculous situation."

Paul quoted the example of Madame Koenitz, a woman whose husband had deserted her for another, even had a child by his mistress. It was something Paul should not have mentioned, but he felt strongly about Madame's situation.

Father Patrice eyed him keenly.

"There I must stop you, my friend," stated the Priest. "Madame Koenitz is a member of my Parish. I owe to her the confidentiality, the secrecy of the confessional. I cannot in any way discuss her situation."

Paul sighed yet again.

"But you would agree that no possibility of divorce creates an impossible situation, a very unhappy one," Paul said.

But Father Patrice remained stolid, and firm in his beliefs, unmoveable!

Paul sighed yet again, inwardly. He hoped Father Patrice would not notice his lack of agreement. There was a certain point where their beliefs clashed. Paul felt he was up against a brick wall, impossible to break down.

"What attracts you about the Catholic Church?" asked Father Patrice in a kindly way.

"Oh, your piety is impressive, so marvellous, as if prayer really means something to you. There is the strength of your beliefs, your convictions, if you like. I can't accept some of them, as with divorce, but yours is a strong faith. In England faith is uncertain at times, and possibly declining, based on values of convenience. There is a spirit of compromise in the Church of England which doesn't help spiritually."

Father Patrice did not comment. They remained silent, facing each other, not knowing in which direction the conversation should go.

"Did you enjoy your visit to Lourdes?" Father Patrice finally asked. It was a conventional question, not very profound.

"I'm not sure 'enjoy' is the right word. But yes and no," replied Paul. "It was a small town, suddenly thrust into the limelight and unprepared for it. The crowds were way beyond its capacity to cope. From the point of view of comfort, human needs, it was singularly lacking. We were therefore tired, unwashed, and the toilet facilities were inadequate. Yet the crowds were huge, and impressive. The Stations of the Cross in the evening by candlelight was unforgettable. The place had a certain mountain beauty. There was tragedy there too, with so many people in wheelchairs, or ill, or incapable."

"Then there is the story of St. Bernadette. The English, as a nation tend to be sceptical. It is a difficulty for us to find acceptance. We have no saints in the Church of England."

"Yes," said Father Patrice, and smiled disarmingly.

It made Paul feel very small, even discourteous in talking as he did. Here he was a presumptuous twenty-one year old, a failed university student, challenging the beliefs of hundreds, even thousands, who believed in the sanctity of St. Bernadette. He suddenly felt it was hopeless talking to this rather enigmatic Father. Their minds didn't meet, and he was getting nowhere.

He rose, politely made his excuse about supper, and walked back to La Refaudio.

When he got home, Madame asked him how he got on.

"It wasn't terribly helpful," Paul admitted. "No meeting of great minds," he added jokingly, with a smile.

"Eh bien," said Madame, "we go to Montauban." She s smiling. "I have been busy, I have arranged for you to see Père Franchaud. He is a good man, very pious, but he is or local priest like le Père Patrice."

Paul expressed his gratitude.

"When will it be?" he asked. "In the evening?"

"The day after tomorrow," explained Madame.

"And transport?" queried Paul, conscious there was

"Why is that?" asked the priest.

"She is already married and won't or can't give up her husband, because of her faith," explained Paul.

"Ha," said the priest, and was silent a moment. Then he spoke, but in a kindly way,

"You mean Madame Koenitz?" the priest asked directly.

"Yes." Was Paul's simple answer.

The truth, the whole truth, and nothing but the naked truth was out. They were both silent for a moment. Finally the priest spoke.

"I thank you for telling me everything. I believe – no, I know – you are a good man. But this is a tragic situation and I feel for you, and even more for Madame."

The priest was silent again, and immersed in thought.

"But this is no time for platitudes!" he said. "You have no hope with Mme. Koenitz. She is loyal both to her husband, and to her Church. If you love her then you are best to leave her. Otherwise her husband, who is no real Catholic, may divorce her because of you, even if you are both innocent. It's harsh, but in this world evil can be harsh. I am sorry, very sorry. It is a tragedy for you, and for Madame!"

Again, the priest was silent, but he continued to smile at Paul. Finally he spoke again.

"Out of a bad situation sometimes good will come. I believe it has happened in this case. Not as a confession, but in conversation, Madame has not actually said so, but I believe she loves you too. She has certainly spoken of you in glowing terms, and how you have helped her, especially with the children. You have given her a new lease of life and she is immensely grateful."

The priest fell silent and smiled again. Then he continued.

"As I have said, I believe good, positive good, comes out of human love. Provided you have respected each other, I see no reason why you can't return to England and cherish this memory, and preserve it. Eventually you will marry somebody of your own age, have children, and yet always remember."

And then he added softly.

"Go with my blessing."

Paul thanked him and went, having thanked him again. It was a strange meeting, entirely dominated by the priest. But it was a meeting Paul was to remember with a feeling of appreciation for the man who was so understanding.

It was not a long meeting with the priest. Paul had to wait around for the brother to come. He spent some of the time in the church adjacent to the presbytery, where he prayed.

It was a muddled sort of prayer, as was often the case. It mainly centred on Madame, or Marguerite he should have said. He prayed that she might resolve her problems, find some peace and happiness. He couldn't see any answer, or how the situation could be resolved. He also had a thought for the children. He couldn't help thinking that a situation without a father was bound to affect them, as it had himself when his father was killed. He felt at the moment a little depressed as if the world was rather a harsh place, overshadowing the love he had for Marguerite, at least for the moment.

Paul sighed and left the church to wait for the brother.

# Chapter 18

*Harvesting!*

When Paul got back to La Refaudio, he said nothing to Madame until the following evening when they were sitting out on the balcony.

"How did you get on with Le Père Franchaud?" she asked, not for the first time that day.

Paul was rather cagey. He didn't really know what to say!

"He says he believes, or he thinks that you love me," Paul said. He sounded a bit aggrieved, but didn't mean to.

"Oh," said Madame, a little taken aback by his directness.

It was the truth Paul wanted to put to her. He had found that this worked so much better with Father Franchaud.

"I cannot talk of love, I must not, I cannot," was Madame's stressful comment.

"Why?" asked Paul somewhat ingenuously.

"Oh, Paul, you know as well as I do," Madame pleaded. "We've already talked about it. I am not free. I am married. I have five children. I just can't. My faith won't allow me. Please, Paul, try and understand. Besides I am so much older than you."

Paul was silent for a moment. Then he nodded, struck dumb by Madame's directness.

"I'm sorry," he said contritely, feeling in fact genuinely sorry, knowing what Father Franchaud had said. He felt in a muddle, rather a crazed muddle, like a spoilt child not having his cake. Madame was behaving much more maturely than he. Madame leant forward and touched his hand.

"I like you as a loyal friend, Paul," she said. "You've made such a difference for me since you arrived. I'm immensely grateful."

With this, Paul had to be content. He did say, however,

"It was the practice in the nineteenth century for girls to have dance cards, and they wrote the man's name down on the card against the dance he wanted. It's no longer used now. I was only joking, but I seriously want to dance with you, all night if possible."

"Why then do you ask me? There are plenty of pretty girls for you to dance with," Madame said teasingly. "I joke, but you know I'm no longer young. I can't dance all night, sadly!"

"I dance only with you," insisted Paul. "But when you are tired, do tell me, and we will sit out."

"Naughty boy!" she scolded him, tapping him playfully on the wrist. "But I don't think we dance together too much. Remember I have a duty to everyone. I think if we dance too much people will talk, and I can't allow that."

"Nonsense!" exclaimed Paul. In turn he tapped her reprovingly on the arm. Under the stars, in the artificial light in the area in front of the Salvetti house, she looked incredibly beautiful and slim and what was more, young. It was not an occasion one could dress up for. She wore a green skirt – green was her favourite colour. People said her eyes were green, but Paul did not, or could not notice. He was just that little bit colour blind!

She had no stockings on; in fact for most of the summer she hardly ever wore stockings; she had such lovely legs. On top she wore an attractive cream coloured, decorated blouse. She never wore jewellery. She also had a light green cardigan, in case it got chillier later on. Paul thought she was delectable, even adorable. He felt life for once had treated him kindly in finding such a freshness, such a rich feeling of love, something he felt he could never have experienced before. It was almost overwhelming.

Paul had the first two dances with her. The music came from a wireless and an amplifier. Madame, after their two dances, whispered to Paul, repeating her early remark that these were her people, and she did not want to cause gossip. She must be free to dance with others.

## Chapter 17

*Priestly Encounters*

Conversation, or instruction, began with le Pere Patrice three days later in the early evening before dinner. It was not entirely a good time for Paul. He came back to La Refaudio from looking after the children by the river. He washed and changed, and then, supperless, went down to the Presbytery.

Father Patrice was a quiet, kindly man with something of the austerity of his profession. He spoke no English. They had to converse in French, which by now was no problem for Paul.

"I understand from Mme. Koenitz you are considering entering the Catholic Church," he said, smiling kindly at Paul.

"Well, not exactly," countered Paul. "I am impressed by your church and would like to know a little more about it first."

"What exactly would you like to know?" asked the priest.

"Well, in what way does it differ from the Anglican Church, the Church of England?" Paul stated.

Father Patrice was quiet for a moment, and then he began to run through some of the historical and religious differences, most of which Paul knew, having studied history at Oxford.

"We recognise the Pope as the Head of the Church, the direct descendant of St. Peter by the laying on of hands. The head of the Anglican Church is the King, or the elected Archbishop of Canterbury."

Paul nodded in agreement. Father Patrice went on in a way that almost sent Paul to sleep. Finally Paul asked a crucial question.

"Why do you not accept divorce?" he said.

"Marriage is a Holy Sacrament," said the priest, "therefore unchangeable; marriage is for life."

"Therefore," challenged Paul, "if the marriage breaks down, even to mutual hatred, or disloyalty, no love left, man and wife still have to remain together. It's an impossible situation!"

"Yes," said the priest.

Paul sighed.

"That I cannot accept!" he stated. "One has to continue in a loveless marriage which has no meaning. It's a ridiculous situation."

Paul quoted the example of Madame Koenitz, a woman whose husband had deserted her for another, even had a child by his mistress. It was something Paul should not have mentioned, but he felt strongly about Madame's situation.

Father Patrice eyed him keenly.

"There I must stop you, my friend," stated the Priest. "Madame Koenitz is a member of my Parish. I owe to her the confidentiality, the secrecy of the confessional. I cannot in any way discuss her situation."

Paul sighed yet again.

"But you would agree that no possibility of divorce creates an impossible situation, a very unhappy one," Paul said.

But Father Patrice remained stolid, and firm in his beliefs, unmoveable!

Paul sighed yet again, inwardly. He hoped Father Patrice would not notice his lack of agreement. There was a certain point where their beliefs clashed. Paul felt he was up against a brick wall, impossible to break down.

"What attracts you about the Catholic Church?" asked Father Patrice in a kindly way.

"Oh, your piety is impressive, so marvellous, as if prayer really means something to you. There is the strength of your beliefs, your convictions, if you like. I can't accept some of them, as with divorce, but yours is a strong faith. In England faith is uncertain at times, and possibly declining, based on values of convenience. There is a spirit of compromise in the Church of England which doesn't help spiritually."

Father Patrice did not comment. They remained silent, facing each other, not knowing in which direction the conversation should go.

"Did you enjoy your visit to Lourdes?" Father Patrice finally asked. It was a conventional question, not very profound.

"I'm not sure 'enjoy' is the right word. But yes and no," replied Paul. "It was a small town, suddenly thrust into the limelight and unprepared for it. The crowds were way beyond its capacity to cope. From the point of view of comfort, human needs, it was singularly lacking. We were therefore tired, unwashed, and the toilet facilities were inadequate. Yet the crowds were huge, and impressive. The Stations of the Cross in the evening by candlelight was unforgettable. The place had a certain mountain beauty. There was tragedy there too, with so many people in wheelchairs, or ill, or incapable."

"Then there is the story of St. Bernadette. The English, as a nation tend to be sceptical. It is a difficulty for us to find acceptance. We have no saints in the Church of England."

"Yes," said Father Patrice, and smiled disarmingly.

It made Paul feel very small, even discourteous in talking as he did. Here he was a presumptuous twenty-one year old, a failed university student, challenging the beliefs of hundreds, even thousands, who believed in the sanctity of St. Bernadette. He suddenly felt it was hopeless talking to this rather enigmatic Father. Their minds didn't meet, and he was getting nowhere.

He rose, politely made his excuse about supper, and walked back to La Refaudio.

When he got home, Madame asked him how he got on.

"It wasn't terribly helpful," Paul admitted. "No meeting of great minds," he added jokingly, with a smile.

"Eh bien," said Madame, "we go to Montauban." She said smiling. "I have been busy, I have arranged for you to see Le Père Franchaud. He is a good man, very pious, but he is only a local priest like le Père Patrice."

Paul expressed his gratitude.

"When will it be?" he asked. "In the evening?"

"The day after tomorrow," explained Madame.

"And transport?" queried Paul, conscious there was no car.

"Pas de problème – no problem. M. Salvetti, comme toujours – as always – is too kind!"

So Paul waited with anticipation. Madame spoke so highly of this man! He wondered if any man could be so remarkable!

The day arrived. It wasn't M. Salvetti who took Paul but his talkative brother.

"You go-a to talk with Le Père Franchaud. He is-a a very good man, very friendly!" the brother explained.

Paul nodded.

"That's what I've heard," he agreed.

"You become-a Catholic?" asked the brother.

There was no end to the lively curiosity of the Italians!

"Madame Koenitz is-a very good Catholic! Verra nice woman!" stated the brother simply.

The Italian probing continued unabated, always with an innocent smile!

Paul nodded in agreement, but said nothing.

When they arrived, Le Père Franchaud had the customary elderly housekeeper who greeted them at the door.

"I'll be back-a in an hour or so," said the Italian.

Paul was led into a darkened room where sat Le Pere. A single lamp on his desk lit up the face of Paul's host. It was an older face than Father Patrice's, with a crop of white hair and a welcoming countenance. He was the first priest Paul had met with a twinkle in his eye, giving hope of a certain sense of humour. Their conversation was in French. Like Father Patrice, he had no knowledge of English. He appeared so kindly, Paul almost instantly warmed to the man.

"Ah, the young Englishman interested in Catholicism! An unusual situation! Why is this so?" was the priest's greeting with a smile.

Paul decided to throw caution to the winds and tell only the truth, or as near the truth as he could. Perhaps that was the problem with Father Patrice. They hedged around the truth.

"I love – I admire – a Catholic girl, a French girl," admitted Paul tentatively.

"And you wish to marry her?" asked the priest.

"Yes, – er – but I can't," admitted Paul.

"Why is that?" asked the priest.

"She is already married and won't or can't give up her husband, because of her faith," explained Paul.

"Ha," said the priest, and was silent a moment. Then he spoke, but in a kindly way,

"You mean Madame Koenitz?" the priest asked directly.

"Yes." Was Paul's simple answer.

The truth, the whole truth, and nothing but the naked truth was out. They were both silent for a moment. Finally the priest spoke.

"I thank you for telling me everything. I believe – no, I know – you are a good man. But this is a tragic situation and I feel for you, and even more for Madame."

The priest was silent again, and immersed in thought.

"But this is no time for platitudes!" he said. "You have no hope with Mme. Koenitz. She is loyal both to her husband, and to her Church. If you love her then you are best to leave her. Otherwise her husband, who is no real Catholic, may divorce her because of you, even if you are both innocent. It's harsh, but in this world evil can be harsh. I am sorry, very sorry. It is a tragedy for you, and for Madame!"

Again, the priest was silent, but he continued to smile at Paul. Finally he spoke again.

"Out of a bad situation sometimes good will come. I believe it has happened in this case. Not as a confession, but in conversation, Madame has not actually said so, but I believe she loves you too. She has certainly spoken of you in glowing terms, and how you have helped her, especially with the children. You have given her a new lease of life and she is immensely grateful."

The priest fell silent and smiled again. Then he continued.

"As I have said, I believe good, positive good, comes out of human love. Provided you have respected each other, I see no reason why you can't return to England and cherish this memory, and preserve it. Eventually you will marry somebody of your own age, have children, and yet always remember."

And then he added softly.

"Go with my blessing."

Paul thanked him and went, having thanked him again. It was a strange meeting, entirely dominated by the priest. But it was a meeting Paul was to remember with a feeling of appreciation for the man who was so understanding.

It was not a long meeting with the priest. Paul had to wait around for the brother to come. He spent some of the time in the church adjacent to the presbytery, where he prayed.

It was a muddled sort of prayer, as was often the case. It mainly centred on Madame, or Marguerite he should have said. He prayed that she might resolve her problems, find some peace and happiness. He couldn't see any answer, or how the situation could be resolved. He also had a thought for the children. He couldn't help thinking that a situation without a father was bound to affect them, as it had himself when his father was killed. He felt at the moment a little depressed as if the world was rather a harsh place, overshadowing the love he had for Marguerite, at least for the moment.

Paul sighed and left the church to wait for the brother.

# Chapter 18

*Harvesting!*

When Paul got back to La Refaudio, he said nothing to Madame until the following evening when they were sitting out on the balcony.

"How did you get on with Le Père Franchaud?" she asked, not for the first time that day.

Paul was rather cagey. He didn't really know what to say!

"He says he believes, or he thinks that you love me," Paul said. He sounded a bit aggrieved, but didn't mean to.

"Oh," said Madame, a little taken aback by his directness.

It was the truth Paul wanted to put to her. He had found that this worked so much better with Father Franchaud.

"I cannot talk of love, I must not, I cannot," was Madame's stressful comment.

"Why?" asked Paul somewhat ingenuously.

"Oh, Paul, you know as well as I do," Madame pleaded. "We've already talked about it. I am not free. I am married. I have five children. I just can't. My faith won't allow me. Please, Paul, try and understand. Besides I am so much older than you."

Paul was silent for a moment. Then he nodded, struck dumb by Madame's directness.

"I'm sorry," he said contritely, feeling in fact genuinely sorry, knowing what Father Franchaud had said. He felt in a muddle, rather a crazed muddle, like a spoilt child not having his cake. Madame was behaving much more maturely than he. Madame leant forward and touched his hand.

"I like you as a loyal friend, Paul," she said. "You've made such a difference for me since you arrived. I'm immensely grateful."

With this, Paul had to be content. He did say, however,

"It was the practice in the nineteenth century for girls to have dance cards, and they wrote the man's name down on the card against the dance he wanted. It's no longer used now. I was only joking, but I seriously want to dance with you, all night if possible."

"Why then do you ask me? There are plenty of pretty girls for you to dance with," Madame said teasingly. "I joke, but you know I'm no longer young. I can't dance all night, sadly!"

"I dance only with you," insisted Paul. "But when you are tired, do tell me, and we will sit out."

"Naughty boy!" she scolded him, tapping him playfully on the wrist. "But I don't think we dance together too much. Remember I have a duty to everyone. I think if we dance too much people will talk, and I can't allow that."

"Nonsense!" exclaimed Paul. In turn he tapped her reprovingly on the arm. Under the stars, in the artificial light in the area in front of the Salvetti house, she looked incredibly beautiful and slim and what was more, young. It was not an occasion one could dress up for. She wore a green skirt – green was her favourite colour. People said her eyes were green, but Paul did not, or could not notice. He was just that little bit colour blind!

She had no stockings on; in fact for most of the summer she hardly ever wore stockings; she had such lovely legs. On top she wore an attractive cream coloured, decorated blouse. She never wore jewellery. She also had a light green cardigan, in case it got chillier later on. Paul thought she was delectable, even adorable. He felt life for once had treated him kindly in finding such a freshness, such a rich feeling of love, something he felt he could never have experienced before. It was almost overwhelming.

Paul had the first two dances with her. The music came from a wireless and an amplifier. Madame, after their two dances, whispered to Paul, repeating her early remark that these were her people, and she did not want to cause gossip. She must be free to dance with others.

"And you must find a pretty girl," she said to Paul, grinning. He pulled a face, and tried to say she was the only pretty one present, but she had already slipped away.

When they broke apart M. Salvetti's brother claimed her. He danced well and Paul was envious. He also seemed to have the Italian capability to make her laugh. Paul's dances with Madame had been mostly silent! They didn't need to talk; they talked so much on the balcony! During the dance it was a moment of silent enjoyment, of motion, of physical rapport.

After the dance with the Italian Madame chose to rest, and sat with Madame Salvetti. They chatted. Paul felt a little out of it, but seeing Anne-Marie alone, he took pity on her, and asked her for a dance. She was not the most attractive of girls, but he liked her; she was so loyal and helpful to Madame and the children. And for some reason she was good with François, and able to talk to him.

All too quickly, the evening began to draw to a close, and people began to drift away home. Paul had a last dance with Madame, and just for a moment she danced close to him. He felt her body in wonder, and held her tight. Just for a moment it was unforgettable. Then she broke away, smiled shyly at him, and went to say her goodbyes. Paul and Anne-Marie also gave their thanks to the Salvettis.

At the house they relieved the elderly lady who had looked after the children. Only Jean-Pierre had come down to supper. But once he had eaten, he went back to the house.

The climax for Paul came when they got back to La Refaudio. Anne-Marie went to her room in the basement. Madame whispered to Paul to wait for her in the sitting room while she checked on the children, and said goodbye to the elderly babysitter.

Paul sank down in one of the comfortable fireside chairs. When Madame came down she said.

"I play for you."

She played a hauntingly beautiful tune. She said it came from Mozart's 'Così Fan Tutte'. Paul remembered his mother had played it sometimes at home when she was sad and missed her husband when he was away during the War.

When Madame finished, she paused, shut the piano quietly, and came into his arms. He held her tightly, overwhelmed with longing for this lovely woman. He whispered to her.

"I love you, Madame. Everything in me aches for you."

She drew back, touched his lips with her finger and said.

"Those are words I do not hear. Dear Paul. Be content with what you have, and do not speak of love. That is impossible."

She gave him another kiss, slipped out of his arms, smiled and went upstairs, leaving a dazed and longing young man.

The second harvest supper came three days later, at the third large farm near the river. The smaller farm by La Refaudio grew only vegetables. Besides, the tenants were elderly.

Although Italians, they had never had a harvest supper on the second farm for as long as anyone could remember, according to Madame.

The harvest supper Chez Les Bertolis did not measure up to the one at the Salvettis. For one, M. Bertoli was a morose man and lacked the Italian exuberance. The pleasure and the food came nowhere near what Madame Salvetti gave. The food he supplied was merely basic, the wine not so generous. But there was still the inevitable chicken.

But it followed in the same pattern as at Salvetti. One ate, one drank, and then one danced.

Julie, their daughter, enjoyed the dancing. She was a little tipsy, and got highly excited. Paul, obeying Madame's instructions, spread his favours and had one dance with Julie. When their dance was over Julie said a little impishly,

"Now, do I dance as well as Madame?"

He was so surprised that he failed to answer. But thinking about this remark afterwards, he suddenly realised how much his situation with Madame was being discussed in the village. It gave him qualms for Madame, and he only danced with her once more. But then he was forced to dance with her a second time. The incident was rather strange.

There was a short, dark-haired man, about the same height as Madame. She was not noticeably tall for a woman. The same man danced twice consecutively with Madame, and was unnecessarily vigorous and demanding. He swung her round and round, and Madame at the end looked as if it was almost too much for her. When he went up to her for a third dance, Paul saw Madame hesitate. Paul quickly stepped in and said politely.

"I believe, Madame, you promised me this dance."

Madame smiled and acquiesced. He quietly danced her away, and did not see the scowl on the man's face. But Madame did and was afraid. The man had been drinking!

"Paul," she whispered. "I'm tired. Would you mind if I went back to the house. The Salvettis are leaving. I'll go back with them. You follow immediately with Anne-Marie. I am anxious for you, please, Paul. That man is angry, bien fache." She indicated the sullen man.

When Paul got back to La Refaudio Madame was waiting for him.

"I'm sorry, Paul," she said contritely. "It wasn't so much being tired; I disliked that man so much, I just wanted to get away. Thank you for intervening so quickly."

"Knight to the rescue," joked Paul, with a smile.

Madame smiled in turn, but said no more. After a brief hug she went up to bed.

The evening had not been a great success, compared with the Salvettis! Paul felt a pang of disappointment. His feelings were churning up his young heart.

# Chapter 19

*'Home'*

It was nearing the time Paul had to return home, but there was a certain formality he had to overcome before doing so. His passport allowed him to stay in France three months, but he had already exceeded this by over four weeks.

To rectify the situation Paul went to the Police Station in Montauban. But they just shook their heads, shrugged their shoulders, and opened their hands as if it was all hopeless. There was nothing they could do.

Paul had visions of being stopped at the Passport Office of the French port when leaving the country, being arrested for over-staying his welcome, finally being prevented from returning to England. It was a horrible thought, especially as it might stop him from being at the school the day before term started, as he had promised.

He spoke to Madame about his predicament, and wondered if she could help.

"N'ayez pas peur – don't be afraid," she said. "I will come with you tomorrow to Montauban."

When the next day came, Paul was surprised to see Madame dressed up to the nines! She had put on her best green dress, a dress Paul loved, with high collar, a mild cleavage, and showing off her figure to the best advantage. She had also put on perfume and make-up. She was dressed to kill, as Paul remarked.

"But why such a lovely dress, Marguerite?" he asked. "You look more lovely than usual, or perhaps I ought to say, your dress enhances your beauty!"

But she just smiled and winked.

The problem of the car had been solved. The Koenitz family had sent her money to buy her own car, which she had done. When they got to the police, Paul began to realise why Madame had dressed up. He nearly burst out laughing. The policeman was all over her with charm, patting her hand that she left resting on the counter. He was full of positives, very different from the remote, negative manner of yesterday.

"Oui, Madame!" "Certainement, Madame!" "Bien sûr, Madame!" he continued to say, repeating over and over again his willingness to help.

Within half an hour, Paul had the letter he wanted. It wasn't a carte de séjour, but Madame explained it would do the trick if he was stopped at the port.

Paul wondered if a situation like Madame's flirtation could happen in England. He thought not; it was an aspect of French character which seemed peculiarly un-English. But he wasn't sure; women used their wiles the world over!

The last few days at La Refaudio were sad for Paul and Madame.

"Will you come and see me?" she asked.

"Of course," Paul assured her. "Wild horses won't stop me. Prep schools have a month's holiday at Christmas and Easter. How will you manage with the children?" Paul asked finally.

"I don't know," said Madame rather sadly. "But God will help me. You were an answer to a prayer, Paul, and it was such a nice answer!"

"I wish I had your faith," Paul remarked.

"The faith is there, Paul," she said. "You've only to ask for it," reassured Madame.

Paul thought a moment.

"I'd like to become a Catholic," he said. "Le Père Franchaud said I needed further instruction, which I will seek when in England."

Madame breathed a happy sigh.

"I should be very, very happy, dear Paul, if you did become a Catholic," she said with an encouraging smile. "You have my sincere prayers and thoughts. Oh, Paul!" and she sighed again.

"Is there a godmother in Catholicism?" asked Paul. "You know, one of those people who promise to support you in your Christian life."

"Why, yes," said Madame.

"Well then, I will ask you to come and be my godmother when I am baptised," said Paul with a happy smile.

"Ça me fait grand plaisir," said Madame. "That will give me great pleasure, and happiness!"

Madame smiled at him. She got up from her deck-chair and moved over to him. She kissed him long and lovingly on the lips. She began to move reluctantly away, her hand lingering on his arm. A few moments after she had left the balcony, Paul heard the soft notes of the piano, and then her singing in the balm of the evening, despite the noise of the crickets. It sounded exquisite, soothing, and made him sigh with longing. He got up, went into the house. He sat down in one of the fireside chairs and listened, enthralled.

When she finished, he got up, stood behind her, and embraced her, his arms wrapping around her. In this position he felt the swell of her breasts and sighed.

For a moment Madame leant back against him, enjoying the strength of his clasp.

Then she gently extricated herself.

"No, Paul, you naughty boy, you mustn't," she said in a kindly way.

"I wish you wouldn't call me a 'boy'," grumbled Paul mildly.

"I'm so much older than you," said Madame. "I wish I had known you when we were the same age." And she sighed.

Paul wanted to ask her why they couldn't cuddle each other, but he knew why.

"Goodnight, my dearest. Thank you for everything," she said softly.

And she slipped away!

Paul decided to go home on the twelfth of September. It was cutting things fine, but it would give him time to go home, collect his things and clothes for the winter, and see his sister. Then he could get down to the school at Motherton in

Somerset by the evening of the fourteenth, ready for the beginning of term on the fifteenth. He had written to the headmaster telling him of his plans. He received a grudging acceptance.

The letter implied that there was a lot to do before term began. The headmaster would excuse him.

Paul rather resented the tone of the letter. After all they had agreed on the fourteenth. No mention had been made about pre-term work. Paul wondered whether he should have arrived earlier than the evening. But again no mention had been made. He felt the term would be starting for him under a cloud.

On his last evening sitting on the balcony with Madame, she spoke, completely out of the blue,

"Paul, two days after you leave, I go into hospital for an operation."

Paul was shocked.

"Oh Marguerite, I never knew. Is it serious? What is wrong with you? How long will you be in hospital?" he asked in anxiety.

"How long I just don't know, Paul. It's not serious. It's just one of those things that happen to women after childbirth, after bearing children," she explained rather vacantly.

Paul didn't know enough of women to realise what she might be saying. But beyond that she would not explain. As Paul, at twenty-one, knew little of the mysterious illnesses that inflicted women, he had to be content.

But he was concerned!

"I wish you had told me earlier. I would have stayed longer. Who, for instance, will look after the children?" he asked.

Madame smiled, and said,

"It's precisely why I didn't tell you," she admitted smiling. "I was afraid you'd cancel everything and stay on, and spoil your plans for the future. You see, Paul, I know you and ......"

She suddenly stopped and didn't continue for a moment. She looked almost in tears. Finally she said.

"The children will be all right," she said reassuringly. "My sister is coming down tomorrow with her husband, André. They will stay a few days, and then take the children back to their home. It's a village, a few miles from Paris. She has a big house, bigger than La Refaudio."

"And you, Madame, who will look after you?" Paul asked.

"Oh, Paul, stop worrying about me," Madame chided. "You break my heart, you are so kind. But I'll manage."

She smiled wanly at him, but there was a glistening of tears in her eyes once again.

"No, Paul, I'll be okay," she continued. "As soon as I am out of hospital, my sister will come down with the children and stay while I convalesce. Anne-Marie will be here also. She's a real treasure."

Paul pondered sadly for a moment. All these plans had been made without any mention to him. He felt hurt and left out of Madame's life.

"I'm very sorry to be leaving you at such a moment," he said slowly and sadly.

"Oh, Paul, don't be silly," she chided. "It's only an operation. After a month or so I shall be all right, as good as new. At least I hope so."

Paul looked sadly at her.

"Will I be able to come at Christmas?" he asked.

"Of course, Paul. I shall be unhappy if you don't come," she said reassuringly. "Stop looking so worried my dear. You look as if the whole world is on your shoulders. There's nothing to worry about, really there isn't! It's an operation common to a lot of women," she explained as cheerfully as she could.

For Paul, the agony of saying goodbye at the station of Montauban was increased by the memory of four months ago. Here he had sat alone for half an hour waiting for M. Koenitz. Now he was waved farewell by five children, and Madame looking so beautiful on a warm beginning of an autumn day. M. Salvetti had helped bring all the children, plus Anne-Marie.

"I wish-a you a happy return," M. Salvetti said, beaming. "Be-a good boy and think-a of us."

Madame said nothing, merely 'bon voyage', looking sad and forlorn. It was little Nano who touched Paul's already over-burdened heart. Nano came up to him, grinning all over his impish face and planted one damp kiss on his cheek. Paul gave him a hug and nearly cried. In the end he embraced everybody, Madame last. He went on board the train with a heavy heart.

At Paris, he had a two hour wait for his connection, the boat train to Dieppe.

In that time he wrote a letter to Madame, acting very much on impulse.

*My dear Marguerite,*

*I'm sitting in a cafe in Paris, drinking coffee, missing you so much, worrying about you and this mysterious operation you won't tell me about, and – and – loving you so much. The past summer has been one of the happiest times I have ever known, or ever had!*

*Please, please, Marguerite, will you marry me? I want you so badly. I feel miserable without you. I have nothing to offer you, no money, no house, but I will work my fingers to the bone to support you and the children. And who knows perhaps one day we can have our very own child.*

*Let's pray it will be a daughter, a lovely daughter!*

*You talk a lot about God, and duty. It makes God seem a very strict, hard being. I believe God is love, and he helps those who truly love, as we do.*

*Oh, Marguerite, I miss you so much. When you are better, please write and give me your answer.*

*Bye, dearest. I hope and pray all goes well with you.*

*Fondest love Paul, and many of these xxxxxxxx*

Paul re-read the letter, put it in an envelope and posted it.

When Paul got to London, he went straight to his sister's flat.

"Hello, Frog," was her cheerful greeting. "I hope you haven't forgotten how to speak English."

This was a reference to Paul saying in a letter he spoke nothing but French, even dreamt in French.

During the evening he told Sis of Madame's operation.

"And Madame, as you call her, are you still fond of her?" Sis asked.

Paul had written to Sis in some enthusiasm about Madame.

"Immensely," replied Paul. "I love her, and have asked her to marry me."

"You've what?" asked Sis astonished.

"To marry me, you know, hand in marriage, wedlock," advised Paul, grinning.

Sis continued to look astonished.

"You are a little ninny," she said.

"Why?" it was Paul's turn to be astonished.

"Have you ever thought what Madame's illness might be?" She asked.

"No, she wouldn't talk about it," admitted Paul.

"Women don't!" she advised. "Well, from what you say I imagine she's going to have a hysterectomy," explained Sis.

"A hysterectomy? What on earth's that?" asked Paul in his innocence, surprised.

"It's the removal of the womb," she explained. "It means a woman can no longer have children. Women usually don't talk about it very much, especially to men."

Paul looked astounded.

"A hysterectomy!" he repeated.

"Have you never heard the word before?" asked his sister, marvelling at his innocence.

"No, never. But remember I miss so much in conversation, my hearing being what it is," explained Paul. But he could almost laugh at himself. He had proposed marriage and suggested children to a woman who could no longer have children seemingly. No wonder she called him a 'boy'!

His lack of hearing was Paul's invariable excuse for all his misdemeanours!

"Oh, Paul," said Sis, seeing Paul's woebegone face. "I'm sorry. You have fallen flat on your face, I'm afraid!"

Paul suddenly laughed.

"And I've told Madame we can have children!" he confessed. "She must think me an idiot!"

Sis smiled. The atmosphere was suddenly lightened.

"Well," said Paul, "she said she would never divorce her husband. Her Catholic faith won't allow it."

"But you still hoped?" queried Sis curiously.

"Yes, I felt she loved me," Paul said, "but could never bring herself to say it. Her Catholic faith again!"

"You admire her faith?" asked Sis.

"Yes," said Paul, "It gave her great strength in time of difficulty."

But Paul did not refer to his own wish to become a Catholic. His sister would have opposed it, had he done so.

The next day Paul went to his mother's. Nothing was said as to recent events. Mother was mostly delighted that he looked so well, but expressed the same concern as Madame about his choice of teaching.

The next day Paul travelled to Somerset to begin his new career. While at the school Paul received a letter from Madame. She wrote as she talked. Her voice sounded out realistically from her letter.

*My very dearest Paul,*

*I'm sorry I've been so long in writing in answer to your letter. It was brought to me while I was in hospital. I was at first too woozy, too uncomfortable to be able to reply. But now it's better, and I go home soon.*

*However, Paul, I was deeply touched by your letter, and flattered you love me. I love you too, more than I can put in words. But you know it's impossible. I went through the sacrament of marriage, and it's God's wish I should abide by the vows I took. I'm so sorry, Paul. You will understand better when you become a Catholic, and I do pray that it will be so!*

*I must stop, Paul dear, the stuff they have given me makes me so sleepy.*

*Come and see me at Christmas when I will be better. Despite everything I want to see you and remain your friend.*

*Bye, my dear, my prayers and thoughts always. Marguerite. xxxxx*

When, one evening, Paul told the Chorleys he would be going to France at Christmas, Mrs Chorley, the interfering old cow, said,

"I advise you not to go. We recognised the situation there."

Paul was dumbfounded. What situation had they recognised? Neither Paul nor Madame had spoken of anything. He concluded that it was none of their business! He was offended she tried to interfere!

Meanwhile Paul was starting to take religious instruction. But it was a little unconvincing. Catholicism seemed a part of French culture, of France itself. But in England it was a different story. Nowhere was there the support, or the piety, or the faith he had experienced in France. The English priest was a man of negatives. Not so much 'thou shalt', but more a whole list of "thou shalt nots".

Thou shalt not use contraceptives, thou shalt not abort one's child, thou shalt not eat meat on Fridays, thou shalt not divorce, and so many others.

The priest himself was a thin, dark, tight-lipped man, intent on the negatives rather than presenting the joyous love of God.

How Paul longed to be back in France, its excitability, its joyous love of life, its restless attitudes, its seeking for the beauty of life. The story of St Bernadette of Lourdes was typically French. It could never have happened in England. The story was of youth, innocence, the longing to create something beautiful, part of so wonderful an existence.

Paul longed to get back to France, to a country where the Catholic faith seemed to mean something. To that end he wrote to Madame and asked if he could go to a religious retreat for three days while visiting her at Christmas in Paris. She wrote back and said she would be happy to arrange it.

# Chapter 20

*Teaching Disaster!*

Teaching at the school run by Mr. Choley was not the happiest of experiences. For one thing it was not a Prep School as Paul had believed. It took all pupils, both boys and girls, regardless of educational ability and intelligence. There was one boy who could not read. There were just a few boarders, all boys, among the one hundred and thirty pupils. The school gave the impression of being overcrowded. The most alarming feature was that the school was not fully recognised, and an inspector was coming in October, towards the end of the month.

The staff were a hotch-potch. Apart from Mr. Choley, who did very little teaching (he seemed to regard teaching as beneath him) there were only two full-time teachers, Paul and Peter Boswith. The rest were part-time teachers. There was an attractive lady who taught art one day a week, and dancing one afternoon a week to the girls only. She seemed to have a phobia about men - all intent on taking advantage of her. She told one story about the local dentist. Once she had an anaesthetic. When she came round he was whispering naughty suggestions in her ear. Paul had difficulty believing her story when he got to know the dentist concerned. There was a P.E. teacher who came twice a week, but only for the boys.

The strangest teacher was Peter Boswith; Paul grew to like him.

"I'm sixty-nine," he told Paul. "I should have retired four years ago, but hadn't the finance. On my c.v. I admit to being fifty-nine, but don't you dare give me away, or I'll throttle you."

Paul wondered how he got away with it in this increasingly bureaucratic age since the Labour government had come to power in 1945. The other surprising thing about him was that he was married to a dark-haired girl who must have been over thirty years younger than him. She was young enough to be Peter's daughter! They had a baby girl, a little sweetie.

Peter was a real cynic. To Paul he commented unfavourably on the Choleys, the school, the government, and people. But he wisely kept his opinions about the school married quarters to himself, apart from grumbling that they were sub-standard.

The building was a wooden structure, consisting of two rooms, a bedroom and a sitting-room, with an added kitchen and bathroom, also of wood.

"The roof leaks," Peter told Paul. "The wood is rotting in certain parts. The whole structure has not been maintained over the years. Choley promised to have the building refurbished, but that was two years ago, and nothing has been done. The bloody man is a skinflint."

Paul found the building warm and comfortable, but it was mostly because of the wife's, Teresa's, hard work with a paint-brush. The heating came from a boiler in the kitchen, and warm pipes leading from it. But Paul wondered how they survived in a bitter winter.

"We get by," muttered Peter, "but it's no thanks to that bloody man, Choley."

He was full of his 'bloodies', was Peter. But it must be worrying for him, and for all of them, with a baby.

The inspection, when it did come, was a disaster for Paul and for the school, as Peter had predicted.

The build-up was a frantic effort by the Choleys to get the place in order. It wasn't apparently their first inspection. Equipment was brought out that Peter remarked had never been used before. A slide projector was produced, with slides showing various countries. A dilapidated horse box was repaired for the P.E. teacher. But when it was used it was obvious the children were not accustomed to it.

Paul suffered badly on three counts. The inspector commented unfavourably on an essay title – 'Queen Victoria's Reign Was A Happy One'. The inspector disliked the word 'happy'. Paul was trying to get the children to write down the more successful aspects of her reign, after reading about it in class.

But the worst humiliation was a remark made by Mrs. Choley to the inspector, which Paul couldn't help overhearing. She had a loud, carrying voice.

"Oh, he's only a stop gap," she said offhandedly. "He's leaving at the end of the summer term."

This leaving was news to Paul, but he didn't say anything. He was giving in his term's notice at Christmas to leave at Easter. What upset him was the apparent cruelty of the Choleys. The first incident concerned a girl in Paul's class who had been disruptive and not particularly hard-working. He had mentioned this to Mr. Choley, intending to take his advice as to what to do about it. The next thing he knew was that the girl was summoned out of the class by the headmaster. He talked to her severely and caned her on both hands. She came back into Paul's class, weeping and clutching painful palms. Paul was so stricken that he swore to himself that he would never mention any difficult pupils to Mr. Choley again.

He would have to deal with them himself, and not seek advice from a head who seemed to be a bit of a sadist. The girl was supposed to apologise to him, but she never did. When asked, Paul told Mr. Choley that she had. It was a lie, but Paul thought the girl had suffered enough.

The other incident that upset Paul concerned a nine year-old boarder who was rather finickety about his food. So Mr Choley took his cane and stood over the boy until he had finished every scrap on his plate. The boy held out for nearly an hour, blubbing pathetically away. When he did finish his food he was sick all over the floor. Paul rather hoped that the child would be sick over the menacing Mr. Choley, but the Head seemed blissfully unaware. Was this from previous experience, Paul wondered?

Paul thought there were other ways of getting a child to eat other than bullying. The whole incident upset him, and seemed typical of the sadistic Headmaster.

It was not a happy school by any means, for pupils and staff!

But by far the worse was Mrs. Choley.

She seemed never to have a kind or compassionate word for anyone. Her enormous bulk made her look formidable.

Like many overweight women she seemed to lean slightly back to counterbalance the weight in front of her. Peter thought of her as a tank, with her breasts like two guns firing downward. Teresa, in her gentle way, protested at this description as unnecessarily cruel, but she had little to do with Mrs. Choley as she did not work at the school. She had been a legal secretary before the arrival of the baby. Trust Peter to find an intelligent, loving girl!

What, Paul wondered, did she see in him?

What did any girls see in men? But she obviously loved Peter. Teresa seemed to regard his open cynicism as an expression of truth, even though she didn't always agree with it. Paul thought her a rather a lovely girl, both in character and appearance. He wondered whether Peter had been married before.

There were two things that made life bearable, apart from Peter and Teresa. One was the choir. He was encouraged by a parent to join the local choir that met once or twice a week. Paul really had no singing voice, as the choir master soon realised. But Paul enjoyed the social life. He found, as he often had done, that regular singers had good speaking voices, always clear and well-articulated.

The other asset was the Sunday school walk. Paul and the young matron, Joan, took the boarders for an outing, provided the weather was fine. Joan was nineteen, engaged to a newly qualified doctor and saving her pennies towards her marriage. She was a sensible, equable girl, who kept herself very much to herself in the school. But like Paul she found the walks were fun. The boarders were supposed to walk in solemn, crocodile fashion in pairs. But once in the country, the children were allowed to break free and they ran around enthusiastically like wild animals. For some lucky reason the Choleys never heard of this excited disorder. The children seemed to realise that the

Choleys must never know. They played tag and hide and seek, and were amazed that Joan could run.

"Golly, Miss," they would say, "you can run!"

"Of course," Joan would say. "I'll race you to that tree."

She always won! It seemed in child minds men like Paul could run, but not girls!

"Who could run the fastest, you or Miss?" they would ask Paul.

"Well, let's have a race," Paul challenged Joan.

The children set out a course, and Paul, ever the gentleman, let Joan win.

"Cor," went the children, amazed, and rather admiring of Joan.

Paul and Joan joined in all the games. Then they all, adults and children, collapsed down on the ground, breathless.

Joan distributed sweets, which she and Paul combined to buy.

Then came the lengthy task of brushing themselves down so that the Choleys would never know. On the way back there was a drinking fountain in the main square and they all queued up for a swig.

The crocodile walk back was full of excited chatter. Paul and Joan had to hush them as they drew near the school.

They were out for two hours, but Paul felt the walk was a great relief to his depressed spirits.

There was another incident which disillusioned Paul about the school. This was small in itself but it was typical of the Choleys. Paul was initially put in charge of the football team. They only had two matches that first term.

"I want to know the team," insisted Mr. Choley.

Paul couldn't understand why, but he dutifully handed in the team sheet before the first match. It was then he realised that Choley had favourites, always the children of his wealthiest parents. He changed three names in the team, including, crucially, the goalkeeper. Paul's own choice was a bit of an inexperienced pick, but he felt that he had chosen the best team possible. The Head's replacement in goal was hopeless, and they lost badly. Paul was about to protest he must have a free hand for the next match, but to Paul's astonishment, Choley said to him.

"I'm giving the football to Mr. Wyatt. It was a bad loss. Mr. Wyatt has more experience of football coaching than you."

Mr. Wyatt was the part-time P.E. teacher, and Paul felt he did not have the time or involvement to give to a team.

Paul stood open-mouthed at this snub. Luckily he didn't lose his temper. When he thought about it, Paul realised he ceased to care. They won the next match and the original choices were fully restored to their positions, much to their delight.

Peter remarked cynically.

"Choley's a bloody coward. He can muck about with you who have had no experience and were too young, but he wouldn't dare it to Wyatt who's a stubborn sod. He'd probably walk out if he was treated as you have been."

Peter's words were harsh, but Paul realised their truth. He just longed for the day when he could rid himself of the Choleys.

"For God's sake," said Peter, "get a qualification before you do any more teaching, or you'll be chivvied unmercifully. Believe me!"

Paul nodded. He was coming to the same conclusion!

# Chapter 21

*Return to France!*

France was not quite the same. It was cold, wet, and blowy in Paris, where Madame was now living with her sister. It seemed like an extension of England! There were no hot summer evenings sitting on the balcony in deck chairs. Madame greeted him at the station. She looked as beautiful as ever, and perhaps smarter – yes definitely smarter! No longer the casual summer dresses, or the skirt and blouse and no stockings. She wore a blue suit, matching skirt and jacket, with a little blue scarf at her neck, and surprise, surprise, a hat, a little coquettish bit of blue material with a tiny veil. She looked surprisingly well, and Paul realised it had been over three months since her operation.

"Oh, Paul, I am glad to see you," was her greeting. She was the same old Madame under that smartness. Paul wondered why she was smart. It never occurred to him that she dressed up for him! He too was in a suit, no longer summer clothing, no shorts and sandals. They were both presenting a smart image different from the time at La Refaudio.

"It's the same for me. I couldn't be more pleased," he said enthusiastically. They embraced, and then quietly she led him to her car, and a trip to a village about thirty kilometres outside Paris. On the way they talked. Paul asked after the children, and was told they were all well. Madame asked after the school and teaching.

"The school I shall be leaving at Easter, rather as you predicted. It's been very disappointing," he explained. "The teaching has been fine, but I'm very inexperienced."

He told her of various instances which had upset him. She smiled sympathetically, and then told him something of her life in or near Paris, She enjoyed being back at Paris, which she had hardly seen since her marriage.

Paul stayed with a friend of Madame's, only half a dozen houses from Madame herself. Madame explained that her sister's house was full to the brim, and apologised, explaining that he would be staying separately. The village was very rural, but half closed up as if they were afraid to open their front doors. Madame explained that most of the inhabitants lived and worked in Paris, and only came down for 'le weekend' in the country.

The next day Paul, after a good night's sleep, went round to have lunch with Madame's sister, and Madame of course. For some strange reason, the children were not there, and Paul wondered why.

Le dejeuner – the lunch – passed affably. Paul happened to mention that his father was in the rearguard while the soldiers were being evacuated at Dunkirk. The sister's, Jeannette's, husband was a thin rather intense man in his late forties. He launched into a defence or excuse for the French army.

"The Germans were so well equipped, so fast, and with tanks superior to ours, we hadn't a chance," he explained sorrowfully. "We fought as if it was the First World War. The Germans had other ideas, more advanced than ours."

He didn't, unlike many French men, blame the catastrophe of 1940 on the British. For that Paul was grateful!

Jeannette was older than Madame, a stouter, bigger version. She was possibly of a more decisive character, as events were to prove.

After lunch Jeannette asked Paul and Madame to come up stairs. She wanted to have a private word with them. She looked so serious, Paul was puzzled and it seemed Madame was too.

Jeannette came straight to the point.

"I don't think you, dear sister, and Paul should be together. I think you ought to separate immediately."

Madame was astonished, as was Paul.

"Why?" asked Madame.

"You know why, Marguerite, as well as I do," stated Jeannette firmly. "Jacques has recovered from his breakdown. He's now on the prowl. He wants his children. If he can find any excuse to take them away, such as your relationship with Paul, he will do so."

"But Madame has done nothing wrong." Paul couldn't bring himself to say her Christian name, Marguerite. "Nor have I for that matter. Madame has always described our relationship as platonic. I like to think it was friendship. That man has nothing on us."

Madame nodded in agreement.

"Whether he has or not, I don't think you should give him the opportunity. It's what is known as tempting providence," Jeannette said seriously.

"Well," Paul said, "I'll do whatever Madame says. I've said it before on many occasions."

"Oh, stop calling her, 'Madame'. She's Marguerite, nothing else," muttered Jeannette.

"That depends on Madame as to what I call her. I love her and because I love her, I want to do what she wants." He was beginning to get a little irritated by Jeannette, sister or not. He had come all this way to see Madame, and now Jeannette was telling him he couldn't see her.

"Don't get angry, Paul; my sister's only trying to help me. She is on my side, and I'm grateful," pointed out Madame, and she smiled kindly at Paul. "There are plenty of people who could say we spent a lot of time together. I hope they won't, but there are."

"So I am to leave, give you up," concluded Paul, real disappointment on his face.

"I'm afraid so; my faith tells me so!" said Madame softly.

"I don't admire your faith which keeps men and women together when they cease to love each other, or when marriage vows are broken by infidelity and strange behaviour," Paul said bitterly. "In your case it condemns you to a life of anxiety and unhappiness. It cannot be right. It can't be what God wants!"

Madame was quiet and, even, sorrowful.

"Don't be angry, Paul!" she begged. "My sister is trying to help me, or to warn me. There are plenty of people around La Refaudio who could say we were very close. We danced together, remember. We even stayed in the same hotel, in the same room even in Lourdes."

"But ..." Paul began to protest.

"I know, Paul, we did nothing wrong, but tongues will wag!" pointed out Madame.

Paul put his head in his hands and sighed desolately.

"So, I come to France, can't see you, and must go back home," he said, feeling in total misery.

"I am sorry," Madame said gently, "but stay and go to the retreat I've booked for you, and pray that all may end well, and we can meet again, in the future, as friends."

Jeannette left the room quietly, leaving Paul and Madame in a last embrace.

Paul did go to the retreat, but it meant nothing to him. Suddenly he had lost that spark of faith, and everything seemed dead. He tried to understand Madame. She had put her children first, and the loyalty to her husband. He admired her for it, but he couldn't help feeling a sense of desolation and loss.

But it left him in the cold!

He looked back on those three days of voluntary incarceration as one of the worst times in his young life.

At the retreat he was shown into a small room with a single bed. Apart from his meals, and a daily visit from a priest, he was left alone.

Apart from the toilet he was left to prayers and contemplation in that dismal room. Even the priest was no help. All that had happened was too recent a shock for him to confide in anyone. Prayer had no meaning, and he wasn't sure that he wanted to become a Catholic, especially after the negative instruction he had received in England. The retreat was supposed to be a joyous affirmation of his new faith. But he just felt abandoned and miserable. The priest was kindly, but he seemed to be puzzled by Paul's lack of communication.

Paul was disappointed that he didn't get to meet any others of the community, or even to attend their services.

The priest talked of God's love and understanding, but in Paul's present mood of misery, it meant little.

Madame met him with two of the children, Nano and Marc as he left on the third day. She said the others were with Jeannette.

"How did the Retreat go?" asked Madame.

Paul shrugged, and said.

"It didn't! I was too miserable."

Madame looked closely at Paul.

"I'm sorry, Paul," she said sorrowfully.

Paul shrugged again and said feebly.

"I'm not used to the contemplative life. I wasn't even allowed out for a walk, It was lonely, and my thoughts were muddled. I couldn't concentrate."

Madame looked unhappy but didn't say any more. It was a silent walk to the station, broken only by Nano's chatter.

At the gare, Paul kissed Nano, shook hands with Marc, the boy he least knew. Like Jean-Pierre, Marc was growing up to be a serious lad. Paul embraced Madame and then entered the carriage without saying a word. Any sweet memories of La Refaudio were far from his mind.

When he got back to London, he told Sis about what had happened. She said two surprising things.

"Poor Paul, love often ends in tragedy. The story of Romeo and Juliet, and the opera 'La Traviata' are examples. Yours is not that intense a tragedy, but it has its sad, human side."

She thought for a moment and then continued rather seriously.

"There is no future with your Madame. She's so much older and cannot have children because of her operation. I can't be an aunty unless you have children. You wouldn't deprive me of that pleasure, would you?"

Paul confirmed that Madame's operation had been a hysterectomy. She had finally admitted it.

"She told me rather reluctantly," Paul confessed.

"You know, Paul, this operation Madame had, was really a blessing," Sis said. "It put a definite end to your relationship with her. You could never have had children. You can only now be friends, and even that might be dangerous for her."

Paul nodded reluctantly.

"What's going to happen?" asked Sis.

Paul could not hide his disappointment. He shrugged and said dismally.

"I'll have to go back to Somerset to serve out my notice. Then I think I will apply to go back to Oxford. I'm no longer afraid of French Prelims. It'll be easy now."

"Good for you," she remarked. "Think positive. That's the spirit. You're bound to find a lovely young woman of your own age, capable of having children."

Paul said lamely.

"I suppose so."

To which his sister replied.

"I know so!"

Paul hesitantly and bashfully said.

"I wrote a poem about Madame. May I show it to you, but please don't laugh, I beg of you!"

Sis nodded. Paul produced it from his pocket and gave it to her.

### IN MEMORY OF MADAME

I loved Madame
so I am damned
Never forget
my mind is set
Her lovely voice
It was my choice
Listen closely
my mind brightly
Lovely green eyes
I know not why
I was enthralled
so enchanted

Rise of her breasts
She was so blessed.
Her tinkling laugh
Such a bright laugh
She so teased me
As one were we!

Sweet lips so soft
I kissed them oft
It was a dream
or so it seemed
Wish unfulfilled
so I willed
Perfume lingers
Body tingles
Scent entices
Here my head lies
our flesh entwines
The love of wine
So lifts our mind.
We are one kind
Oh, how I love
Heavens above!
Such deep longing
Always mingling
with hopes and fears
and many tears!

To be one flesh
that is my wish
to touch, embrace
our hearts do race.
Love does not last
it's such a task,
but we will win
our minds a twin.

"That's beautiful, Paul," Sis exclaimed. "I didn't know you wrote poetry. It's rather fanciful, as if you are dreaming or wishing. Have you shown it to Madame?"

Paul shook his head.

"The trouble is it's in English and she doesn't speak our language," Paul pointed out. "But I think she knows somebody who would translate it for her."

"Well, there you are," concluded Sis, smiling kindly. "There is a quotation rather apt in your case – 'Better to have loved and lost than never to have loved at all.'"

# Chapter 22

*Return to School*

Paul returned to Motherton with a heavy heart. But somehow the daily routine did much to settle him. In the evenings Peter and Teresa were still as welcoming, the choir was in cheerful voice, and Joan was still around for Sunday walks. It was cold but the children did not seem to mind the weather. They still rushed around enthusiastically and wildly on Sunday afternoons.

The teaching lacked the intrusion of an inspector. The classes seemed to go much more smoothly. The problem was the wide spread of ability. There were in Paul's class those who had difficulty in reading, and those who were quite fluent. The classes were maintained on an age basis, not aptitude. The most difficult to fit in was a boy who spoke with a strong regional accent. He was maliciously nicknamed 'Oick'. His accent Paul had difficulty in understanding at times. Paul liked the lad. He was always smiling, and had a very genial personality. Paul got to know the parents who were just as kind. Paul started taking the boy for an extra lesson after school. He had no remuneration for this.

Not unsurprisingly it led to trouble with Mr. Choley. Unknown to Paul, Choley started charging the parents for extra tuition. When Paul discovered this, he was furious.

Why didn't you tell me you were charging Bert's Dad?" was his angry confrontation with Mr. Choley. "I gave the lesson without charge to help the lad."

Mr. Choley eyed him coldly.

"What I do is frankly none of your affair," he remarked. "You are employed by me. Whatever you undertake in my school is a charge."

"Can one not help a handicapped pupil of one's own free will?" enquired Paul.

"No!" was the abrupt answer.

"In that case," challenged Paul, "I will not help him in the school, but will go round to their house. I don't think the father can manage your charges. This is why they brought up the whole matter with me. The father is only a farm labourer, though his wife works as well. They are anxious their son has a good education."

You don't interfere in school matters," said Choley coldly.

"But I do," challenged Paul. "This was a private matter of my own choosing. I am amazed you take it to your financial advantage without consulting me."

Choley's face became apoplectic with rage. He didn't like to be thwarted.

"Look, young man," he said, banging the table. "Let me remind you you're only here on sufferance due to your inexperience. If you continue to oppose me you will be out of here as quick as a flash."

"If you do," challenged Paul. "I'll have you up for unfair dismissal."

Mr. Choley waved a furious hand at him to leave the room.

Paul sought consolation with Peter that evening.

"I admire you for wanting to help our oicky boy," Peter said. "But I wonder whether Oick himself is worth the struggle. To me his brains are in his strength. He's happiest at manual labour. That is where he is most content. School work means nothing."

Paul felt there was truth in what Peter said, but he still thought he'd like to see whether he couldn't try and inculcate a little reading and writing into Oick. Perhaps he would marry a girl when older, a girl who would make up for his lack of fundamental education, as he rather understood his father had done. Oick was a good-natured boy; he would make somebody a wonderful husband, if she could bear his lack upstairs.

"Be careful," advised Peter. "That bloody Choley is a vindictive bastard."

Paul accepted what Peter said. It was his own assessment of Choley's character, but he still persisted in going round to Oick's home to do what little he could for the rest of the term. Any charge by Choley was dropped. Paul asked for no money, but was occasionally offered a meal. He found their food was far better than school grub. After the quality of French food, Paul longed for a good meal. School food was very basic. Paul felt it was another of Choley's false economies.

His relationship with the Choleys continued on very shaky grounds for the rest of the term.

The other instance that affected Paul was that Peter had a heart attack at the end of February. He was rushed to hospital. He recovered but was never quite the same again. Paul took over Peter's French classes which he much enjoyed, and Choley found a retired teacher to take over for the time being.

Teresa was left neglected by Mrs. Choley, so Paul and Joan found time to spend with her and cheer her up. It meant Paul had to give up the choir, but he didn't mind. Teresa seemed to bear up remarkably well.

When it became obvious Peter was never going to teach again, Teresa, Peter and the baby moved to be with Teresa's mother. Peter was sorely missed in the school. Choley tried to persuade Paul to stay on to fill the gap in French, but Paul was determined to leave. He felt Choley only offered him the job because he would be a cheap option.

Once term was over Paul packed up, dumped his things at his sister's and rushed to Paris. He and Madame had decided to meet in secret, and nobody would know, even her sister. It was only for an hour or so at the Louvre, or in the Tuileries if the weather was fine.

It was all very innocent. Madame never seemed to get over the fact he had actually proposed marriage to her, even though she never mentioned the proposal again.

"You can't have paid a woman a nicer compliment," she said but only once.

Paul grinned happily. It was nice to hear it, though he had been turned down. But he accepted the situation in time. They were now entering a period of genuine friendship.

Since he had left La Refaudio, Madame had gradually changed. She had lost her fresh bloom, and was becoming slightly gaunt and thin. She kept her lovely figure, but she looked wasted somehow, and of course her clothes were different, more suitable for Paris.

In the Easter holidays in Paris, Paul had joined the French courses at the Sorbonne; these were specifically intended for foreign students, like the 'Teaching English as a Foreign Language Courses' in England. It meant he could only meet Madame after lunch. Then it was but for a short hour as Madame had to hurry back for the children coming out of school. It was disappointing, but there was no alternative. Madame did take him on one glorious evening to the opera, an event Paul found unforgettable. It was a wonderful performance of 'Così Fan Tutte' by Mozart. It was one of the operas of which Madame had sung excerpts at La Refaudio.

The main reason for the French course at the Sorbonne was that Paul had applied to a Prep School in Sussex as a teacher of French. Incredibly he had been successful. The school was Woodford, a recognised I.A.P.S. school in beautiful grounds. It had not been the main Scholarship French Paul was given, but the normal Common Entrance French. Paul was delighted. It was a start, just what he wanted. It meant Oxford was put on hold for the time being.

The interview with the Headmaster was strange. He was a Welshman and Paul had been warned never to trust a Welshman.

But the man had talked only of cricket for most of the interview. This suited Paul who loved cricket, and followed Test and county cricket in the newspapers and on radio.

What worried Paul was that Choley had given him a bad reference. He voiced his concern.

"I'm afraid I didn't get on with my previous Head," Paul admitted. "I fear he may have given me a poor reference."

But the Head shook his head. His name was Ashley-Jones, a double-barrelled name, but for ordinary purposes he stuck to a dull and simple Jones. He was not a boastful man who tried to present a favourable image. Paul liked him, a contrast to Choley.

"I never ask for references," he stated. "I prefer to make my own judgement."

Paul was relieved, and even more so when he was offered the job which he accepted at once. The salary was a genuine one, far, far better than in Somerset.

"Well," remarked Madame when he told her about his new school and position, "You've done wonderfully."

"Entirely due to you," stated Paul firmly. "You've done two things for me. You've helped me with French, thereby reviving a language which I once disliked, and given me a new faith which as yet I've done nothing about. But there will be time for that. You've also helped my confidence."

Madame looked at him thoughtfully.

"What gives me concern is your hearing," stated Madame. "You're wearing your hearing aid which you hardly did at La Refaudio. I notice now you sometimes have difficulty hearing people. You're all right with me, but ...."

Her voice trailed off, as if she didn't want to upset him.

"Oh, Madame," began Paul. But he was quickly interrupted.

"Paul," she stated firmly. "Stop, for Heaven's sake, stop calling me Madame. I don't call you M'sieur. I'm Marguerite, and will always remain so, as far as you are concerned."

Paul apologised.

"You're always Madame to me," he said. "It's the respect I owe to an older person."

"Stop it. Paul," Madame exclaimed. "I know now I'm middle-aged. But you don't have to rub it in. If you call me Madame again, I shall walk away and not come back, so there."

But she smiled, taking out the abruptness of her words.

"That would be a tragedy, Madame, oh sorry Marguerite!" said Paul grinning "I'll know now how to get rid of you, Marguerite!"

Marguerite saw the impish grin on his face, and exclaimed.

"Oh, Paul, you're incorrigible!"

Paul bowed his head, and said.

"I'm very sorry. We're so serious sometimes, I want to tease you. But don't worry, you're not old to me. They say a man in love, carries always the image of his loved one when they first met. That transcends the years."

"As far as I can remember I wasn't particularly welcoming and kind when we first met," explained Marguerite.

"Anger sometimes enhances the beauty of a woman," commented Paul. He had no idea that a woman's beauty was enhanced by anger, but had read it somewhere.

"Oh, Paul, how on earth do you know so much about women? You are so young," explained Marguerite. But she smiled.

"Well, I have a wonderful sister," said Paul. "I hope you will meet her one day."

Marguerite nodded.

"I hope so," she said. "But not if she is as rude as you."

"She's very outspoken," said Paul grinning.

Somehow this little repartee lightened the atmosphere, and Paul was grateful. Life was a little hard on them at times, but particularly so on Marguerite. Paul was beginning to see some prospects of happiness, but for her there was only an estranged marriage and a lonely future, except for the children. It was all she had. Paul felt immensely sorry for her.

Marguerite sighed and rose from the table.

"It's been lovely seeing you, Paul, and a chance for a frank talk," she said. "I'm afraid I can't see you for the next three days, there's so much happening, and Easter is approaching. I'll be back here in four days. Behave yourself and watch out for Parisian girls."

Paul grinned and got up to embrace her, and then watched her hurry away. She would never let him accompany her. He sighed; it was such a secret relationship. The next few days would seem very empty.

# Chapter 23

*Catholic Growth!*

Paul's new school did much to restore Paul's keenness to become a teacher. Woodford was an established school of some fifty years, going right back to the beginning of the century.

The first noticeable fact was that the staff were young. It was as if the headmaster favoured a young staff. The Latin master was the only elderly gentleman. Like Peter in Somerset he was openly critical, even cynical of life and people, but unlike Peter he lacked human feeling. He was unmarried and appeared to be an unhappy, lonely figure. He was a man to be feared as he had a sharp, biting tongue. The lady who took Scholarship French was also a lonely, middle-aged personality, and Paul found it difficult to establish any relationship with her. The rest of the staff were in their twenties or early thirties. The matrons were also young. It made for an enjoyable evening. At the end of a long day, they would walk down the drive and congregate in the pub, only a hundred yards or so away.

It meant Paul had peers who shared a common interest. After the elderly staff at the Choley school, and the company of Marguerite, Paul found young company a pleasant experience, though not one he could often be involved in.

The most interesting of the company was a young matron of eighteen who was a Catholic. Her name was Michelle. It was generally felt that she had the remote qualities of a nun. But Paul found her interesting. She did much to restore his waning faith and interest in the Catholic Church. On Sundays they would cycle to eight o'clock mass, and be back for breakfast at nine.

But the incident that really cemented their friendship in a funny way occurred one summer Sunday in early June. Michelle, normally impatient to get to church early, would set off first. On this occasion she had pedalled away, with Paul following a few minutes afterwards. He had only gone part of the way down the long drive just before the playing fields when he found Michelle lying on the ground, obviously in pain. Her bicycle lay on the grass verge beside her. Paul thought she'd had a fall.

"What happened?" he asked anxiously, not certain what to do.

But Michelle just groaned.

"What's wrong?" Paul begged.

But there was still no reply.

"Can I help you back to the school?" he asked.

Michelle gave a mumbled 'yes'.

When he tried to help her up, she resisted. Paul looked at her, perplexed.

"I'll have to carry you," he suggested. "Have you broken any bones?"

He remembered vaguely one didn't move people with broken bones.

Michelle shook her head.

Paul bent down and lifted her. She put an arm around his neck which helped. She wasn't a heavy girl, but Paul found himself labouring under the weight. In the school he took her up to the sick bay where the school nurse took over.

Can I help at all?" he asked.

But the nurse shook her head. Paul went back to retrieve the bicycles. Later that morning he met the nurse.

"Is Michelle all right?" he asked.

The nurse smiled.

"She's fine," she said.

What's wrong with her?" he asked.

With the usual frankness of the nursing profession, she replied,

"It's only the curse."

Paul was surprised. His sister took her monthly periods in her stride, without fuss or incident. But Paul didn't enquire further. Michelle was at breakfast the next day. She whispered.

"Thanks, Paul," and smiled diffidently.

He didn't have any further conversation with her until the following Sunday. Coming back together he asked, "Are you free on Thursday?" His voice was a little hesitant. Boarding Prep Schools had a six day teaching week, which meant a compensatory half day off during the week.

"I'm free after lunch," she explained.

"Could we meet in town, have some tea?" he asked.

She nodded, with a little smile. They discussed arrangements.

The nearby town was Woodford, a typical, small Sussex town.

They met at half past two at a neat cafe where the proprietor was a keen potter. It was the wife who ran the cafe itself. It was known as the teapot cafe. The shelves were crowded with teapots, made by the proprietor, some eccentric, some traditional, some frankly bizarre. One didn't buy them as teapots but as ornaments. They would have been difficult to use for making tea. Paul just liked looking at them.

Their shapes and sizes were so varied and unusual. Michelle tended to giggle at them, they were so imaginative, so impractical. The one that caught her attention most was in the shape of a locomotive. The boiling water went in through the roof where the driver worked. The tea came out through a nozzle at the front. The rear end had a handle, but it was so small it would be difficult to hold.

"I love this place," said Paul. "It's so unusual, and the cakes are home-made."

Michelle nodded in agreement.

When they had settled and ordered, Michelle asked curiously,

"Why at Mass do you not take Communion? You just stay in your seat."

"I'm not actually a Catholic."

"Oh?" said Michelle surprised.

So Paul explained. He didn't mention that he had fallen in love with a French lady. And he didn't tell her of his time at La Refaudio looking after the children.

"I spent a couple of days in Lourdes," he explained. "I much admired the piety and faith of the true French Catholic. I started having instruction but I didn't continue when I got back to England."

"Why was that?" asked Michelle.

"W-e-ll," said Paul slowly. "I found Catholicism in England not so – enticing, I suppose, as in France."

He explained how he found English priests so full of negatives.

"The ten Commandments are mostly negative," said Michelle. "The only truly positive ones are the first two, full of love."

Paul nodded.

"I also found some of the statements were a little extreme," he stated. "They would insist the Bread and Wine were the actual body and blood of Christ. I've always thought they only represented the body and blood. There was nothing actual about them!"

"It's a question of faith, the belief that you are actually eating and drinking the Body and Blood of Our Lord," said Michelle. "Put it another way, Our Lord said 'This is My body' when holding the bread. He said the same thing with the wine 'This is My blood'. It was actual, not representative."

Paul nodded in understanding. For a moment they were quiet. And then Michelle continued.

"Look, Paul, if you really are keen on taking instruction, why not contact the local priest where we take Mass. He's a relatively young man, and very human. I'm sure he would help."

"I'll give him a try," promised Paul.

After that they talked of other things, school, themselves and life in general.

"I'm leaving at the end of term," said Michelle. "I've been appointed as Matron to a Catholic girls' school in Suffolk."

"I'm sorry to hear that," admitted Paul. "May I ask why you are leaving? I shall miss you."

Michelle shrugged.

"I suppose I'm a little lonely," she said. "Nobody shares my faith. They seem to think I'm some sort of religious – well – prude. I don't mean to be. I mean you all go down to the pub after supper, but I'd much rather rest and read a book."

"That's understandable," said Paul. "I've been in the same sort of position myself. My hearing handicap has made socialising difficult at times. But I like the pub. It's a change of atmosphere from the school. We live and work in the school. We need somewhere different."

"I believe they term me a nun," admitted Michelle.

Paul nodded.

"People can be a bit cruel," stated Paul. "I shouldn't worry. In a way it's a compliment."

But Michelle looked dubious. They chatted more and then Michelle looked at her watch.

"Heavens!" she cried. "I must be getting back. I'm late already."

She bustled off with a smile.

Paul decided to see if he could make contact with the Catholic priest, as Michelle advised.

At the church a woman told him where to find the presbytery. Regretfully the priest was not in, but Paul left a message. Then he decided to go the cinema, rather than going back to the school. He found this relaxing after the hectic life of teaching. He really worked a twelve hour day, from breakfast at eight until the last boy went up to bed, usually about eight.

At the pub he would take his marking and preparation, being careful not to let these become covered with beer stains.

It was a strange thing about Paul, he rarely minded working alone. At university he worked in the library. Letters he wrote in a cafe drinking coffee. He would switch off his hearing aid, and he would be perfectly happy. It seemed unsociable but he never enjoyed talking in a noisy room. His best time for conversation was on a one to one basis, as with

Marguerite on the balcony, or with his sister in her funny London flat. The only other fun he had was playing tennis when he could find time and an opponent. Occasionally this would be another matron, a young amazon called Naomi.

They had some terrific games, but she usually won. He had a devastating serve when it was in court, and a strong forearm, but a weak backhand. She had a better all round game, and would shrewdly concentrate on his backhand. The best thing about tennis was that Paul didn't have to talk except for the scoring. Hearing, or lack of it, was not a handicap, as it might have been in most sports.

Towards the end of term, he had a devastating letter from Marguerite.

*Dearest Paul*

*You're going to hate me, but I'm afraid we cannot meet any more, none of those secret meetings in Paris. The situation for me is quite serious. A legal battle is raging over the custody of the children, particularly Jean-Pierre. Paul, I'm afraid to do anything which may endanger the situation. You may continue to contact me by letter at my sister's but nothing more than that.*

*I can only say that I miss you and our innocent friendship, and the way we talk together. But I do beg of you to understand and not to try and meet me.*

*Life is hard at the moment, but please, Paul, try to understand and pray for me. I shall think of you with love and affection. You've been so wonderful in my life.*

*Please, Paul, find a girl of your own age and forget all about me and my problems.*

*I can't say any more, nor can I write with tears flowing.*
*Much love, and bless you,*

*Marguerite.*

Paul sat in his room for a long time, contemplating this sad letter. Eventually he sighed and tried to write a reply. It took several efforts and discarded paper, before he came up with the following.

*Dearest Marguerite,*

*I do understand, and I accept the situation. I know how much you love your children, and the comfort they give you. I will not come to France during the summer holidays. I can only say that I owe you a lot. You've given me a language I love to teach, and will always love. But you've given me more, much more. The most important is my confidence after my failure at Oxford, and a new reason for living. I hope soon to be received into the Catholic Church, and am undergoing instruction from a very understanding priest. But I don't want to be baptised in England. I want to find a sympathetic priest in France. The Catholic Faith means so much more in France than England.*

*I'll never forget you, Marguerite, nor my happy days at La Refaudio. They have so many precious memories. Give my love to the children, especially that little imp, Nano. If ever things sort themselves out for you and we can meet again, then I will come running.*

*You have my love, my respect, my dearest memories, and there will always be a bit more of me that won't forget you.*

*You have my prayers that all may go well with you, and you may reach a happier, calmer time.*

*Bless you, dear Marguerite. All my love,*
*Paul.*

Paul was feeling somewhat miserable when he met Michelle at the teapot cafe. It must have shown because Michelle said after a while.

"What's wrong, Paul? You aren't your usual self."

"I'm sorry," said Paul. "I've received some disappointing news."

"Am I allowed to ask the problem?" she enquired. "It sometimes helps to get things off your chest."

But Paul shook his head.

"Well, then," persisted Michelle, "am I allowed to hazard a guess?"

"I don't think so," said Paul. "I've never given you any inkling of what's happened."

"Well, yes, I have," continued Michelle. "You've never shown much interest in me as a person, just mild friendship and your interest in the Catholic Church. I can only assume you regard me much as the others do, as a rather remote figure. Or you are in love with somebody else, and that somebody is in France, Your enthusiasm for the French language gives a hint."

Paul looked at her for a moment. Suddenly Michelle gave a giggle and said.

"Naomi thinks your mind is sometimes elsewhere, which is not very flattering for us as women."

Paul sighed.

"You're as bad as my sister, always delving into my mind," grumbled Paul. "Yes, I loved somebody in France, but it's come to an end, sadly. And that's all I can say, or want to say."

"Won't you tell this agony aunt?" pleaded Michelle, with the usual feminine curiosity.

But Paul shook his head. How could he tell a girl that he loved a woman much older than himself, and the mother of five children? She'd only laugh!

"I don't know, Michelle," he said. "I don't want to be discourteous, but I don't want to talk about it. Suffice to say I'm not going to France this summer. Instead I shall be working on the cross-Channel boats, Newhaven-Dieppe."

"Cross-Channel boats!" echoed Michelle surprised. "What a comedown from being a teacher!"

Paul grinned weakly, then said,

"I learn more about life in a week as a steward than I'll ever do as a teacher, or I ought to say as an unqualified teacher."

Michelle looked at him attentively.

"You know," she said softly, "I shall miss you, and these friendly meetings in the teapot cafe."

"I shall miss you too," Paul said gently. "I would have been lonely as a trainee Catholic, if I had not met you on the ground and carried you back."

They smiled at each other.

"I'd like to keep in touch," Paul said, and he meant it quite sincerely.

Michelle nodded.

"Well, you have my address," she said smiling.

They left the teapot cafe for the last time, and never met again once term had ended.

# Chapter 24

*France Again Momentarily*

Paul, funnily enough, looked forward to his new job at Newhaven. He had an uncle with whom he could stay when not working. This was his mother's brother, Tom Walford. Mother had appealed to Tom to intercede when Paul had left Oxford. But Tom had got nowhere. They hadn't quarrelled, but Tom had been forcible in reminding Paul just how much he would miss in life without the backing of an Oxford degree. Paul had just sighed and gone his own way. Nobody seemed to understand the loneliness of a hearing handicap. But Paul liked Tom. They got on well.

Tom was a civil servant working in London, and only coming home at weekends, an arrangement his wife, Joan, seemed to appreciate. They had two daughters younger than Paul. The cousins didn't always get on well. The teenage girls seemed to look askance at their rather quiet relative who wore a deaf aid. One of the problems was that Paul's type of deafness heard female voices less well than male voices. The girls also tended to gabble quickly. They were soon put out when they discovered how little he heard of their conversation. Paul was better on a one-to-one situation, as with Marguerite and Michelle.

"He's so boring," they told their father. "He never seems to understand what we are saying, nor does he join in with what we are doing."

Uncle Tom laughed.

"He's a good bit older than you," Tom told his daughters. "I don't think he's very happy at the moment. Try to be kind to him, my sweet lasses, as I am sure you will."

The girls tried, but it was uphill work. Fortunately Paul was not at home very much while working on the cross-Channel boat. He was usually tired after a shift on the boat.

Paul's first day was a little disconcerting. When he had served before, he had worked in the restaurant. But this time he was relegated to cabin steward and steward to the Captain of the boat. The restaurant was more profitable because of the tips. He assumed he would get some tips from those in the cabins but perhaps not so much.

He was also disconcerted when a steward came up to him, and said rather bluntly.

"You're a teacher, ain't you?"

Paul nodded.

"Then yer not in need of money, just a supplement to your pay as a teacher," the steward stated. There seemed no consideration of reasons why Paul might possibly want to work during the holidays. He was still restless to travel, and that needed money.

Paul felt it was none of the steward's business what he earned, but he was too shaken by the abruptness of the steward's manner to pursue the matter. He found the stewards were a cagey lot, always whispering together. They had been much more friendly and open on the previous occasion. But basically his work as a cabin steward gave him a certain measure of independence.

What disconcerted him even more was the Captain. He was nothing more than a drunken sod, and spent most of his time in his extremely untidy and smelly cabin. It was the Chief Mate who seemed to run the ship. Paul wondered how the passengers would feel if they knew the situation.

The ship itself was a lovely old boat. It had a plaque up saying it had seen action at Dunkirk in 1940. Sadly it was rumoured the boat would soon be taken out of service. But Paul felt, as a historian at Oxford, there was a life story in the boat. It was a sad, lovely old thing.

With his isolation from the stewards who served in the restaurant, Paul felt the onset of his loneliness, which amounted almost to depression. He was partially saved by a strange incident. He was making his way up to the Captain's cabin, when he passed a sailor. They stopped and stared at each other, certainly in astonishment by Paul, and amusement by the sailor.

"Why are you looking as if you had seen a ghost?" said the sailor, smiling.

Paul shook himself as if getting rid of some strange shock. He pulled himself together.

"I'm sorry to stare so rudely," Paul said hesitantly, "but apart from the clothes, you look like my father who died in 1940."

The sailor grinned.

"I could almost say the same for you," he said in a friendly voice. "You're probably younger, but you look like my eldest son. A strange world!"

"I know one is said to have a doppelganger somewhere in the world, but this is pure fantasy," remarked Paul in wonder.

"What's a doppelganger?" asked the sailor, puzzled, but smiling in a friendly way.

"A twin, a look-alike, a double," explained Paul. "It's as if God got tired of creating characters, and decided to duplicate people. Or his brain got fuddled."

The sailor looked at him and his face was suffused by an even more friendly smile.

"Look, laddie," he said. "I've got work to do. Do you live in Newhaven?"

Paul nodded.

Well," said the sailor, "When we're next off, could we meet and discuss this situation? I often go to a pub called the Golden Feathers. Do you know it?"

Paul nodded. They discussed times off, and arranged a meeting.

Thus began a strange friendship, and an unusually warm one.

When Paul finally met the sailor, it was at first an awkward meeting.

"I don't even know your name," Paul said with a half-smile. He had never really come across sailors before. They were a breed that filled him with some uncertainty, he didn't know why.

"That's easily remedied," said the sailor. "I'm Geoffrey Portal, commonly known as Jeff. May I know your name?"

"I'm Paul, Paul Treloar."

"Why are you working on the cross-Channel boats? Jeff asked. "I gather you're a teacher."

"Money mostly," said Paul. "I'm not a qualified teacher. The pay is very poor, mostly in board and lodging. I like to travel, which is expensive."

"You won't see much of the world between Newhaven and Dieppe," pointed out Jeff.

"I appreciate that," said Paul. "At the moment it's restoring my finances."

Jeff grinned.

"Don't we all," he said.

For a moment they were silent. Then Jeff said,

"Why am I so like your father?"

"It's the eyes," said Paul instantly. "They crinkle at the corner when you smile. It's a very warm smile. You're lean like my dad, your hair is dark, though possibly with more grey. But it's the eyes; they are so warm, and yet he had a temper, and could be quite fierce."

"I'm too old and settled now to lose my temper," said Jeff grinning. "But I used to have a certain temper."

"What makes you think I look like your son?" asked Paul.

"Easy," said Jeff smiling. "It's your chin. I imagine you can be quite an obstinate cuss."

"My chin?" echoed Paul surprised. "I used to be called obstinate and pig-headed when I lived in France. Is there any other resemblance?"

"Hair, and face," said Jeff. "But the other notable thing is the way you walk. Like my son you've got short legs."

Paul nodded.

They're the bane of my life," he stated. "I could never sprint. People referred to me as having rugby front row legs."

Jeff grinned.

"That's my son," agreed Jeff and gave his warm smile that made Paul's heart turn over.

"What does your father do?" asked Jeff.

"He doesn't," said Paul. "He died in 1940, when I was only ten."

"I'm sorry," said Jeff.

"Don't be," said Paul. "I think he died proud of what he had done."

"How come?" queried Jeff.

"He was part of the rearguard that made Dunkirk possible," Paul explained. "He won the Military Cross. He and his men made Dunkirk possible by their resistance."

Jeff nodded.

"I was at Dunkirk," he admitted. "You've probably noticed the boat was there."

"Gosh!" exclaimed Paul, full of admiration. "Was it very terrible?"

Jeff shrugged.

"We survived," was all he said.

Paul thought that this was just like his father. He had served throughout the First World War, but would never discuss it.

After that they talked mostly about general matters. It was hoped Paul would meet Jeff's son.

At one stage Paul asked,

"I am concerned about the Captain. He seems to remain in his cabin drinking. He only uses me to get him more alcohol."

Jeff nodded.

"Poor sod!" he muttered. "His wife died some time ago. He just went to pieces. We try to cover for him; the first mate's very good. But the Captain must go sometime."

Paul marvelled at the kindness of these sailors. They were a very different breed to the self-seeking stewards.

How corrupt the stewards were, Paul was not to realise until the last ten days of his stay.

But before that happened, something arose that made Paul very happy. Some friends of the port master at Dieppe asked if they could see round a boat that was actually involved at Dunkirk.

"There's nothing to see," grumbled Jeff. "We were damaged, but it's all been repaired. We're just an old boat soon to be pensioned off."

Paul was asked to accompany Jeff as the only one on board who spoke French.

The visitors were a mother and father and two teenage daughters. The father tried to explain they were interested in the history surrounding Dunkirk. In many ways Dunkirk was a miracle. Jeff, as usual was a little reticent. He had lost two friends in the evacuation. But he showed them parts of the boat where it had been damaged and then made good. The father asked.

"How many soldiers did you rescue?"

Jeff shrugged. Paul had to explain Jeff's comment that in the heat of battle, it was impossible to estimate. But the boat had been so full he wondered whether the boat would capsize. This rather confused Paul; he didn't know the French for turn-turtle or capsize. He had to illustrate it with his hands. Fortunately the French are used to hand language. They just marvelled at this small ship crammed with soldiers, wet, tired and frightened.

"It was like hell on earth," explained Jeff. "The Stukas weren't very accurate but they made a bloody frightening noise."

Paul tried to translate as best he could, but left out the bloody!

An incident happened below decks. When they came to a ladder, Jeff and the father went first. Paul, remembering his manners, stood aside to let the ladies go first. The girls were giggling and not moving. Paul realised his mistake when the mother started going up. She was wearing a skirt as were the girls. Embarrassed, Paul turned away and moved to the other side of the deck. He didn't go up until they had all disappeared above. When he reached the top, Jeff muttered,

"On ship, ladies go down first, and up last."

He winked at Paul.

When the tour was finished, the harbour-master thanked them.

"Unusual for an Englishman to speak French," he remarked.

"I'm not very good," Paul confessed.

As they were leaving, the harbour-master said to Paul.

"Come and see us if you have a moment."

He gave Paul the address. Paul liked the man. He was a short, stocky man who rather reminded Paul of Cornishmen. Perhaps there was a similarity if he came from Brittany. Paul would have to ask him.

Paul's first visit to the harbour-master was brief, as the constant changeover of summer passengers allowed little room for freedom.

But when he did see the harbour-master, he expressed a wish as follows.

"I imagine you are Catholics," Paul asked. "I want very much to be baptised into the Catholic Church in France. It's where it all began. I've received instruction, and can bring a letter of confirmation. I just need somewhere to stay in France during the Christmas school holidays, and access to a sympathetic priest."

The harbour-master looked for a time at this eager young man, with his strange request.

"We are Catholics," he said hesitantly. "I'd have to consult my wife and the local priest, but I imagine it would be all right to come for Christmas."

Paul thrilled at the thought of spending Christmas with a French family. Up till now, his only experience of Christmas had been English, never French.

The harbour-master had only one query.

"What about your family? Would they want to be present?"

But Paul shook his head.

"I've no dad," he explained. "I doubt whether my mother would want to come. She is a fervent Anglican. The only person who might come is my sister, but I think it would only be a quick visit."

"She'd be welcome to stay," was the kind reply.

Back in the boat, Paul began to wonder about his sanity. Why was he so persistent about Catholicism, putting others to endless inconvenience, going against the feelings of his family? He knew his sister would have reservations, and would only come as a sisterly duty.

Why, oh why did he have to behave so strangely, he asked himself. He was a loner, seeking a lonely path. He could blame his hearing, his obstinacy. All he could remember was Marguerite's fortitude in face of adversity. It was as if her faith gave her an unknown strength. It was that strength, that faith which he needed, he wanted. He was beginning to realise that his loss of hearing would mean a lonely path in life. He needed a faith, a support in life. How he wished Marguerite could be there to talk to. The only alternative was his sister. She would laugh at him, but still try to understand.

As he lay in his lonely berth on the ship, he felt depressed, desolate, and couldn't sleep. But he had a hard day tomorrow. He needed sleep. Sleep came, but it was a restless sleep.

## Chapter 25

*Crisis!*

In the days before he was due to finish on the boat, the cashier left suddenly and unexpectedly. Paul was asked to stand in until a more permanent replacement could be found. Paul had been good at Maths at school. He thought he could cope.

But he soon realised it wasn't normal cashier's work.

On the first day he was not only rushed off his feet, but the stewards seemed to think he was in the know as to their scam. They were indulging in a very simple fraud. They would ask harassed customers for the amount for their meal. But they would not issue a bill for the true cost of the meal which the stewards would ask verbally and collect. The passengers were too engrossed in their travel concerns to notice the lack of a bill. When they had gone the steward would make out a bill very much less than the original cost of the meal. The steward would pay that small bill in to Paul and would add a little extra as his reward for turning a blind eye to what was going on.

When the first bill came to Paul, it was for three pounds, plus a few shillings as his reward.

"What is this?" asked Paul. But he was only met by a wink and a gesture to be quiet.

The stewards were absolute fools. They had never checked whether Paul knew about the fraud, or that he would participate with them. But Paul could never hear their whispered conniving! Like all criminals they made mistakes!

Paul never knew the full amount of the uproar that ensued. As he began to suspect, the Chief Steward was involved, but to what extent he never knew. Before he left the boat that day he went to find Jeff and told him what had happened. Jeff thought it was a matter for the First Mate. The latter went to see the Chief Steward and a row ensued. The sailors had little time for stewards, calling them Jew Boys and other uncomplimentary names. The upshot was, the authorities were informed, both by the First Mate and, to save his own precious skin, the Chief Steward. There was an immediate crackdown. All Paul knew when he came on duty the next day were a number of dirty looks, and pointed remarks, but the day was more normal, the right money given in with the right bills. The Chief Steward was ever watchful, and the Assistant Chief Steward. Somebody also came over from Central Office to keep an eye on things. The Office had long been suspicious as takings from the restaurant were mysteriously down.

What Paul could not understand was that two of the stewards went to see the Stewards Union and a strike was threatened. This could not be countenanced at such a busy time. In the midst of it Paul was blamed for making a deliberate mess of his work as cashier. But it wasn't his mistake!

Three things happened. When Paul told Uncle Tom he immediately went to the authorities and pleaded that Paul be moved to another ship. He also, the kind man, came to meet Paul off the ship.

Jeff himself, when the ship docked overnight at Dieppe for an early start the next day, insisted that Paul should sleep with the sailors instead of the stewards.

"Why?" queried Paul astonished.

The bastards will do you a mischief, laddie," was Jeff's comment.

Uncle Tom had said the same thing.

"I fear they'll attack you," was Tom's comment.

Paul was astounded, such was his innocence.

The Chief Steward was just a two-faced hypocrite. He asked to see Paul.

"Paul, my lad, you shouldn't be so judgmental," he pleaded. "The reality of life is that one survives in these times by fiddling. A friend of mine saved a lot of money by building a garage from materials that fell off the back of a lorry."

Paul had heard of this practice before, falling off the back of a lorry, as it was called. But he wasn't convinced by the Chief Steward's explanation.

"What the stewards were doing was a fraud," Paul said. "They were stealing money that rightly belonged to the company. I'm surprised the police weren't called in."

But the Chief shook his head.

"Had they done so there would have been an all-out strike," the Chief stated. "The Union is already involved. The company could not accept a strike at so busy a time. Masses of people are returning from the continent."

Paul remained silent for a moment.

"Well, all I can say is, I shall be glad when my stint behind the cash desk ends," he stated. "The atmosphere is full of hate. I've never come across anything like it. It's very different from the War when people were sacrificing their life to avoid defeat."

He and the Chief Steward parted. They begged to differ. But it left a peculiar distaste in Paul's mind, as if the arguments by the Chief Steward were incomprehensible and not honest.

Paul had never felt so depressed. Though he loved France he was glad to be English. Great Britain had come out of the War, proud of what had been achieved. But his depression was worse because he seemed to be involved in evil. There was Marguerite's husband who was either mad or evil. He had ruined life for her and for his children. And now Paul was involved in a fraud situation which affected passengers and the company. And worse still the power of the Unions made it impossible for justice. And he had to face the dislike on people's faces. It was much the same dislike as he had seen on Marguerite's husband's face. Oh why, oh why was he involved in so much unhappiness caused by others?

But nothing happened over his last few days. He didn't know it, but Jeff had threatened retaliation if anything happened to Paul.

"What will happen to these Jew boys as you call them," Paul asked Jeff. He shook his head.

"I suppose the company will find ways of getting rid of them," he surmised. "They say the new ship will have a completely new staff, including women working in the restaurant."

"Not women sailors also?" queried Paul jokingly.

But Jeff just smiled.

"That'll be the day," he said. "They could never do the heavy work. Their breasts would get in the way!"

Paul thought incongruously he had never seen a naked woman's breasts, except in the occasional picture, not even his sister's! He was in his twenties and he hadn't yet enjoyed that experience. He had felt Marguerite's breasts pressed up against him under her blouse, but he had never dared touch them.

Sadly, Paul never saw Jeff again when he left the ship. Their lives just went in different directions. But Paul never forgot the man who reminded him of his father!

## Chapter 26

*A French Christmas!*

Paul would never forget that Christmas he spent in France, in Dieppe, with such a kindly family.

But first he had to cope with his outspoken sister.

"Really, Paul," she said when he went to see her in London. He had mentioned his plan to enter the Catholic Church in December. "You complain about being a loner, being alone in the world. But you put yourself in situations which only increase your loneliness."

Paul looked puzzled. He had expected his sister's attack on Catholicism, but not this. So she explained.

"Look, little brother, most people go with the tide of feeling. But not you. You get smitten by a lady twice your age almost. I'm sure she's a lovely lady, but why can't you fall in love with a girl your own age and nationality? Worse still you want to become a Catholic, a religion not exactly part of English culture. We're Protestant, or part of the easy-going Anglican Church."

Paul shook his head.

"As far as girls are concerned, it's what I have said before," said Paul sadly. "They've only to look at my cumbersome hearing aid behind my tie, and the wire going up to my ear, and they immediately conclude I'm dull."

"I don't think you are dull," said Sis. "In fact I rather admire you. Leaving Oxford as you did would shatter anyone, but you didn't whine. You found a job in France, you learnt a language you'd previously found difficult, and started teaching it. Your complication with a woman does credit to your heart, but not to your brain."

She paused and smiled at her brother.

"Oh, dear, I've upset you," she said kindly. "Shall I tell you something which will please you?"

Paul nodded, curious.

"Well, you remind me of Dad," she said. "He was always a positive man, and, like you, he was unlucky. He spent his early manhood in the First World War. When he came out of the army, there wasn't much opportunity for an untrained soldier in life. But he worked on his great asset, namely maths, and eventually made it into the bank. What's more he never complained. Mother told me all this."

Paul looked at his sister with warmth. She couldn't have said a kinder thing. Paul had always been proud of his dad.

Sis gave a little sigh.

"Well, that's enough of this nonsense," she exclaimed. "I'm hungry. I can make Spaghetti Bolognese. Will that do you? And I have a last bottle of wine. Now there seems no more wine in the shops, sadly, due to that silly war of which we are still feeling the effects."

Paul nodded, smiling. Sis busied herself with the cooking while Paul laid the table.

Sis had one more go at him, when they had settled down for the meal.

"Paul, if you become an R.C. I will never speak to you again!"

Paul just grinned. He had heard this threat before.

"And another thing," she continued relentlessly. "If you are to become a teacher, then I suggest you do something about getting qualified."

"Yes, boss," said Paul, still grinning, happy to be with her. But he recognised the truth of her words.

Paul arrived in Dieppe three days before Christmas. He expected to see Jeff on the boat, but he was not there. He did his best to avoid the stewards, and did not enter the restaurant. When the boat docked he made his way to the harbour-master's house. It seemed a strange building.

Everything seemed to centre on the kitchen. Then Paul remembered how the Italian farms near La Refaudio had as their main room the kitchen. It seemed a habit, not only of the Italians but the French as well to make the kitchen the most important room in the house. In a way it was sensible. The kitchen was always the warmest place; food was easily transportable and served hot; it was also the most convivial room, in winter the warmest and most cosy. Then television began to dominate, to change habits. It was just beginning in England. It hadn't yet reached the stage when people began to realise it was turning them into mental cabbages. Paul's reflections were based on the installation of a television in the school. In the evening all the staff gathered round the television and watched spoon-fed entertainment, instead of going down to the pub.

Jacques, the name of the harbour-master, a name Paul associated with Marguerite's husband, had two teenage sons, both short and stocky like their father, though they had some filling out to do. One of them, Pierre, took Paul down to the beaches where Canadian forces had fruitlessly tried to land.

"They were shot to pieces," Pierre told Paul. "They hadn't a chance."

"The English newspapers quoted the raid a success," Paul remarked.

But Pierre shook his head.

"It achieved nothing," he said. "Dad sheltered one of the Canadians for months. He was a French Canadian. He naturally spoke French, but some of his vocabulary was different from ours.

"Your dad took a risk," commented Paul.

"He was lucky," Pierre said. "The Germans never suspected."

The other visit Paul had to make was to the local priest, a quiet, saintly man. He spoke no English. The letter that Paul provided, which stated that Paul had taken instruction, meant nothing to him. Paul had to translate.

"It's enough you wish to be a Catholic," the priest commented. "Normally you would have to make confession, but I imagine it would be difficult for you because of the language."

Paul was a bit hurt by the slight on his proficiency in French. But secretly he was relieved. He remembered when at fourteen he went through Confirmation in the Anglican Church, the priest who instructed them had asked them individually to come to his room and make confession. But nobody had gone. They seemed to feel such an act was not English. It was perhaps lucky because the priest was later prosecuted for interfering with boys.

A date after Christmas was fixed for the baptism. He wrote to inform Marguerite knowing she would be unable to come.

Paul was disappointed with Christmas in France, but in another sense he was pleased. There was none of the commercial razzmatazz that existed in England. No cards, few presents, no decorations or tree. All it consisted of was Mass, a good meal and Yule logs made outwardly of chocolate and sponge in the middle. The log was decorated on top with greenery. It tasted delicious, well up to the standard of French cakes. In a way he was thankful that Christmas was so quiet. It concentrated much more on the celebration of the birth of Christ, rather than of personal enjoyment.

When the day of baptism came, Paul was delighted when Marguerite appeared, totally unexpectedly. But his heart went out to her. She was thinner, more gaunt and had lost some of her fresh beauty. But it was a joy she was there. Her presence gave the short ceremony a certain justifiable formality.

"How are things?" Paul asked after he had introduced her to Jacques and the family.

She shrugged her shoulders in that exasperating French way.

"Could be better," she said quietly. "The children are all thriving, and Nano sends his love."

But then Marguerite turned to speak to Marianne, Jacques' wife. She explained how she came to know Paul, how he had stayed with her and helped look after the children. In a way Marguerite was such a lady it helped to make the whole occasion legitimate or credible with Jacques. Paul knew Jacques had doubts about the baptism, wondering why none of Paul's family were present.

The actual service was over in a few brief minutes. The priest gave absolution, followed by a watery cross on Paul's forehead. Another quick prayer, and it was all over, like an anti-climax. The priest chatted for a moment with Marianne and Marguerite. Then they went back to a celebration lunch to which Marguerite was invited. For once she seemed happy and smiling, revealing something of her old self.

Afterwards Paul walked with her to the station.

"It's been good of you to come, Marguerite," Paul said. "I'm immensely grateful."

Madame shrugged. Paul was never to forget that Gallic shrug. It seemed so memorable of the many French gestures.

"It was nothing," she said sadly. "It was the least I could do."

"You've changed," Paul said, worried. "Has life been very difficult?"

Madame nodded hesitantly. It was not in her nature to complain.

"Come," she said. She took his arm and led him to a cafe within sight of the station.

"Your train?" Paul queried, not wanting her to miss the train.

"No matter," she said. "There'll be another train. I need to talk, if only to get it off my chest."

Paul looked at her. There were tired lines in her face, around her eyes. She had become almost middle-aged, no longer the lovely woman of La Refaudio.

They ordered coffee. It quickly came. Marguerite leaned on the table and poured out her heart, in a way she had never done before.

"Oh, Paul, it's been such a lovely day here, to see you baptised. It's a time I've longed for, prayed for." Her tone was sad, almost tearful.

"Tell me, Marguerite, what's wrong?" he pleaded. "You've changed. You're not the same."

"No, no," she exclaimed. "I must not talk of myself on such a happy day for you."

Paul looked at her, not knowing what to say.

"I don't matter, Marguerite. It's you I'm worried about. I wish I could help."

His plea was so heartfelt that Marguerite began to cry quietly. Paul just sat, not knowing what to do. Like most men a woman's tears made him uncomfortable, so ridiculously ill at ease. He thought of his sister, so lacking in feminine tears.

After a while, Marguerite began to speak, dabbed at her eyes, sipped her coffee.

Life's been a constant battle for the custody of the children, especially Jean-Paul," she explained. "Jacques has even taken me to court. I won, but the experience was devastating. He did his best to blacken my name, and my capability as a mother. He was a mass of untruths."

She fell silent, her whole demeanour cast down. Paul didn't know what to say. He could think of nothing to say to this unhappy woman.

"Eventually, under pressure from his family," Marguerite explained. "I agreed he should see Jean-Paul for a weekend."

Why do the family exert pressure?" asked Paul.

"They thought it would do Jacques good," explained Marguerite. "He was still mentally an unwell man."

She paused and for a moment looked sadly at Paul. Then she continued.

"It was a disaster. Jean-Paul was very reluctant to go, but he consented in the end. He was due back on Sunday evening, but didn't arrive. I was in agony."

She stopped looking miserable.

"What did you do?" asked Paul gently.

"I did everything I could," explained Marguerite. "I contacted the Police, and his family, and went to see my lawyer. We were about to go to court, when Jean-Paul was brought back by that young priest you met. It was three weeks later. The priest didn't say much, and you know how quiet Jean-Paul can be. He only said he would never go to his father again. I tried to comfort him, but he still said very little. I just resolved never to let the children out of my sight again."

What support have you had?" asked Paul.

"Well, always my sister," Marguerite explained, "but she tends to be very outspoken. She blames me for ever marrying such a man. She wants me to end everything by seeking a divorce, despite being a Catholic."

Paul smiled wryly.

"Why do you smile?" she asked.

"I know all about outspoken sisters," he said. "I've one in London. I love her very much, but she can be very critical."

They were silent for a moment, and then Marguerite said, standing up.

"I must see about trains. I won't be a moment."

Paul offered to go but she shook her head and hurried away, telling him to wait a moment in the cafe.

When she came back, she said.

"I've got twenty minutes, then I must go to the station."

For a moment they did not know what to say. Then Marguerite said.

"Paul, write to me if you have a moment, but write as a friend, not of love. It's too dangerous. I'd like to know how you get on, what you are doing, girls you meet. Have you any special girl?

Paul shook his head.

"There was a girl at school, working as a matron, but it came to nothing. She suspected I had a friend in France."

"Oh, Paul, forget me," pleaded Marguerite. "I'm no good for you. I'd like nothing better than if you found somebody of your own age, married her, and had children of your own."

"Uhm," went Paul doubtfully. He didn't say he found girls difficult to know. But then at the school he had got to know Michelle by accident, and he had played tennis with Naomi.

"I'll try," he added vaguely.

"You will, you must," insisted Marguerite. "Just look at me as a happy incident in your life, an incident nothing more, though it's been very precious to me. It's been a wonderful friendship!"

Secretly she vowed she would never write to him again. He must forget her, and she had enough on her plate to have no moment for him. But it was a resolution she failed to keep.

They looked at each other, and Paul slowly began to realise his life with Marguerite was a thing of the past. For her sake he could never see her again, at least not until her life stabilised, or until she no longer had any fear of losing the children.

They walked slowly together to the station. He kissed her, gave her a hug, and then watched as she mounted the train, and it slowly moved away. He was not to see her for some while. But she remained a happy memory of that place La Refaudio in the South of France.

# Chapter 27

*Facing up to Reality!*

Paul returned to England with a heavy heart. He had never felt so sad or depressed before, despite several difficult moments. It should have been a happy time. He was now accepted into the Catholic Church in France, which is what he wanted. He felt the Church should have given him comfort, but it didn't! He found himself wondering what his father would have thought of him, probably the same as his sister. The thought made him even more miserable.

He did a strange thing for a man. When he arrived at his sister's flat, and she opened the door for him, he fell into her arms, and cried, tears that shook his whole being.

"Here, here," she exclaimed. "What's all this about?"

She drew him into the privacy of the flat, shut the front door, and led him gently to where he could sit down.

"I'm sorry, I'm sorry," he mumbled.

She gave him a handkerchief, and then waited patiently. Her heart was stricken; she was fond of her brother, even though he exasperated her with his strange doings.

When Paul had quietened down and drunk a cup of coffee, Sis asked him kindly,

"What's upset you so much? It's unlike you to be so upset."

It was a long time before Paul managed to reply.

"Marguerite has come to an end," he managed to say.

Sis heaved a sigh of relief.

"Well, that's a step in the right direction," she said simply, and with a quiet, gentle smile.

"But there's more to it than that," Paul said quietly. "Coming back I just felt an overwhelming depression. My life seemed so useless, beginning with failure at Oxford, failure to get on with people, and wherever I go, I seem to walk into trouble. It began with Marguerite's husband, continued with a lousy job in a tinpot school in Somerset, then trouble on the cross-Channel boat. Moreover I couldn't help thinking of Dad; I don't think he would be very proud of me. I seem to be doing everything he would not agree with, Catholicism, love of France over England. It's as if some devil in me makes me do things which are different from normal English thought. I can even feel people shake their heads over me, as if I was some imbecile."

He was quiet for a moment, and his sister said nothing, unusual for her.

"Mother always felt I should be brought up as a normal boy," he continued. "She would never send me to a school for the deaf. Yet I'm not normal. There's something in me that separates me from people. I go through life seeking a normal situation, but never can. I thought I had found it with Marguerite, but that came to nothing. The only person I can really talk to now is you, Sis, but it's not fair on you. I just feel I am going through life as a loner, trying hard to be a normal person, but I'm not. There are just moments when I feel I belong, but then something happens, and I don't, I really don't."

He lapsed once again into sad silence, and his sister continued to say nothing. But then she got up, settled down on a chair next to him, put an arm around his shoulders, gave him a gentle shake, and said,

"You know, Paul, we were lucky. We had a very brave father who gave his life for his country and won a medal for bravery. Do you remember we went up to Buckingham Palace to receive his posthumous medal from the king? Mother wouldn't go because she was afraid she would cry. Well, dear Paul, it's silly saying it, but you've got to be brave like Dad. There's only one thing you can do, go back to Oxford, and show the world you matter."

She fell silent, and then suddenly laughed.

"Personally I would tell the world to go to, well you know where it should go," she said defiantly. "Hold your head up high, and be damned to everyone else."

They were silent again, and sat contemplating the electric fire which warmed the room on this cold morning.

"You will go back, won't you, Paul?" she persisted. "You need have no fear now of French Prelims, and you know how hard you can work when you want to."

Paul came out of his self-indulgent reverie, and said,

"I'll go," he said simply. "It means I'll have to give in my notice to the school and leave at Easter. They won't be pleased. In a way, it's a pity because it's a good school with a good head."

He paused and then added.

You know, Sis, it will only mean a Pass degree."

She nodded. She knew the reason.

"Though I suppose a Pass degree is something," he mused. "And it would mean I could then take a Certificate in Education, post graduate."

Sis smiled, and said only.

"Atta, boy,"

# Chapter 28

*The Dreaming Spires Again*

Returning to Oxford was very different from his previous existence. For one thing he did not seem to be part of the college. He was given a tutor to whom he seemed to have no relevance. The tutor's only concern was that Paul had an academic tutor. Beyond that he seemed to have no interest in Paul, except he vaguely said that if Paul had any difficulties he was to come and see him. Paul felt that, as before, Oxford left men to find their own way. It was a good policy as men had to move out of a helpful school life, and stand on their own two feet.

Paul's most helpful academic tutor was his old history tutor who was a man who went by the ordinary name of Mr. Smith. He had a double-barrelled name of Templeford-Smith, but he rarely used it. He said, defying the snobbery of Oxford, that he was proud to be a 'Smith'. He was Paul's original history tutor, a talented, kindly tutor, who was largely instrumental in introducing Paul back to Oxford.

Paul's first problem was money. He had managed to make some savings, but it wasn't nearly enough. He really had to find a job, one that would fit in with his studies.

He found one as a night porter at Oxford Railway station. It was laughable, an Oxford undergraduate working on the railways, even if he was only taking a pass degree. But the coursework wasn't onerous. Once Paul had taken the French Prelim in June, he sailed through easily. He had read so many books in French since starting in France and Marguerite had been a good tutor. The autumn was a period of history which he knew well. It involved reading, which he could do while on night duty. The porter's job was not difficult. When a train came in, normally a goods train, it was just a question of unloading the parcels. Then there was a moment of quiet until the next train came in. They weren't very frequent. The worst unloading was the fish train between five and six in the morning. The fish were always smelly and the boxes dripping wet. Paul's clothes smelt to high heaven of fish. Then he was free to pedal back to his digs. Paul had lodgings in Walton Street, and he was blessed with a kind landlady, a middle-aged widow. She was used to dealing with undergraduates, but never one so complicated as Paul.

Paul never spoke of his night work to anyone in the university. He wondered whether anyone else worked as he did.

When Paul got back after the fish train, he would strip off his clothes, leave them out for his landlady to wash, then have a quick bath. He was usually in bed by a quarter to seven. He would then sleep until nine, get up, have a quick breakfast supplied by his kind landlady, quickly make sandwiches for lunch, and then pedal off to the library. Mr. Smith had given him a list of books to read. He would stay in the library until five, apart from a saunter out to stretch his legs. He was also capable of the occasional drop-off, but he didn't mind. It cleared his head. At six his landlady gave him supper, his one big meal of the day. He would then slump into bed from seven until about half past nine, get dressed quickly and then pedal off to work. His bike was invaluable, one which he had rescued from home.

In this peculiar life he owed much to his landlady, Mrs. Betty Austin. In fact Paul wondered how he could have managed without her support. It was strange how he tended to get involved with older women.

When Paul told her of his plans she was horrified.

"You can't!" she exclaimed. "Oxford is for men of leisure."

"But I've no money," stated Paul. "I used to have a grant, but not now."

Mrs. Austin was astounded, but when she realised he was having meals out, or taking food up to his room she announced,

"Look," she said, "you need proper meals, if you are working as you intend to do. I will feed you with a proper breakfast and supper."

But I've no money," pleaded Paul, "or very little."

He only paid her for the room.

"No matter," said Mrs. Austin firmly. "I hate cooking just for myself. It will be a pleasure to cook for somebody."

They argued some more, but gradually Paul succumbed. He was overwhelmed by her kindness. But she was also a decisive woman.

"Look my son," she said. "My husband's dead, my daughter's married and living in Scotland. I've nobody to care for. Besides I rather admire you. It's nice to see a student standing on his own feet. They're a useless lot until they go out into the wide world and have to fend for themselves. Then I suppose they find a wife to look after them, the poor dears."

She seemed to have a certain contempt for the Oxford male undergraduate.

They had the same argument over the washing of his clothes, but Paul likewise had to give in.

"You're spoilt," remarked Sis, when he told her of his good fortune. "Us women have to feed ourselves and do our own washing of clothes. You men are spoilt, and we do the spoiling."

But gradually Sis seemed to become grateful he was falling on his feet, even if it was a strange existence for a student.

Paul enjoyed the weekends. He had two nights of deep and lengthy sleep, on Saturday and Sunday nights. On Saturday he did little but read and talk to Mrs. Austin. His life didn't allow him time to make friends, so he found himself making a friend of Mrs. Austin, and after a while calling her Betty. On Saturday they would often go to the cinema. He found Betty an intelligent person to talk to, and something of a cinema buff. She also had decided views on life, and was not afraid to voice them. She was an avid reader of the Daily Telegraph. Paul was astonished at what she had to say. She was a Christian, an avid Anglican, and seemed disappointed Paul was a Catholic.

"The Catholic lives on fear," she would say, "fear of doing wrong, as if it constrains people from doing anything. The Church of England is a benevolent institution, intent on being positive."

She would smile kindly at Paul, who felt he should be defending Catholicism, but didn't know how. He didn't want to talk about Marguerite's faith or of the Catholic Church in France. It would seem disloyal to England. On Sundays he would go to Mass at eight, say a prayer for Marguerite, express his thanks to God for the way Oxford was working out. Then after breakfast he would go for a long cycle ride, while Betty went to her church. They would have Sunday roast about four p.m. when Paul got back from cycling. Then it was a peaceful evening of reading in Betty's sitting-room, interrupted by occasional murmurs of conversation by them.

He would have another night's good sleep, and then off to study on Monday, much refreshed.

Once the French Prelim was over in June, Paul looked round for a summer job for the months of July, August and September. It had to be a day job, to fit in with his night work.

And he found it!

It was a swimming-pool attendant at the local pool. It wasn't arduous work. It was merely giving out hangers, taking them back with the clothes attached, and then giving them back when wanted.

Betty was horrified.

"You can't," she cried, when she heard of his plans to undertake a double job, night and day. "You really can't. You'll kill yourself!"

Paul grinned. He expected this outburst from the rather maternal Betty.

"I can, you know," he reassured her smiling. "It's not difficult work. I'll be home by five-thirty, and I'm still free at weekends."

But Betty still shook her head.

"It's too much," she said anxiously. "It won't do your health any good."

"Let me try," pleaded Paul. "If I find it too much, I can always give it up. But it will make all the difference to my finances. I can even take you out to Sunday lunch!"

"You'll do no such thing," she exclaimed.

"It's only a way of saying thank you for all you do for me," Paul said, still smiling.

But Betty shook her grey hair.

"We'll see how it goes," reassured Paul.

The matter was left, but Betty did eventually agree to Sunday lunch, but at first only once a month, then once a fortnight, finally once a week.

Paul recognised that Betty was lonely. There were two other undergraduates lodging in the house, but they were rarely in, except to sleep. They had all their meals in the college. They disappeared at the end of term. Only Paul stayed, thinking of it as a mother/son situation. Certainly Betty jokingly called him a foster son. Her only child was so far away. Paul had to recognise he owed her a lot, and was grateful. His problem was how to thank her when he had so little money. All he could do was to share his few moments of leisure with her. That was no hardship as she was an interesting, thoughtful woman, and well educated.

But the luck was all on Paul's side, and he was grateful. Paul wondered what it was about him that found companionship in older women. Was it some bizarre trait in his character, or the lack of relationship with his mother? He didn't know. His sister provided a possible answer.

"I believe somehow, Paul, close relationships may be with opposite characters," she stated thoughtfully. "You are too like your mother in outlook. You got on well with Dad, certainly better than I did. I'm like Dad, I've always believed. But the delightful thing between us is that we are opposites. You are sensitive and inward looking. I like to think I am the opposite."

She paused a moment and grinned at that brother of hers. Then she added,

"Oh, it's impossible to make generalisations about character. It can be so misleading. But I hope you understand."

Paul nodded. He'd always missed his father, oh, so much. Seeing Jeff on the cross-Channel boat had opened many heart longings.

But Paul had to get on with life, and he was really too busy to think about human character too closely.

On the whole he enjoyed his busy situation. He got on better, both with the men on the railway, and the men and women working at the swimming-pool. Certainly there were none of the secretive attitudes of the boat stewards.

On night duty the most interesting man was an Indian. He was an immense man, unusually strong. He had fought at El Alamein under Montgomery, part of a contingent of Indian soldiers. Paul never knew the full name of this Indian. He had mentioned it, but it was not pronounceable. He was called several nicknames by the other porters, the most prominent being 'darkie', but he didn't seem to mind. Sometimes he would reply in kind – 'Hey you, whitey,' he would say. He was married to an English girl. He had one child, and another on the way. Paul couldn't help wondering what marriage between two varying nationalities and cultures could produce in the way of offspring. Certainly such a liaison was unusual at the time.

Darkie, for want of another name, was so strong he could carry the fish boxes straight out to the waiting vans. The other porters loaded them on trolleys and wheeled them off, including Paul. The difficulty was getting them off the train and onto the trolleys without getting wet. The boxes just dripped fishy water. When they got to the vans, there was help.

The only memorable incident on night duty happened when they were unloading the smelly fish boxes. Suddenly there was the noise of a falling box, and a cry of pain. Paul rushed to the spot and found the porter, a youngish man, lying on the ground, holding his leg.

"The bloody box fell on my foot," he exclaimed. "I think it's fucking broken something."

He lay back gasping in pain. Paul took charge.

"Don't move," he told the man. His name was Jim. "You'll only make it worse."

"That's bloody difficult," exclaimed Jim.

Another porter approached anxiously.

"Telephone for an ambulance," exclaimed Paul. "In the office!"

The man nodded and hurried off.

Within a short time an ambulance arrived, and Jim was carted off on a stretcher. Because of the incident Paul was late getting back.

He found Betty in a dressing-gown, preparing breakfast.

"You're late," She accused sharply, just like Sis.

So Paul explained.

"Well, get out of your things," she snapped, "and come down to breakfast, or it will spoil."

Paul smiled.

"Yes, Ma'am," he said mischievously.

When he got down, having showered, and in his pyjamas and dressing-gown, Betty said,

"A foot's nothing. In the war they had their leg shot off, or both legs."

"Times change," muttered Paul, and sat down to his cornflakes. "Whatever it was, he was in some pain."

A similar incident soon after involving an ambulance happened at the swimming-pool, but it was fatal. Paul was busy putting away hangers, when there were cries at the pool. Paul went out, and saw the life-saver swimming frantically to a man, being supported by a woman shrieking for help. Gradually the man was brought to the side of the pool, laid down, and the life-saver began mouth-to-mouth resuscitation, while another assistant ran to the phone. The man was taken off to hospital, where they later learnt he had died of a heart attack. Paul wasn't late home this time, or what he now liked to call home. He told Betty.

"Lordee!" she cried. "You do have an exciting time. Two incidents in a few days."

"Usually it's been very quiet," said Paul. "The only other incidents have been these wretched glass bottles."

This referred to notices in and around the swimming-pool, stating that no glass items were to be taken onto the premises. But people invariably ignored the instructions. They would lie down by the pool to sunbathe, take out a bottle from their bag and proceed to drink. The poor pool assistant then had to intercede, take the bottle, and explain why. The reason quite simply was that broken glass meant the pool had to be emptied, cleaned out thoroughly, and then refilled. The whole process meant a day's swimming was not possible. But people still argued.

"I'll be very careful."

Or

"I never break things."

Or, worse still, usually men.

"I resent this interference. I can take a bottle and drink where I like, so fuck off!"

The customers seemed to be unaware of how easily accidents could happen. But on the whole they accepted the situation. The difficulty came with women with small babies or very young children. Paul had to suggest they had a drink outside, which caused resentment.

But the children needed a drink and were too young to understand rules. Paul only had one uncomfortable moment with a woman. She was so difficult that Paul had to summon the supervisor. Usually he left such incidents to the other staff. There was one male member of staff who loved asserting his authority.

When September came, the weather proved somewhat inclement. Few people came for a swim. The council started winding down staff numbers, and Paul was the first to go. He couldn't grumble. In fact he was rather pleased. He could revise for his history exam at the end of November.

So, back to the library! And peace and quiet! Betty was pleased.

"You've hardly had a summer, or a holiday," she exclaimed kindly.

Paul wasn't concerned. He felt he had a year of hard work, and then he would have a degree, even though it was only a

Pass Degree. It was then he could relax, if relaxation was in his nature.

"I've got a suggestion," Betty said. "Can you get a week off from the railways? We have time before term begins in October."

"I don't know," admitted Paul. "Why do you ask?"

"Well, I'm going down to Cornwall to see my elderly mother," she explained. "Why don't you come with me? I'm going next week. It would give you a break, and it would solve the problem of your meals while I am away."

"Golly!" exclaimed Paul, overwhelmed by the generosity of her offer. "You're very kind, more than I deserve."

He thought a moment.

"I really don't know," he said thoughtfully. "I don't want to lose my job on the railways. It's a life-saver for me. The other problem, as ever, is money. I don't know whether I can afford it. I hoped to make enough money to give up the railways in the summer term. It will leave me free for the English exam at the end of June. It's the exam I'm least confident of passing." Then he added. "I've made a silly mistake. I've always been told never to end a sentence with a preposition. I ought to have said, 'the exam of which I'm least confident.'"

"Go on with you, you bookworm," exclaimed Betty. "You've no need to worry about money, you really haven't! You worry too much about the filthy lucre."

"I have to," said Paul. "I've no support except my sister, and she's not that well off!"

Betty looked at him with a glint in her eye.

"Look, my lad," she exclaimed firmly. "You've really no need to worry about money. I won't charge you for that week I'm away, and I know my mother won't charge you either."

"But what about railway fares and food, and any extras," protested Paul. The rail itself is expensive. You have to go to London, then change onto a direct train to Cornwall."

"Getting to Cornwall is no problem," Betty explained. "I'm driving down. As for food you're my guest for that one week!"

"Oh!" exclaimed Paul. He had forgotten that Betty had a car. She hardly ever used it. Driving in Oxford was fast becoming horrendous, the streets were so crowded, and parking was difficult. Far easier to go by bike or Shanks' pony. Oxford was a fairly compact city, unless you wanted to journey down to Cowley and the motorworks. But undergrads had no interest there.

"Oh, golly!" said Paul, feeling ashamed. "Why am I so dependent on women's kindness?"

Betty laughed.

"That's because women like you, for some unaccountable reason," she said smiling, and then teasingly. "Perhaps it's because you are so hopeless a man. You need mothering!"

Any offence in her words was taken away by the twinkle in her eyes. Paul did not know what to say, but eventually he came out with the words.

"I'd love to go to Cornwall. It's the county I enjoy the most, perhaps because of my Cornish ancestry. I'm very grateful."

He returned her kindly smile.

The next day he checked with the railway superintendent.

He seemed reluctant, but hesitantly he agreed, but hastened to say,

"I don't think you've worked long enough to be entitled to holiday pay."

Paul was disappointed, but he'd half expected the decision. He didn't mention the situation to Betty.

The drive down to Cornwall was uneventful. It took longer than Paul had thought as Betty was not a particularly fast driver, but they got there by supper time. Granny was a somewhat elderly and bowed, but mentally alert person. It was obvious Betty got her forthright character from her mother.

Granny lived just outside Penzance in a comfortable pre-war bungalow that had three bedrooms. After supper Betty had a straightforward talk with Paul.

"Look, Paul," she said seriously, "Would you mind amusing yourself? I don't see much of my mother. I'd like to spend the week with her. I'm very sorry. I should have spoken of this before, but my mother is much more frail than before."

"No problem," said Paul cheerfully. "I expected you would want to be with your mother. If I could make some sandwiches after breakfast, I'll disappear until supper. I know the area. We used to spend our holidays here before the War."

"You must have been very young," observed Betty.

"I was nine when last I came here. We had two earlier holidays when I was seven and eight, and another when I was very young, but I don't remember that very well. Dad was very fond of Cornwall. I'm not so sure about Mum."

Betty nodded.

"Well, I can desert you with a clear conscience," she said smiling.

It was on his second day in Cornwall that his holiday changed dramatically.

On his first day, after walking round the town, he strolled in the direction of Land's End. He always liked using a stout stick. To find one, he searched a small area of woodland away from the coast, and eventually found what he was looking for.

It was a stick of the right length, strong and stout. He went happily on his way. He was pleased to be on his own. He didn't have to make troublesome conversation, which he didn't enjoy. People seemed to talk a lot of repetitive inanities. His hearing difficulty had made him into a loner, happy with his own company, something he tried to explain to Betty. She wasn't convinced, arguing he made his handicap an excuse. It was the kind of remark Sis would make.

He didn't get very far in his walking. It started to rain, so he turned back.

On the next day he walked along the coast in an easterly direction. He was looking out over the sea, admiring the view.

In the distance were two white-sailed yachts which hardly seemed to move in the vastness of the water. Then a girl passed him along the coastal path. She gave him a quick half smile, and hastened on. He hardly seemed to notice her, except she appeared to be dressed entirely in brown, both matching jacket and skirt. She seemed to be too well dressed for a walk along rough terrain.

Paul settled down on a rough grass patch and took out his sandwiches. It was a perfect place for a picnic in the September sun, still warm.

Suddenly he heard a scream nearby, and then another of anguish. Quickly he picked up his stick, and rushed to help, thinking the girl may have fallen.

When he emerged over the brow of the path, he saw an astonishing sight. The girl was struggling on the ground, a man kneeling over her. He had pulled off her skirt and knickers. She was still struggling and kicking frantically. He slapped her hard.

"Keep still, you bitch," he growled.

For a moment the girl was still. Then she started to struggle again, trying to turn on her hip. In his effort to keep her still, the man did not notice Paul as he quickly advanced.

Paul raised his stick and brought it down on the man's arm with all the force he could muster. The man gave a cry and toppled over sideways off the girl. Paul noticed his trousers were round his ankles.

The man looked up at the menacing figure of Paul over him.

"Fuck you," he growled. "You've fucking broken my arm."

"Good!" snapped Paul. "I'll break the other arm if you don't clear off."

The man struggled to get up. It was almost funny watching him pulling up his trousers with one hand, cursing away. Paul didn't offer to help.

He thought it safer to keep his distance from the wretched man. When he had finally gone, Paul looked down on the girl exhausted and in shock from her struggle. He noticed her nakedness below the waist. She struggled up and twirled her fingers, indicating he turn round.

"Sorry," muttered Paul, and turned to look out to sea. After a few minutes she called out.

"I'm decent now!"

When Paul turned she was brushing down her skirt.

"I'll escort you home," he said, "just in case that man troubles you again."

"He won't!" replied the girl, "not with a broken arm."

Paul hastened back to collect his rucksack and the remains of his interrupted lunch. On rejoining her, he said,

"What is your name, if you don't mind my asking?"

"Annabel, but most people call me just Anna," she replied.

"The beautiful Anna," mused Paul.

"Why do you call me that?" she asked. "I'm hardly beautiful at the moment."

Paul looked at her. Her face was flushed and marked by the blow the man had given her.

"Bel," he explained, "means beautiful in French, Anna beautiful."

She smiled and changed the subject.

"May I thank you for the way you dealt with that horrible man?" she asked. "You saved me."

Paul grinned and looked abashed. He muttered something about 'damsel in distress'."

Well, you were certainly a knight to the rescue, and I couldn't be more grateful," she said.

Paul muttered in reply.

"It was nothing. But I really feel you ought to go to the police."

"Please, no," she said strongly. "It would be the last thing I want."

"Supposing he attacks another girl," he argued. "She may not be so fortunate. The man deserves punishment."

But she still shook her head. Paul remembered there had been reluctance for women to come forward in rape cases. Perhaps it was the publicity.

He didn't pursue the matter.

The girl seemed to walk in discomfort. He longed to take her arm in support but felt he should not. A man's touch might be abhorrent to her at this moment!

They talked on as they walked. She told him she was a nurse in London, on holiday staying in a boarding house.

Paul said he was on holiday with a friend, staying in the mother's house. He felt saying he was on holiday with his landlady would need some explaining.

"What do you do?" she asked.

"Well, at the moment I am struggling for a degree at Oxford," he explained.

"Oxford!" she exclaimed. "That's marvellous. I wanted to do my nursing training at Oxford, but landed up at a London hospital."

Further exchange of information was interrupted by their arrival at the boarding house.

"Look," said Paul. "May I see you again?"

"Yes, I'd like that," she exclaimed.

"Would you feel well enough to meet me in a pub?" asked Paul.

"I should think so," she remarked. "I'm only bruised. Bruises soon mend."

Paul didn't know it, but this was a typical nurse's disclaimer. Their tendency was to make light of injury. They had seen so much in their work.

So they parted, but not before she had once more expressed her thanks.

Paul later returned to Betty's house, feeling rather elated. 'Elated' may be the wrong word, because the incident Anna had suffered was tragic. But he felt content he had done the right thing for once in his useless life, and rescued her.

"What are you looking so pleased about?" remarked the ever observant Betty.

So Paul told her briefly what had happened.

"Lordee," said Betty. "It takes an incident of major proportions to get you to ask a girl to go out with you. But why didn't she want to go to the police?"

"I suppose it was all about the personal questioning," observed Paul. "I gather it can be quite embarrassing."

"Hmmm," went Betty. "I suppose I might have felt the same. But I still think the man's a menace and ought to be punished."

Paul met Anna the following evening as planned. She looked wan and a little tired as if she hadn't slept well. Paul's heart went out to her.

Immediately she said rather sorrowfully.

"Paul, would you mind if we only went out for a short while, say half an hour. Yesterday took more out of me than I realised."

"Not at all," said Paul. "A quick drink and then home to our beds."

She smiled. Paul took her to the only pub he knew in Penzance, near the seafront.

But it was fatal!

They had no sooner entered, than a man approached with his right arm in a sling. Paul could feel Anna shrinking back behind him.

"Ha, the bloody sod who broke my arm," he said in savage triumph, "and the stupid bitch with you. I've a score to settle with you both."

He was looking at Paul grimly. He took his arm out of the sling, and began to advance. His right arm was covered with heavy plaster, a potent weapon.. Somebody was trying to hold him back but he was shaken off.

Paul reacted in a way that afterwards surprised him.

I'm the one who has a score to settle!" he shouted in genuine anger. His fist shot out. The fierce blow caught the man full in the face. He went over backwards, blood spurting from his nose.

"Take that!" Paul said sharply, but he couldn't help clutching his knuckles, now in pain. "You don't call a lady a bitch after what you tried to do to her."

The barman came up to Paul.

"I should go quickly," he advised encouragingly, almost hissing. "I'll deal with this; you're not to blame. I don't want any further trouble."

Paul went, Anna holding on his arm. Once in the street, Paul released her hold on his arm. He took her arm in his turn, and they hurried away, almost running, putting as much distance as they could from the pub. After a while, Anna said.

"Paul, let go my arm; you're hurting my bruises."

"I-'m sorry," said Paul quickly. "I didn't realise I was holding you so tightly."

"It's not you," said Anna, smiling. "It's my bruises."

Paul let go of her. Instead she slipped her arm into his. As they walked along, more slowly now, Anna, whispered quietly,

"Paul, thank you for dealing with that dreadful man. It's the second time you've stood up for me. I feel so very grateful."

"I'm afraid I lost my temper," admitted Paul.

"Don't worry, he deserved it," Anna remarked, and then she added, "where are we going?"

"To my friend's house," he told her. "It's the only quiet place I know, where you can relax."

"Will he mind?" Anna asked.

"It's a she," he explained. "She's my landlady at Oxford."

"Your landlady!" she echoed in surprise.

So Paul explained about his strange life at the university. He could see she was puzzled. But before she could ask any more questions, they arrived at the bungalow. Betty greeted Anna with open arms.

"So, you're the girl who's been through an unpleasant ordeal," observed Betty. "Paul told me of the incident yesterday."

Anna nodded. Paul could see she was a little disturbed at being discussed. But Betty's pleasant character soon reassured her.

The only drink in the house was sherry, Granny's favourite tipple. But it was a drink that opened up everyone. Paul felt happier as he saw Anna relax. Despite her wan and tired face, he was beginning to realise what an attractive girl she was. Her light brown hair came down to her shoulders. It glistened with health under the artificial light of the evening. Her green eyes shone, as the evening progressed. She was wearing another light brown skirt. Brown seemed to be her favourite colour. She had on a cream coloured blouse covered by a brown cardigan. She had a young, shapely figure. Paul couldn't help looking at her, well, not looking, but glancing from time to time.

They told Betty of the incident in the pub, mostly from Anna, as Paul felt embarrassed by the affair and his quick temper.

"Well, Paul," Betty said in a teasing voice, "I never knew you had a temper."

"The man spoke so rudely, I had to do something," Paul said quietly.

Betty, horrified by what had happened yesterday and today, said in a kindly but firm voice.

"Anna, you really must go to the police. The man's a menace to women. He makes me shudder that someone like him should be in England. Our manhood during the War did us so much credit. His behaviour is so shameful."

But Anna remained reluctant. Betty looked at Paul.

"This, Paul, is women's talk," she said. "Do you think you could leave us for a moment?"

Paul nodded and went upstairs to the books he had brought to study. He was still feeling somewhat shaken up by what had happened. He realised it was far worse for Anna. Yet he rarely lost his temper; he felt he couldn't help it.

He didn't know what the girls discussed, but the outcome was positive.

"We've rung the police," Betty explained. "Somebody's coming to see us. Anna has agreed."

Paul felt relieved. He was against hushing up everything.

In fact two officers came that evening. One was a W.P.C. who retired with Anna and Betty into the kitchen. Paul remained with the constable and told his story. After about forty minutes the police left, extracting a promise that Anna and Paul would come to the station the next day to make their statements. Betty pleased Anna by saying she would go with her.

Afterwards Betty said firmly to Anna.

Now, dear, you are coming with me in the car, and Paul as support, to your boarding house to collect your things. You're staying here with us. I think you could do with a few friendly faces around you, and you'd be much safer."

Paul looked at Anna. He could see her interview with the W.P.C. had shaken her up, though Betty remarked later that the woman had been very kind and understanding.

He wondered about sleeping arrangements. The bungalow had only three bedrooms. But Betty told him Anna could go into her room, and she would go in with Granny. Paul protested he could sleep on the sofa, but he couldn't argue with Betty's masterfulness.

The journey to the boarding house didn't take long. They were soon settled back in the bungalow. After a warm drink, they retired to bed. Paul couldn't sleep for a while, his mind going over and over events. His hand still hurt. Anna had made him promise he would go to the hospital after the visit to the police station. She was concerned about his fist in case he had broken something.

The next morning they all looked a little droopy-eyed. Betty mentioned that her mother had kept her awake with constant restless movement. Paul imagined that Anna had suffered even more than he had done. He felt better after breakfast and a cup of coffee. He reflected he had felt worse than after night duty on the railways.

But matters went fast after that. After their statements the man was arrested. The police had visited the pub and learnt his name and where he lived. Somebody leaked events to the newspapers. Anna promptly proposed she went back to London. The police consented and she parted that very afternoon, but not before promising to visit Paul and Betty in Oxford. Paul sadly said goodbye to her at the station. All he had left was the memory of a lovely girl and a hand that hurt, but was not broken. What haunted him was the memory of her nakedness.

He struggled hard to rid his mind of that wicked thought. How he longed to see her again in all her young beauty. He sat down and wrote to Marguerite, telling her of Anna. She wrote back, more than delighted, and hoping all would go well.

The eventful week came to an end, and they drove the long journey back to Oxford, to be embraced by that teeming, beautiful city.

# Chapter 29

*Back to Work and Study*

Paul felt unduly reluctant to return to work his first Monday back. The station seemed dark, drab, even dirty. But the quiet cheerfulness of the men began to overcome his reluctance. The powerful Indian smiled at him, and asked if he'd had a good holiday. Paul returned the smile, and said he had. He said nothing of events, ever memorable in his mind. He gradually got caught up in the routine, as train after train arrived to disgorge its contents. The last fish thing was a little distasteful, with its cold, smelly wet boxes, but he managed. He went back to Betty's more tired than he could ever remember. But Betty cheered him up, and the library gave him peace. However, he found it difficult to concentrate. An image of Anna would prey on his mind, her loveliness, her quiet smile, and her nakedness. He tried to shake it off, and concentrate on his study. He couldn't remember whether he had seen a woman before, her living, naked flesh. He had played a game with his sister of going to the toilet together, but she saw more of his bits than he ever saw of hers. Mother stopped their communal visits as soon as she realised what was happening.

In the afternoon he went to see his tutor, Mr. Smith, who gave another list of suggested books he might read. Paul asked for a tutor to help him prepare for the summer exam in English. It was his least confident subject.

On Wednesday, he and Betty received letters from Anna. Paul was overjoyed.

Both letters were really to thank them for all the help. But at the end she asked if she could come to Oxford not the coming weekend but the one after.

'I'll come early Saturday morning,' she wrote. She gave the time of the train. 'Would it be possible for me to stay the night? I'd be so pleased. I love Oxford. Then I'll go back late Sunday evening.'

"She's got it all planned," commented Betty drily. "But it would be lovely to have her. I'll write."

Then she looked at Paul and said teasingly.

"I don't suppose you'll be writing, will you?"

Paul replied in kind.

"I suppose I just might," he said. They looked at each other and grinned.

When the weekend arrived, Paul met her at the station. His heart was beating in expectation. Anna gave him a warm smile as she emerged from the platform. Without hesitation she ran to him, and they embraced.

A porter who knew Paul from a bout of night duty shouted "hey, hey!" in a rising note of amusement. Anna giggled. They broke away and hurried out of the station, then walked into the city. Paul took her to his favourite cafe just off the Broad. Lingering over their coffee, Anna noticed that he was wearing a hearing aid. Paul explained about his handicap.

"Why weren't you wearing it in Cornwall?" she asked.

Paul shrugged.

"People think I'm dull the moment they see my aid," he explained.

"I don't!" said Anna forcibly. "I've seen you in situations where you are far from dull, in fact rather fierce."

She thought a moment, then said,

"In my work I meet rather a number of people who wear hearing aids. They tend to be rather introspective. But they are thoughtful and kindly when you get to know them, together with other handicapped people."

Paul's heart gave a jump of delight. She understood! Eureka!

He changed the subject.

"What would you like to do in Oxford?" he asked gently.

"Well, if it's possible, I'd like to go punting. It's quite a warm day for September. Do you punt?"

"You bet!" said Paul with a touch of enthusiasm. "It's a relaxing form of exercise."

Anna smiled. "When I came to Oxford for my interview, I went punting with a friend who was also new. We were all over the place. We couldn't manage the pole and had to use the paddle. I hope you will teach me."

"Not in those clothes," Paul said. "The lady lies in the boat, languid and lovely, so the punter can admire her beauty."

"Not this lady," said Anna firmly. "Can we go to Betty's so I can change?"

"She's expecting us for lunch," explained Paul.

Oh, good!" said Anna pleased. "I can also get rid of this bag."

She indicated the bag lying beside Paul.

So they rose and wended their way to Betty. On the way they passed Worcester College.

"That's my college," said Paul with a touch of pride.

"I'd like to go in when we have a moment," said Anna with interest. She suddenly took his arm and gave it a squeeze. "Oh, there's so much I'd like to do."

Her eyes were shining.

Paul grinned.

Betty welcomed Anna with open arms. They were soon sitting down to a pleasant lunch, chatting happily.

"Don't eat too much," warned Paul. "We're taking you out to dinner tonight."

"Wow, it's all happening," exclaimed Anna. "But I must pay my whack."

"No need," said Betty. "I'm the one with the money, Paul's always broke, and I don't suppose you get well paid under the new health service, Anna."

"It's all right," said Anna loyally. "We get by. But supper out is a lovely idea. Let me pay for the drinks."

But Betty was insistent.

After lunch, the two children, as Betty rudely called them, set off for Magdalen Bridge, and the punts. Paul was feeling a little tired for punting but he saw the joy in Anna's eyes, and pulled himself together.

He took the pole first. He was a practised punter from his early days in Oxford. But he hadn't often a girl as lovely as

Anna lying on the cushions. She had changed into what she termed an old skirt and jumper. The skirt was a dull brown but it had a pattern of green woven into it. The jumper was fawn. She had changed out of stockings.

After a while Anna begged to have a go.

Well," said Paul teasingly. "The tradition is that we stop for a canoodle first."

He shouldn't have said it! Anna suddenly became serious.

"Paul, would you mind if we didn't – er – canoodle, if you mean what I think what you mean by canoodle?" she said anxiously. "After what happened in Cornwall I'm not particularly happy about men touching me."

"I'm sorry," murmured Paul, feeling rather ashamed.

"Don't be," said Anna. "I'm told it's a normal reaction, and one gets over it. I saw the psychiatrist at the hospital."

They did stop at the bank but only to change over.

"Now," said Paul. "Punting is almost an art. You relax, let the pole drop through your hands until it touches the bottom. Then you give a heave which is the effort bit, then you straighten up, and let the pole trail in the water. It acts as a rudder. Allow the pole to drift to the left, the punt glides left. Same to the right. When the punt is straight, you repeat the process."

"That sounds fairly simple," said Anna laughing, "but I don't know whether I can manage that huge pole. I'd much prefer the paddle."

"That's infra dig in Oxford," said Paul. "Everybody will look down their snooty noses. The paddle is for losing the pole, or when you fall in."

"Fall in!" she echoed. "Do many fall in?"

"Not many," admitted Paul. "The only time I've seen it was during a heat wave. The falls were deliberate to cool off."

He grinned at her.

"Have a try," he said. "If you fall in I shall be there to rescue you."

"Oh, you!" muttered Anna. "Give me the pole, damn you! I can't go through life being rescued by you."

She suddenly realised what she had said, and blushed.

"I'd love to go through life rescuing you," exclaimed Paul, laughing, "provided I can have a canoodle afterwards.

But Anna didn't reply, taking her embarrassment out by sudden energy with the hefty pole.

She struggled for a while, veering all over the river, then she gave up, frustrated. Paul took over. Her frustration was further increased by seeing a girl poling along quite happily.

"Don't worry," reassured Paul. "It takes a lot of practice. I floundered a lot at first."

But Anna merely grunted, peevish anger all over her pretty, reddened face.

When they returned the punt she had calmed down. She had even enjoyed the relaxed feeling a punt engenders, her fingers trailing in the water.

"What would you like to do now?" asked Paul.

"Tea, definitely tea," she replied firmly.

Over tea, she said.

"Paul, I'm sorry I'm so – well – frigid at the moment."

"Not to worry," Paul said gently. "You had an experience no girl would want. How are the bruises?"

"Recovering!" she admitted.

She smiled wanly. Then she added seriously.

"I'm sorry, Paul," she said. "I've been selfish. I thought you were looking a little tired while punting. I forgot you've been on night duty. I suggest we go back, and you have a little rest while I talk to Betty. You'll feel refreshed for dinner."

Paul nodded gratefully, and made a motion of going to sleep among the tea cups.

"Not now, you idiot," laughed Anna. She stood up, took his arm and dragged him out of the cafe. Then she remembered they hadn't paid, hastened back, leaving a dazed Paul to keep awake, standing outside.

Betty woke Paul at nearly at seven with a cup of tea.

"Get this down you," she ordered. "Then get your glad rags on. You're taking the two of us out." Paul rubbed his eyes, smiling, and complied. Downstairs he met two lovely ladies, also in their glad rags. Anna almost took his breath away. She had put on a simple green dress.

'Green, thank goodness,' thought Paul.

The only ornaments she had on were a small black belt round her waist, and a little gilt necklace around her neck. Her perfume was alluring, without being too prominent.

"You look so wonderful," Paul exclaimed, "I could almost eat you."

Anna blushed but seemed pleased. Betty wore a blue skirt, and a white blouse, and a necklace she said her husband had given her. The beads were a pale blue to go with her skirt.

"I'm honoured to be taking out two such lovely ladies," said Paul sincerely.

"Get on with you," said Betty, making light of the compliment. "We're late."

They drove to the restaurant in Betty's car, even though the restaurant was only just off the Woodstock road.

The evening was a delight, both girls determined to enjoy themselves, and both became just a little tipsy. Paul couldn't help feeling how much his life had changed from earlier days at Oxford.

Then he had been lonely, friendless, even mildly depressed, and unable to study. Now he felt alive, confident and with such charming companions. Life was good!

"What are you two children doing tomorrow?" Betty enquired, smiling.

Paul looked at Anna enquiringly.

"It's your weekend," he said to her, leaving her the choice.

"No," said Anna firmly. "I've had a lovely day. What would you two like to do?"

They thought a moment.

"I didn't think to be included," Betty said.

"But you must," insisted Anna.

Paul felt a little jealous of the closeness between the two women. It was obvious they had been discussing him while he slept. Anna now knew he had taken on two jobs during the summer. She knew also that his father had won a medal for bravery. All this had come out during the meal.

Paul sighed. He wanted Anna to himself. She was beginning to grow on him. He loved watching her as she struggled with the punting, the movements of her body and legs.

"Well," said Betty, interrupting Paul's reveries. "You are welcome to come with me to Woodstock, to Blenheim Palace. We could have a picnic. I'll take Jenny, my dog, for a walk. She loves it there. You two can go round the Palace, if you're interested."

"I'd love it," said Anna, pleased. "I've never been there. How would you feel, Paul?"

"I saw Blenheim when I first came to Oxford," Paul admitted. "But I wouldn't mind going round it again. It was a very brief visit."

"There's one thing that concerns me," said Anna. "I wanted to see round Paul's college."

"Well, I think we could do that after Blenheim," said Paul. "The other thing, I often go to the Chapel there for evening service. It's an unusual Chapel. But I'm not certain whether there is a service outside term time. How do you feel about going to Church, Anna? We've never discussed our religious feelings."

"That would round off our weekend nicely," said Anna smiling. "But aren't you a Catholic?"

Yet another thing she must have learnt from Betty!

"I'm a Catholic in France, but tend to be an Anglican in England," Paul explained. "But we'll have to talk about it sometime. I feel I owe a loyalty to my school and college, which were Anglican."

Already he felt the influence of Marguerite was beginning to lessen. He didn't feel he would ever forget her, but he was beginning to plan his life away from France and her. The person influencing him most was this lovely young girl sitting near him in the restaurant.

"How do you feel about Catholics, Anna?" asked Betty.

Paul felt it was a naughty question. It was just like his sister, to bring everything out in the open.

"I've no objections to Catholics," said Anna. "I have one or two nursing friends who are Catholics. But I do object to some of the principles of Catholicism."

"Why?" asked Betty.

Paul wished Betty would shut up.

"Well," Anna began, "birth control for instance. The world is getting over-populated. Then the ruling in mixed marriages that the child must be brought up as a Catholic. That's monstrously unfair on the non-Catholic. I like the Anglican Church with its more open-minded principles. Finally the refusal to accept divorce. There are too many unhappy marriages. It's wrong to insist couples stay together in a loveless marriage."

"Uhmm," went the mischievous and slightly tipsy Betty. "How do you feel, Paul?"

"I'm not answering," said Paul. "It would be a pity to spoil this lovely dinner with religious arguments. One day when Anna and I are alone, I will discuss the very personal question of faith."

And with that he shut up, and refused to discuss the matter further. Betty just grinned at him, not at all offended by his bluntness.

"I'm sorry, Paul," Anna said, more sensitive to the situation. "I shouldn't have spoken as I did."

"No worry," said Paul. "But let's talk about it at a quieter moment. This restaurant is very noisy on a Saturday evening. I've a difficulty in hearing. My hearing aid picks up all sorts of extraneous noises."

So nothing more was said on this subject until the next day.

Later they walked home, Betty feeling she couldn't possibly drive as she felt she had had too much to drink. So Paul asked permission to leave the car in the car park until the next day.

The proprietor grinned.

It's not the first time it's been requested," he said. "I can get a taxi."

But Paul shook his head.

In fact it was a lovely walk back. The coolness of the evening helped to soothe their minds. The girls linked arms either side of Paul.

He was the king-pin that helped to support them. During the walk Anna squeezed his arm and whispered.

"That was a lovely meal, Paul. I enjoyed it."

"I should thank Betty. She was the host," Paul said, which they did when they got back to the house.

Betty kicked off her shoes, gave a big "oof", and announced she was going to bed. Her final sad words were,

"Harry would have loved this evening. Good night, my children."

Anna whispered when she had left the room.

"Who's Harry?"

"Her husband. She's a war widow."

"Oh," said Anna.

"I'm sorry, Anna, I couldn't discuss Catholicism," said Paul softly. "I'm a bit confused myself. It's so personal a question, could I leave it until tomorrow? I'm feeling very tired."

So they parted, Paul asking whether there was anything she wanted, but Anna shook her head.

Paul longed to kiss her, but didn't, mindful of her earlier remarks.

# Chapter 30

*A Relaxing Day Out*

They were a bit jaded the next day. But the weather was pleasant for September, so they embarked for Woodstock after preparing a picnic. They were a little lackadaisical and somewhat late setting forth.

The view from Blenheim Palace was breath-taking.

"Wow," exclaimed Anna. "I wish I'd worked in Oxford, instead of London. Everything's so beautiful!"

"Why did the Radcliffe turn you down?" asked Paul.

"Simple, really," replied Anna. "I had rheumatic fever as a child. It concerned the Radcliffe, but strangely it didn't worry the London Hospital I applied to."

"Why is rheumatic fever a problem?" asked Paul.

"Well, with some people it can have after-effects," explained Anna. "But I've been free of any complications, thank goodness."

As they had planned, Betty went off with Jenny the dog wagging its tail excitedly. Anna and Paul went round the Palace.

Paul loved the place, redolent as it was of English history, from the eighteenth century to Churchill in modern times. Anna loved the beauty of the magnificent building and what it contained.

They met Betty for lunch. A blanket was spread on the ground, and they reclined Roman fashion to eat. Afterwards Betty said she was going to have a snooze. Paul and Anna set off for a walk, with Jenny again showing excitement. She seemed a tireless dog. After a while, Paul said,

"Anna, do you think we could find a spot to sit down. I feel I ought to talk to you, or rather, I feel I owe you an explanation."

Anna smiled. They chose a grassy spot overlooking the lake. Paul sat, fondling Jenny's ears, while Anna sat with her knees hunched up to her chest, her arms wrapped round her knees.

"You know, Anna, about my leaving Oxford early. Well, I went to France. There were three reasons, but I won't bore you with them. The job I got was with a family near Montauban, looking after five children. The mother was a lovely woman. You wouldn't believe it of a woman who had given birth to five children, but she had kept her figure. Her breasts were a little too big, but I felt it was because she had fed five children, all boys."

"Five boys!" exclaimed Anna. "She must have longed for a daughter."

"That was part of the trouble," said Paul.

"Why do men concentrate on women's breasts?" asked Anna surprisingly.

"I don't know," said Paul. "I think it's to do with maternal feeling. Our first human contact is with a woman's breasts."

Paul wondered whether the man who had attacked her had fumbled with her breasts. But she probably would never tell him.

"I felt sorry for the mother," continued Paul. "Her husband was rarely home. When he came there was always a quarrel and tension in the family. I felt he must have a screw loose. He told me he had a mistress in Paris and she had given birth to a daughter. He wanted both families to live together in the house near Montauban."

"Together!" echoed Anna. "No woman would accept that, or not in our civilisation."

"Hmmm, Marguerite certainly didn't," admitted Paul. "I just felt sorry for her, and that sorrow grew as incidents multiplied. But the real thing is that I went to France rather lonely and depressed after Oxford, and Marguerite's kindness did much to restore my confidence, even happiness. It happened in several ways. Not only was she a lovely woman, but also very talented."

"She belonged to the Paris Opera before she married. Most evenings she would sing and play the piano. She said it relaxed her after a busy day. She was a mezzo-soprano, and I was fascinated. But another thing happened which drew me closer to her. The weather was very hot that summer. I'd never before experienced such heat. In the evenings, once the children were settled in bed, Marguerite would take two deckchairs onto the balcony. We would sit outside. The summer evenings were fantastic. We'd watch the night sky, listen to the murmur of the crickets, and talk and talk. I'd never known anything like it, an attractive woman talking to me as a friend. Except with my sister I'd never really communicated with a woman as we did. My French improved by leaps and bounds. It was wonderful, almost miraculous. The funny thing was that the local farmers seemed to think we were in love. The French are much more romantically inclined, and sympathetic than in England; yet I never touched her, or rather we only embraced quietly when it was time to go to bed. She was my employer, and I thought about fifteen years older. She never told me her age, and I never asked."

Paul stopped and looked at Anna. Then he asked.

"I'm sorry. Am I boring you?"

Anna shook her head and said.

"I'm wondering when we're going to get to the Catholic bit."

"It's quite simple really," mused Paul. "I couldn't understand Marguerite. She never criticised her husband to me or to anyone else. She was completely loyal to him, and said her faith did not allow divorce. In that part of France the faith seemed very strong. The little village church was unbelievable. Every Sunday it was packed. Men and women were segregated, men sitting on the right, and women on the left. The whole atmosphere reminded me of the War when the churches were packed. There's been a falling off since in England. I knew enough Latin to follow the service. I had sessions of discussion with two priests, both of whom were very pious, especially the last. It was a kind of saintly piety which touched and affected me. We went for two nights to

Lourdes, which was an incredible place, especially the torchlight procession of The Stations of the Cross at night. It seemed as if millions of people were there, and the procession snaked for miles, or so it seemed. I began to read the lives of French saints, and Marguerite herself was like a saint. I became drowned in Catholicism. It affected me deeply."

He paused and thought to himself, half smiling at the memory.

"Then I think my feelings to Marguerite began to change. I began to look on her as a very desirable woman. Don't laugh, a mother of five children and much older. Such a feeling was unbelievable. It began with dancing. I'm not much of a dancer, but Marguerite was fantastic. We visited a plage by a river where they danced during the day, sometimes wearing just a bathing costume. It was then Marguerite's breasts got in the way. She was a dancer who nestled up to one."

Anna for some reason began to giggle, whether from the mention of breasts in the way, or from closeness, Paul didn't know.

"Don't laugh," pleaded Paul.

"I began to look on her as a desirable woman. Moreover she seemed attracted to me. They were only little signs. I know I'm not a particularly handsome man, but ...."

"Don't belittle yourself," said Anna, smiling. "You're not a bad looking bloke, as blokes go."

Paul smiled uncertainly at this sort of compliment.

"Oh, I forgot where I was," he pleaded.

"Dancing," Anna reminded him.

"Oh, yes," remembered Paul. "There were two other occasions of dancing, at the harvest supper at two of the farms. Marguerite was a wonderful person to dance with. I wanted every dance, but she said it wasn't very proper. I had to dance with other girls who weren't nearly as good."

Paul paused a moment, and then continued.

"Anyway, in September I returned to England to take up a post as a teacher. I left France, very much in love with Marguerite and determined to take instruction to become a Catholic. Just after I left, Marguerite wrote and said she was going into hospital. She didn't say what was wrong, only that it was a woman's thing. I missed her so much that I wrote and asked her to marry me. It was so stupid. I had no money, and no real job. I was an unqualified teacher in a lousy school. My sister also increased my discomfiture, by telling me I had proposed marriage to a woman who was having a hysterectomy. She thought it very funny, until she saw how upset I was. Marguerite sensibly told me marriage was not possible. She repeated her commitment as a Catholic. She was very nice about it all, and said kind things."

Paul paused and looked at Anna. He saw she was smiling.

"Oh, you're as bad as my sister!" Paul exclaimed. "You women make fools of us men. I know it all sounds ridiculous and I behaved stupidly but I really did love that woman. As for Catholicism it began to go badly downhill. My instructor was not a pious man, not like the French priests. He was full of negatives, thou shalt not. He made it appear such a measly faith. At Christmas, things got even worse. I was told not to go near Marguerite. Her husband was seeking grounds for divorce, and I could be a possible target, even though Marguerite and I had done nothing. I was going into a Catholic retreat in France, but the whole occasion meant nothing to me. It was Marguerite who dominated my thoughts."

"So, your interest in Catholicism came to an end," observed Anna.

"Well, not exactly. I seem only to get to know women who need rescuing, or are in trouble. There was you and Marguerite, and another girl, called Michelle."

"Was she French?" queried Anna.

"No English, pure English, despite her name," mentioned Paul. "It was funny. It was another example of my complete lack of knowledge of women. She was a matron at the Prep School where I was teaching. We used to go to eight o'clock Mass together on Sunday."

"I was still not a Catholic, but Marguerite dominated my thoughts. We still wrote discreetly to each other. Anyway, one Sunday Michelle set off for church before me. When I followed I found her on the ground, clutching her stomach, obviously in pain. I didn't know what to do. Anyway I finally picked her up and carried her back to the school and the sick bay. She wasn't a heavy girl. I didn't know what was wrong with her, but the school nurse told me cheerfully she was having her period, nothing to worry about. I was amazed! I didn't know a period could affect a woman so badly. She was a funny girl, a very devout Catholic, almost like a nun in her primness. We became friends. We luckily had the same half day off.

She introduced me to a priest. He wasn't particularly pious, but he instructed me in the Catholic faith a little more positively. That Christmas in France I was accepted into the Catholic faith and I was baptised. Marguerite came. I didn't know how she managed it, but it was marvellous to have her there. But the same day she told me we must stop writing. She was going through a bad legal time with her husband. She was really saying how our friendship must come to an end. I went back to England heartbroken, no Marguerite and no Michelle, who was now Matron in a girl's school."

"My Catholicism rather went downhill. I realised it was bound up with Marguerite. It seemed so un-English. I also began to think about my dead father whom I much admired. He would not have tolerated Catholicism, as my sister didn't. Then Oxford seemed a world away from the strict rules of the Catholic Church. There is so much of open thinking here at the university. Though I told Betty I was a Catholic, gradually I seemed to be drifting back to the Anglican Church, my early background. This is where I am now, a confused, uncertain man."

"Uhmmm," muttered Anna thoughtfully, "Your life seems to be ruled by your heart."

"Exactly what my sister said," Paul remarked, laughing ruefully.

"I should like to meet her," was Anna's comment.

"Certainly," agreed Paul. "It won't be difficult. You both live in London. I've got an idea you'll get on well."

Anna got up.

"We'd better get back to Betty," she said. "I'd still like to see your college."

Paul got up. Jenny the dog looked as if she was ready for another walk, instead of having to listen to those lumps of adults chattering continually in the background.

"Poor old girl," muttered Paul. "You haven't had much exercise.

As they walked back, Anna said sincerely.

"Thank you, Paul, for letting me know about your Catholicism and events surrounding it."

"In retrospect it was a very happy time, which did me much good," said Paul. "I shan't easily forget it."

Anna thought a moment. Then said,

"You know, Paul, you don't have to get to know women just by finding them in difficulty. All you have to do is give a smile and show kindness and understanding, and they will come flocking, hearing aid or no hearing aid, believe me."

"Uhmm," went Paul doubtfully.

Anna almost shook him.

"Paul, dear," she said. "Women are human beings, just like men. You get on with men all right, except when you punch them on the nose or break their arm!"

She smiled cheerfully at him.

They arrived at the car. Betty looked at them.

"What have you been arguing about?" she asked.

"We haven't been arguing," said Anna happily. "Just trying to knock some sense into this hopeless, young man."

Betty smiled maternally.

"He's very obstinate," she said.

When they got back to Oxford, Paul showed Anna around Worcester College.

"It's heavenly," exclaimed Anna. "Once you get into those gates, you seem to be entering a different world."

"It was a Benedictine monastery at one time," he observed.

"That would explain the sense of peace," remarked Anna.

"Wait until the undergrads arrive," Paul remarked. "It's pretty noisy and vibrant then."

When they left the college, having seen the grounds and the chapel, Anna said,

"You know, Paul, you're very lucky to be part of such a place."

"Well, yes, I agree," said Paul. "But when I first arrived, I didn't appreciate it as much as I should. I've had more sense since. My history tutor said in his blunt way that my absence has done me good. I've matured, he thinks. The only trouble is I can't take an Honours degree, only a Pass degree. I've gone past the statutory time limit."

Anna nodded. He'd already explained the reason.

After a quick meal at Betty's, he took her to the station. They stood awkwardly on the platform, not knowing what to say or do. Goodbyes are always awkward. Paul longed to take her in his arms, but resisted the impulse. It was Anna who broke the silence.

"Paul, could I say something?" she asked quietly. "You may not understand as a man, but what happened in Cornwall made me feel unclean, besmirched me. I've taken baths, but that's only outward cleanliness. I feel dirty inside. But could you give me a hug, and a gentle kiss that I could remember as clean and sweet?"

Without hesitating Paul took her in his arms and held her gently. Their lips met for one lovely moment and then they parted.

"Thank you, Paul," she whispered. And then she seemed to pull herself together, and said in a normal voice,

"There's one other thing. Would you come up to London one weekend soon, and may I meet that sister of yours?"

Paul grinned, and said,

"Nothing would please me more! But you'll have to put up with a rather sleepy man after night duty. But you can talk to her while I have a snooze on her sofa."

"Oh, I can put up with that, I think," said Anna laughing.

At that moment, the train arrived.

"I'll write," Anna said quickly. "I'll have to look on my duty roster."

And with that they parted.
It had been a wonderfully pleasant weekend.

# Chapter 31

*To London*

In the days that followed, Paul almost forgot Marguerite, and even the Catholic Church. He still remembered to pray. Though Anna was uppermost in his mind, he felt guilty. He was like politicians, constantly changing his mind to suit changing needs. He couldn't help talking to Betty about it. She just laughed, which hurt, but she did say one thing which Paul felt helped him.

"Paul, dear, you're young, a wonderful time, but beset by anxious change," she said smiling. "Take the word of somebody of middle years. You're finding your feet. Life will go on changing until you find your way of life that will suit you, and your feelings and thoughts. You are a basic Englishman, and Catholicism, which is basically a Latin culture, will never fit happily on your shoulders. You were brought up an Englishman. I should remain one. But that is not to belittle your experience in France. It will give you a wider knowledge of the difference in people and their culture. God made many different peoples, and we must try and understand them. Does that make sense? What I'm really trying to say is, don't be afraid of change."

"You'll change in any case if you continue with a girl like Anna, and I hope you do. She's a lovely girl, the best thing that ever came into your life."

Paul nodded and smiled.

"Wherever did you get your wisdom from?" he asked teasingly.

"Oh, it comes with the years, and with experience," she admitted. "I've had my times of change, the biggest being the loss of a husband, much loved. I could have happily died with him, but couldn't. I had to change!"

Paul thanked her, and felt humbled that her life had been so much more painful and changeable than his.

Two weeks later he went up to London. He came off work, and caught the next train to the capital. He went straight to his sister's flat. There, waiting for him was Anna, dressed as ever in various shades of brown. Even more wonderfully, they embraced without hesitation. Sis also was there, smiling as ever.

"Hey, I'd like a hug," Sis exclaimed.

Paul embraced her with a laugh and enthusiasm.

When they parted, he observed, smiling.

"So you two have got to know each other."

"Yes, Anna rang me," Sis said. "We've got on like a house on fire, including discussion of a certain wayward young man."

Paul groaned.

"I might have guessed," he grumbled.

The girls sat him down for breakfast, and then packed him off to bed.

"We're going out shopping," announced Sis. "We've got it all planned. We'll be back in a couple of hours."

Paul pointed out plaintively that he'd already had a sleep on the train. But the nurse in Anna stated firmly it was not enough.

"Sleep tight," she said encouragingly, as they slipped out of the door. Paul was left to enjoy some much needed sleep. In fact the girls didn't return until nearly lunchtime.

"Why didn't you wake me?" he grumbled.

"We felt you needed it," excused Anna smiling.

"More likely to avoid your grumbles," announced Sis pointedly. "You're like a bear with a sore head unless you have a sleep!"

Paul could see his weekend being organised by feminine wiles. Somehow he didn't mind. It was relaxing!

At lunch the girls told him what they planned. In the afternoon they would walk to the National Gallery and wander around. Then back for tea. Afterwards they were going to the theatre.

"What to see?" asked Paul.

"It's a concert at the Albert Hall," explained Anna. "At the hospital we sometimes get free tickets. I snapped them up, knowing you were coming."

I'll probably fall asleep," muttered Paul.

"You'd better not," said Sis. "My boyfriend is coming."

"Your boyfriend?" queried Paul, surprised. It was the first time Sis had mentioned a boyfriend for quite a while. It made him feel rather ashamed. Sis took a helpful interest in his female friends, but he never in her boyfriends. It seemed a selfish, one-sided interest by him!

Sis nodded at his query.

"Good grief," exclaimed Paul. "You never told me."

"You know now," said Sis.

"Tell me more," begged Paul.

"You'll see him this evening," pointed out Sis. "His name is Brian, Brian Penrose. And we're to be married in the spring."

"Congratulations!" exclaimed Paul, and then he added grinning, "I'll have to keep awake this evening to tell him all your disagreeable ways."

"Don't you dare," muttered Sis, "or I'll tell Anna how horrible you can be."

"I'll keep poking you, Paul," Anna said smiling. "I've hardly had a word out of you so far."

The afternoon was an occasion, a happy occasion with all their banter. This helped to enlighten the rest of the day, indeed all the weekend.

"Does Mum know about Brian?" asked Paul.

Sis nodded.

And Mum's pleased you're back at Oxford," she added. "But not the Catholic circumstances."

Paul muttered he must go and see her, but when was the problem.

Sis told him a little more about Brian. He was a bit older than her. He had lost a leg in the War and now worked for

Barclays. Paul couldn't help thinking it was typical of his sister to take on a man with a disability. It did her much credit.

Paul couldn't exactly say he enjoyed the National Gallery. He followed the girls around, feeling still a little weary. He wondered what he would have done, had he had the choice. Probably just sitting around the flat catching up with everything. The girls obviously enjoyed the viewing, and Paul admired his artistic sister for her knowledge. Eventually he retired to a bench, admitting he was more tired than he'd realised.

"Poor you!" said Sis unsympathetically. "If you will do these unsocial jobs!"

She was really trying to tease, but to Paul it did not come across.

Anna took a kinder tone.

"Why don't we have a sit down somewhere and have a cup of tea?" she suggested. "I think I've seen as much as I can cope with today."

Paul nodded, pleased, but Sis said she would stay on another half hour or so, and meet them back at the flat.

It gave Paul a few precious moments with Anna, which is what he longed for.

"I'm sorry I'm so tired," he said once they were settled over a cup of tea.

"Not to worry," said Anna smiling. "I've done night duty in the past. It suddenly hits you after a while. I do a twelve hour shift from eight to eight, four hours more than you!"

"Anyway," said Paul softly. "How are you now, I mean, after Cornwall? I haven't had time to ask you."

"On the whole much better," admitted Anna. "It certainly sets one back, what I experienced. But life is returning to normal, thank goodness. I feel more forgetful of the incident."

"I'm glad," said Paul, and reached for her hand.

After a while Anna asked.

"Paul, you said something about going back to France after your degree and Dip. Ed. Why is that?"

"Basically I shall have a poor, very poor degree," admitted Paul. "The only way I can rectify that so I can teach at Secondary level is to go to France and take another degree in French language and Literature at a French University."

"But won't that take another three years of study?" protested Anna.

"Well, no," said Paul. "If I already have a degree in England, the French will excuse me the first two years of study. I only have to do the final year. I'll have to keep up my French in the meantime by spending the vacations in France."

"Oh," said Anna thoughtfully. "I don't think I can wait that long."

"What do you mean?" asked Paul surprised.

"Simply, I want to marry you," said Anna with devastating openness.

"Marry?" exclaimed Paul, astonished out of his wits. He'd only known her a short time.

Anna nodded, looking serious.

"But I thought the man had to make that suggestion first," said Paul, his mind fighting with astonishment and pleasure, two contradictory reactions.

"I don't see why," stated Anna. "Marriage is an equal partnership. Why can't a woman pose the question first, especially when men are so slow."

"Good Lord!" exclaimed Paul. "I've heard the War emancipated women, but never to this extent! Shouldn't we wait? I feel we hardly know each other."

"No, Paul, I love you. You make me feel safe. I know you, I feel I can trust you." Anna was speaking with sincerity and yet with a radiant smile on her pretty face.

Paul looked at Anna, at first not knowing what to say. Finally he spoke with the same sincerity.

"Anna, I'd love nothing more than to marry you, but I've no money, no degree and no worthwhile job. Above all I'm handicapped with poor hearing. I'm all right with one-to-one talking, but in a group I'm lost. I'm not much of a catch at the moment for any girl!"

"Oh, Paul, stop hiding behind your poor hearing," Anna exclaimed with exasperation. "Sis said it was the most annoying thing about you."

"Have you discussed me with Sis?" asked Paul.

"Not really," said Anna. "But I can tell you something - that sister of yours is very fond of her little brother. Though she teases you she's completely loyal to you. If she wasn't your sister, I'd be jealous of her. As for too soon, I've loved you since you struck that wretched man in the face. My heart jumped with joy. I wanted to cheer."

"I've loved you ever since seeing you at the side of the path outside Penzance, so unfortunate, so helpless, even though you were half naked."

Anna blushed.

"You can see the whole of me now, the way I feel," she said. "But perhaps it's better we wait until we are married. We should keep to the proprieties."

"Oh, Anna," said Paul, "I could get up and hug you. But we're so public here."

They both laughed and looked round in case anybody was listening.

"I must say you chose a most unromantic spot to propose to me," admitted Paul laughing. "You didn't even go down on your knee to me, which is traditional. But could I ask, why the hurry?"

"I'll go down on my knee to you willingly when we are alone," said Anna grinning. "I'd even profess undying love, and all that nonsense. As for the hurry, I can't allow you to go to France and fall in love with another of those terrible French women. I'd be biting my nails in anxiety. That's why!"

"French women are not so terrible," said Paul loyally. "They're human like English women."

"That's really my point, or my anxiety," admitted Anna, smiling. "It's not that I don't trust you, I don't trust them!"

They grinned happily at each other. Finally Anna said.

I'm going to learn French, so we can converse together, and I won't be a hindrance," said Anna smiling. Then she added. "May I tell that wonderful sister of yours we're engaged?"

Paul nodded.

"She'll guess in any case, if you continue to look as cheerful as you are doing," he told her. "She's very perceptive. You're grinning like the proverbial Cheshire cat!"

"Oh, Paul, can we go somewhere alone together tomorrow?" she asked. "We've so much to talk about."

Paul nodded.

"I don't think she'll mind when she knows the reason," he said. "In any case Brian is going to be around tomorrow. She'll want to be with him."

"Oh, Paul, this has all been so sudden and so unexpected, I feel like crying," Anna admitted.

"Well, if it's been so sudden for you, imagine what I must feel," exclaimed Paul. "To use another expression, you've quite taken the wind out of my sails. But I bet you planned this, thought it all out beforehand."

But Anna shook her head.

"I'm not saying," she said with a touch of feminine mystery.

"Well, it makes sense," said Paul thoughtfully. "They say two people living together can live much more cheaply than apart."

"Paul, can we go?" pleaded Anna, "and find somewhere I can go down on my knee to you. It'll ruin my stocking, but it'll be worth it."

Paul nodded.

"If we go down the lane at the side of Charing Cross, there's a small park down on the left," explained Paul. "It might be quiet, or I hope so."

They left the cafe and went to where Paul had suggested. They found the tiny park and a bench, somewhat sheltered by hedges. It was difficult to believe such a place existed in so busy an area of London.

"Down on your knee, woman," said Paul, teasingly.

"But I'd rather a cuddle and a kiss," said Anna, predictably changing her mind.

This they did, their lips sweet and soft, and Anna's body pliable and young, stretching out to Paul with longing.

"We'd better go," said Paul after a while, "before we're had up for indecent behaviour."

Smiling they reluctantly parted. It was a heavenly moment.

Slowly they walked back along the Thames, arm in arm, until they branched off for the flat.

When they entered, Sis said, as Paul had thought,

"My, you two look as if you'd swallowed the cream. What's brought this on?"

"I've asked Paul to marry me, and he said yes," explained Anna.

"You said?" exclaimed Sis, surprised.

"I'm afraid she did," admitted Paul, "and worse still, I did accept. You're the first to know."

"Well, I never," said Sis. "I've repeated many a time that you never cease to surprise me, Paul. This calls for a drink, a celebration, and I've a bottle of white wine. But first, you two love birds, meet Brian, the man I intend to marry."

Brian was a tallish man, Paul thought about six foot, with a very slight limp, as if he had to draw one leg forward with more effort than the other. He had a ready smile, dark brown hair, and a mouth that widened with pleasure. Paul immediately warmed to him.

"May I kiss the happy girl?" he asked, and proceeded to give Anna a hug and a peck on the cheek.

After that it was a talkative, happy time until the moment to go to the concert.

There, Paul felt that he rather disgraced himself by falling asleep on Anna's shoulder. She put her arm around him to give him more support. Paul slept peacefully, only waking when it was the interval and people moved.

"Oh, dear," he exclaimed. "I heard nothing of that concert."

He began to get up. Anna laughed.

"It's only the interval," she pointed out. "You'll be able to redeem yourself in the second half."

"If I stay awake!" said Paul gloomily. "Getting engaged to you has tired me out even more than usual."

Anna could only laugh happily. She saw Brian wink at her. He was a great winker, that man!

Paul dropped off to sleep again during the second half, but managed to wake for the crescendo of the final movement.

"I'm sorry," he mumbled again to Anna.

"You're not the most scintillating of companions," she opined teasingly in a whisper. "But it's just as well you woke up. My arm was getting a little numb. Thank goodness you don't snore!"

When they got back to the flat, Paul couldn't help wondering where Brian was to sleep. The solution seemed to be on a mattress in the sitting-room with him. But he was surprised to see Brian and Sis go quietly into Sis' bedroom. He felt almost jealous of Brian. It looked as if he had lost a good friend, a wonderful sister of many years. He looked at Anna, and she looked at him. Without saying a word he knew instantly what she was thinking. But he didn't react.

Anna did. She came over, gave him a hug, and whispered.

"I'll be along in a while. You can see all of me then."

"You can't," said Paul quietly. "We're going much too fast."

For a moment, Anna said nothing. Then she said quietly,

"Paul, dear, your sister told me you left Oxford because you felt lonely. You'd been a lonely person all your life because of your hearing. You needn't feel lonely any more because I'm here. I not only love you, but I want to be with you, to touch you, to feel you. Besides," and she almost pouted, "you've seen me in the next to nothing, I haven't seen you, and I want to very much."

Paul's answer was to take her in his arms, and lead her to the sofa. When they were sitting, Paul spoke also quietly.

"Oh, Anna, I want you as much as you want me. You're such a lovely woman, I find it difficult to resist you. But I wonder whether we are going too fast and might one day regret it. I have so little to offer. And, besides, you take away my manhood."

"In what way?" asked Anna softly.

"Well, It's all so sudden, so unexpected. You first of all propose to me, and now you are propositioning me, both of which are the duty or prerogative of men, or have been."

"Oh, Paul, don't be silly," said Anna gently. "Your manhood is never in question with me, never will be. Didn't you stand up for me when I was being assaulted? Many a man would have looked the other way. Then you hit him so beautifully when he called me names. You didn't for a moment consider the consequences. Fortunately there weren't any. Your sister also told me you had a father who fought bravely in the War. I can only repeat, your manhood will never be in question as far as I am concerned. The only thing," and she hesitated, "you tend to be slow, to want to ponder things before making up your mind. You're a funny mixture of action man in a crisis, and a slow ponderer at more normal times. We obviously love each other, well let's go for it, but treat me gently."

Paul sat bemused, and then he said.

I'm sorry, Anna. I long to hold you in my arms and feel your loveliness. There are a couple of problems. I've never made love to a girl, and I haven't got any condoms. I imagine you've no wish for a child just yet."

"Oh, Paul, we'll learn together," she said gently, "and I've got what you want! Condoms are easily available in a hospital. We give them out to women who need to persuade their husbands to be more careful."

"You have!" exclaimed Paul, astonished. "Good grief, you think of everything!"

Anna just grinned.

"Give me a few minutes," she said, "and I'll join you."

She left Paul, an astounded man, wondering if he would ever understand women. As he undressed, he wondered how they would manage on the sofa. He was also a little apprehensive, wondering how he would perform. This was something he had dreamt about. But now it was reality.

But Anna, as ever, dispelled his fears. She took one look at the sofa, proceeded to arrange all the cushions on the floor, slipped off her dressing gown and lay down, covering herself with a blanket. She looked up at a gaping Paul and gave her usual grin.

"Come on, slowcoach," she said. "I'm waiting, all expectant."

Paul said something very unromantic.

"Do you mind if I remove my hearing aid. I may not be able to hear you."

Of course, silly," she said, almost laughing. "This is not a time for talking, but for action, and you're good at action, as you've proved."

Paul joined her under the blanket!

# Chapter 32

*Making Plans*

The next day, two very quiet couples sat, drinking coffee and eating a desultory breakfast. The sitting-room was tidy, no vestige remained of the night's cavorting.

"I hope you slept well," said Sis, grinning. Paul suspected she knew or guessed, but wasn't going to interfere.

"I was a bit restless," confessed Anna with a naughty grin.

What are your plans today?" asked Sis. "Brian and I thought we would go to Kew Gardens, if you'd like to join us."

Anna looked at Paul.

"I think we'd rather stay here," she said. "We've got a lot to talk about."

Sis nodded. Paul looked relieved. A restful day was just what he needed.

When Sis and Brian had left, Anna and Paul sat down together on the sofa, over yet another cup of coffee.

"When do you plan the wedding?" Paul asked with the trace of a teasing smile.

"It's not you, but we, when do we plan the wedding?" Anna emphasised. But when she saw Paul's smile, she nearly threw a cushion at him.

"Oh, you!" she uttered. But Paul took her in his arms and silenced her.

"We must be serious," said Anna, breaking free. "I feel we must see my parents first. They're going to bear the financial burden. We must go to them with an idea of a date."

"Well," said Paul thoughtfully, "I'll only make a decision after we've had a cuddle like last night. Sis and Brian won't be back for ages."

Oh, Paul!" exclaimed Anna. "You're like a child who wants his sweets. Perhaps later when we've settled this important question."

Uhmmm," went Paul disappointed. "As far as I am concerned, next summer when I've finished my degree. Then we can spend our honeymoon in France. I'd love to show you what a beautiful country it is."

"But Anna shook her head.

"I'd much rather it was sooner, Christmas or Easter. Then I could support you so you can concentrate on your studies, and not do such tiring work."

Paul looked at her in astonishment. The idea of being supported by her was a further indictment on his manhood. He shook his head.

"Anna, I just can't be supported by you," he said firmly. "It's just not on."

I don't see why," argued Anna. "I've finished my studies. I'm a qualified nurse. I've much more chance of a decent job than you have. I'd love to support you, make life easier for you. From what Sis has told me you've had a raw deal in life, losing your Dad at the age of nine, and with a hearing difficulty. I don't understand how you can possibly teach French with such a handicap. But Sis says you're obstinate. She actually said pig-headed."

Anna grinned teasingly. Paul said, smiling,

"That's what the French called me."

He quoted the French expression.

"Oh, Anna," he continued, "you're taking away the very ground on which I have started to build my confidence. I must get a degree, poor though it may be. On that I've set my heart. I don't want anything to interfere with that. After that we can plan the next stage in our lives, marriage, where to live, what to do next."

For a moment he was silent. Anna too couldn't think of anything to say.

"Anna, dear, could you possibly realise what this degree means to me?" he pleaded. "Since leaving Oxford, everything that has happened to me has gone wrong. I fell in love with a talented, lovely woman, and it created all hell for her. You'll laugh at this, but I actually punched her husband, much as I did your bloke."

"I became a Catholic, and I'm beginning to realise it was a mistake. I took a job on a cross-Channel boat, and was too naive to realise what was going on, the fraud that was being committed. Now two positive rights are happening. I'm back at Oxford, and I fall in love with another lovely girl, this time my own age, and that love is returned in a way that was unforgettable. But I've nothing to offer that sweet and lovely girl who has given me her body. I don't want to spoil those two precious rights as I have done with others. They say men with a hearing handicap are very immature. My history tutor once called me the most immature man he'd ever met. I admired and liked him as a man and wasn't angry. He meant well. But I've never forgotten his words."

Anna took his hand gently.

"Paul dear," she said softly. "You've given me the biggest offer of all, your love and your physical love. I couldn't have wanted anything more. You even defended me, and I shall never forget it."

She paused, and then continued.

"We've now, dearest Paul, to find a way to build up our lives together, which is what this discussion is all about. All I want to do is to help you and be with you. Couldn't we get married in a registry office?"

"Never!" said Paul firmly. "A proper wedding means a lot to a girl. I could never deprive you of that joy! They say a girl is a queen on her wedding day. For men it's just agony, but not for the bride."

"That's a funny way of putting things," said Anna laughing. "I'll leave you out when I get married, and just go up to the altar by myself!"

Paul smiled. He saw her point.

"Incidentally," added Anna, smiling even more. You can't make love to me. I haven't any more condoms!"

"You wicked girl," said Paul, laughing himself. "I'll just have to make love to you without."

He made a grab at her, but she slipped away, and ran round the back of the sofa. Paul chased her. After two giggling circuits, he managed to seize her. They clutched together and kissed. It was a long, sweet kiss. But there was no love-making.

"We'll have to be better prepared next time," Anna said as they broke reluctantly apart. "But you can get those horrid things yourself. People snigger if I do."

Paul consented, not quite knowing how. When they had resumed their seat on the sofa, a little breathless, Paul said seriously.

"I think you may be right, Anna," he said surprisingly. "It's just possible Christmas may be a better time for a wedding."

"Why do you say that?" Anna said, not able to hide her surprise.

"Well," Paul started, and then paused. "The history exam is, I think, early December. I'm not over-concerned about it. It was my best subject at school, and I had a damned good teacher. The same applies to French. I've done nothing but read French books for the last two years, well, mingled with the history. It's the English that concerns me in the summer term. I've spent most of my time reading history and French books, but not English. I feel if I can get marriage, history and French out of the way, I can then concentrate on the English."

"Don't count me as a burden like an exam," said Anna.

"No, no, I hadn't meant that at all," said Paul hurriedly. "It's just when it comes to marriage, there will be pressure, not between us, but relatives and friends. And I haven't seen your parents yet. They may well oppose the whole idea. I hope not but you know how parents are."

Anna nodded.

"Leave my parents to me," she said firmly.

They both sat and contemplated the future silently. Finally Anna said,

"Where will we live initially?" she asked.

"I've been thinking about that," said Paul, glad at last he was making the decisions, and not this modern, emancipated girl whom he loved. "Betty has a flat at the top of her house. It's very small, a miniscule kitchen and bathroom, but it would do just while we're at Oxford. I'll have a word with her."

"I like Betty," commented Anna. "But let me see the flat first before committing ourselves."

Paul nodded. They seemed to be getting somewhere, with some positive solutions.

# Chapter 33

*Parental Visit*

The following weekend Paul and Anna went down to Bognor Regis on the Sussex coast where her parents now lived.

"I'm going to sleep," stated Paul as they got on the train at Victoria Station and settled down. "Would you mind?"

"I should mind excessively," said Anna teasing. "I should regard it as the height of bad manners."

Paul grinned.

"Well you'll have to lump it," stated Paul. "I need some kip to face your parents."

"They're not so frightening," Anna explained with a grin. "Dad's lovely, but Mum may be a bit difficult, I don't know. It all depends whether she likes you or not. Perhaps you ought to get some sleep, just in case. My soft shoulder is available. But it'll cost you!"

"What will it cost me?" enquired Paul.

"A proper cuddle, not the miserable embrace you gave me coming off the train from Oxford," Anna stated firmly.

Oh, dear, was it so miserable?" enquired Paul. "I was a bit worried. I had to rush washing and changing in order to catch the train to London. I was a bit worried in case I smelt fishy. Betty said I smelt as if I had come out of the sea."

Anna laughed.

"No, my sweet, you smelt all right," reassured Anna. "Now stop fussing and get your beauty sleep."

To this Paul complied and he slept for about two hours, most of the way to Bognor.

He woke feeling like a bear with a sore head.

"Golly, you slept well!" exclaimed Anna. "At one time your head slipped from my shoulder onto my breast, and the woman opposite gave a cheeky grin."

"Oh, I'm sorry," apologised Paul.

At that moment, Anna's dad arrived. There was instant liking by Paul. His eyes had much the same friendly twinkle as Paul's dad had. Eyes can be very expressive of the soul!

"Hallo, my love," he said to Anna, giving her a hug. "How's my little girl."

"Not so much the little, Dad," chided Anna teasingly. "I happen to have grown up."

"You'll always be my little girl, I suppose in memory," Dad said.

"Oh, Dad!" protested Anna.

Dad turned to Paul and shook his hand warmly. He was a man of medium height, in his sixties, greying hair, and a wide, smiling mouth.

"So, you're Paul," he said. "I've heard a lot about you from Anna."

"Good, I hope," said Paul, returning the smile despite his thick head.

"Of course," said Dad who put his arm around Anna's waist and led them to the car.

At the house, Anna's mother was a bit more formal, certainly not so warm as her husband. Paul's heart sank a little. He'd heard that if you wanted to know what your love would be like in middle age, then look at her mother. But that couldn't be true! Anna was more like her father.

Anna's mother was probably in her late fifties. She had hair that was dyed, not a trace of grey, her eyes didn't smile, only her mouth, but that was briefly. She just gave Anna a peck.

After a late lunch, they settled down to discuss the wedding issue. But it was not a discussion, more a one-sided pronouncement.

"I cannot possibly agree with a wedding soon after Christmas," announced Mother flatly.

"But why?" challenged Anna.

"I would have thought it obvious," stated Mother firmly. "There's not enough time either for your preparation or for ours."

"Why, Paul and I can get married tomorrow," challenged Anna, rising furiously to the challenge. "Our minds are made up."

"You're not pregnant?" Mother asked, the question shooting out with abruptness.

"Mother!" exclaimed Anna fiercely. "We don't want children until Paul is settled."

"That's another problem," stated Mother mysteriously.

"What do you mean?" challenged Anna fiercely again.

"Well, dear," began Mother patronisingly. "You hardly know this young man. it's not long since your holiday in Cornwall."

"Not long!" cried Anna. "If only you knew!"

Paul, listening anxiously, suddenly realised Anna had not mentioned to her parents what had happened in Cornwall.

"What should I know?" queried Mother, still patronising.

It was here that Dad took part in the argument, in a more understanding, less patronising manner.

"My dear, I'm sorry," began Dad quietly, speaking to his wife. "Anna was attacked twice in Cornwall, once physically, and then verbally. On both occasions Paul came to her rescue very bravely. That cemented their relationship. Anna didn't want me to tell you, but I feel now you should know."

Paul breathed a sigh of relief. It sounded as if Dad was on their side.

"Was she raped?" asked Mother anxiously.

"Nearly, Mother," replied Anna. "Paul arrived just in time. I really would rather not talk about it."

"Yet you talked to your father, not to me." Mother sounded hurt.

There was silence, an awkward silence for a while, Anna not wishing to explain her reasons. Eventually it was Dad who broke the silence.

"I feel, dear, we must support these young people. It's their life, not ours. Anna knows what she is doing. We must let the marriage go ahead when they want, give them our blessing and support." He spoke kindly, softly.

"Some marriage!" spoke Mother with a shade of bitterness. "A man without a degree, no money, and no job, and who wears a deaf-aid. He's got nothing to offer Anna."

The truth was out!

"Mother!" exclaimed Anna angrily.

Anna turned to Paul, speaking kindly.

"Please, Paul, would you mind having a walk for half an hour. I'll meet you by the pier. This is a family matter for me to deal with."

Paul sighed.

"I'd rather stay," he said gently. "Your mother speaks the truth, and I wish I could reassure her that I would do my best to look after you."

"Truth or not, I'd rather you left," pleaded Anna. "It won't be long. There are some beautiful gardens just opposite the pier. I'll find you."

Reluctantly Paul departed. He somehow recognised this was a battle only Anna could fight. There wasn't any support he could give her on this occasion.

He wandered slowly down to the front. The pier looked as forlorn as he himself felt. It had been cut in half during the War so enemy invaders could not land. It had not been mended yet.

Paul crossed the road and entered the gardens, found a bench, and sat down to ponder events. It was curious that Anna used the more formal 'mother', whereas with her father it was always the more familiar 'dad'. He remembered once hearing a father tell his son always to use 'mum' when addressing his mother. It was couched as an order, not a request, Paul never knew why, but he thought mum was bound up with the close attachment one should have for a mother. He also realised that a Christmas wedding was now unlikely, but he reckoned without Anna's powers of persuasion. When she joined him she was smiling all over her pretty face.

"Paul, it's all right," she cried, giving him an ecstatic hug. "We can get married the first Saturday after the New Year. I'm sorry Mother was so beastly. It's really Dad who won the day. He told Mother the wedding would go ahead, even if he had to organise it on his own. Mother bleated about my being their only daughter. My two brothers married where their wives lived. But Dad said if it was so, they should stand by their only daughter. Mother retired complaining she had a headache. It was all too much for her. Dad whispered to me it would all be all right, and packed me off to find you. He's a bit like you," mused Anna, "always standing up for me. But don't think too badly of Mother. She's a bit disappointed in life. She always said Dad ought to be more ambitious in his work. He was just happy to jog along, but she wanted a bit more from life. She imagined me marrying some filthy rich bloke, and living happily ever after. She was disappointed I became a nurse. She imagined me as a doctor or lawyer. Though we argue, she usually comes round to my point of view in the end."

"Uhnn," mumbled Paul doubtfully. "I feel sorry for your mother. She's losing a daughter, and worse still to a not very eligible man."

Stop that!" Anna snapped. "Stop running yourself down. You're very eligible. You remember that always. You're the most eligible man I know. I need you badly, more than you realise."

So there the matter ended. It was still uncomfortable for Paul, but Mother seemed to be coming round slowly as the weeks passed.

# Chapter 34

*Wedding verses Exams*

When Paul got back to Oxford late Sunday evening, he greeted Betty with a cheerful grin.

"My!" she exclaimed, "You look as if the cat's had the cream, if that's the right expression."

"I'm getting married just after Christmas," explained Paul happily.

"My!" said Betty again, looking pleased. "That's quick off the mark!"

"It's Anna really," Paul admitted. "She set the pace."

"Well, you certainly came together like a bolt of lightning," remarked Betty. "But I'm so very pleased! Do you think you could give me a nice kiss to celebrate?"

Paul immediately obliged with warm affection.

"There's something we or I would like to ask you," Paul remarked, the celebratory kiss over. "We wanted to ask you if we could have the top flat as our first married Oxford home."

Betty thought a moment.

"I don't see why not," she said smiling.

"It would be lovely to have you both here. The only thing I would ask is that you moved into the flat at once, or during this week. I would ask the same rent until Christmas. That would leave your present room free for an undergrad. It would also mean that you and I could do up the room for the blushing bride, that is if you are not sleeping your head off."

So, it was agreed. Anna came up the following weekend to view the flat. To Betty's great astonishment, the two also christened the flat by spending the night together. Betty was no prude, luckily!

So began for Paul a fulfilled and busy time working on the railway, studying in the library, and spending the weekend making the flat more presentable. Anna would join him when she could, but she was working off her notice at the hospital, preparatory to helping her parents prepare for the wedding, which was looming large. Anna came to Oxford when she could, not wanting Paul to travel himself because of his study. Otherwise they rang each other daily, and even corresponded.

Paul found the excitement of his present situation did not help his concentration, but two things helped to save the situation. One was that he had a natural interest in history, and much enjoyed the books he was recommended to read.

The second factor was that he teamed up with a girl called Lisa. She had been ill and forced to take the Pass degree like Paul. They made out fact cards, and then tested each other. Paul was surprised how relaxed he was with girls now, after his experiences with Marguerite and Anna. Lisa had a boyfriend, a research graduate, a little older than her. Lisa talked incessantly of Nigel. Paul responded by talking of Anna. The friendship between Lisa and Paul was purely academic and helpful. They tended to tease each other to relieve the monotony of studying.

When the exam came, Paul found it easy, as did Lisa. He regretted not being able to take an Honours degree. He made one mistake, but rectified it at the viva exam.

Lisa invited him to her college Christmas Dance.

"There'll be plenty of pretty girls to dance with," she explained, tempting him.

But Paul pleaded that he was going to visit Anna at her home in Bognor.

When he finally arrived, Anna met him at the station. They hugged and kissed.

"My! Am I pleased to see you!" she exclaimed. "We must talk."

"Oh, dear," exclaimed Paul, "has something happened?"

Anna said nothing, but dragged him off to a cafe nearby. They were really serving lunch, but agreed reluctantly just to serve coffee.

"What's up?" asked Paul gently when they were seated.

"Mother!" exclaimed Anna cryptically. "She's driving me up the proverbial wall. If it wasn't for Dad, I'd be having a screaming fit!"

"In what way?" asked Paul, concerned.

"She keeps changing her mind," grumbled Anna. "One would think she was getting married, and not me. We've had two changes of venue for the reception. The first was for the church hall, which was marvellous. The church ladies promised to do the cooking. Dad was pleased because it reduced costs. But Mother went to look at the hall, and came back saying it was completely unacceptable. We then plumped for a restaurant, you know, the nice one near the front. It had a pleasant banqueting hall upstairs. But Mother insisted the stairs would be impossible for our more elderly relatives. There was no lift."

"Oh, dear," remarked Paul, trying to sound sympathetic. He found it hard to adjust to these predicaments.

"Mother's final choice was the hotel just opposite the putting green. Dad's face blanched at the cost, poor man! But Mother insisted."

"I can understand your dad," commented Paul. He'd heard that weddings were hard on dads.

"Uhmm," murmured Anna. "It's not just the reception. It's the whole bang shoot, guest lists, menus, present lists. The number of guests is completely out of hand, including a number of local people whom I hardly know."

Anna sat back in tired exasperation, thought a moment, and then said,

"Paul, can we go away, for a couple of days. I feel I could scream, or have the heebie-jeebies! What about your sister?"

"Sis is staying with Mother," Paul pointed out. "But it would be good if we could go to my home. Mother keeps complaining she has only met you once, and then briefly. I've been so busy."

"That would be wonderful," exclaimed Anna.

"There is one slight difficulty," remarked Paul. "My mother married again. He's the most boring man possible, a complete contrast to Dad."

"I'm quite used to boring men," said Anna, smiling. "In the wards they take your hand, and tell you endless stories which they think interesting or funny. They're neither. We have a rescue service among the nurses. One will rush in and say you're wanted urgently."

"The man releases your hand. You rush out and have a giggle somewhere private. I prefer the quiet men who look at you with adoring eyes, and are very grateful for all you do."

"I doubt whether I could rescue you on this occasion," mused Paul. "But I'll think of something."

Anna was pensive a moment, and then said.

"Paul, we may be having a row with Mother tonight. I want you not to take part, just keep quiet and not take sides. Will you promise?"

Paul nodded, but couldn't help being curious.

"What's the row about?" he asked.

"You'll see, you'll see," repeated Anna.

But Paul still looked curious, even dubious, but he was learning to trust Anna.

"It's just I'm going to have my own wedding, or we'll leave and have our own quiet wedding elsewhere," explained Anna. "But I don't want to do that; Dad will be so hurt."

"Oh," said Paul, realising the implications of what she was saying.

"Don't worry, Paul," she said. "Everything will turn out all right. I know Mother. We've quarrelled before. I usually get my own way, and Dad backs me up."

After lunch, the two parents had a snooze. Anna took Paul to Pagham, her favourite place during the War. The beaches were all barbed-wired off. There was a small lake, and a number of makeshift holiday cottages. The place was peaceful, but the weather was so cold they didn't stay long. Back at home the parents had aroused. A cup of tea was made and all four settled down. It was then that Anna made her move.

"Mother, I'm afraid I'm going to say something you won't like," she said firmly.

Yes, dear," Mother said, slightly patronisingly.

Dad, who knew his daughter, moved apprehensively.

"Don't worry, Dad," said Anna quietly, making a movement of her hands for him to sit back.

Anna turned to her Mother, who looked mildly happy and, unlike her husband, unaware of what was coming.

"Mother," said Anna firmly. "This is my wedding, and Paul's. I'm going to ask you to step aside, and let Dad, who has the money, Paul and myself decide on everything."

"Yes, dear," said Mother, not fully comprehending what might be coming. "What arrangements were you thinking of?"

"Several," said Anna firmly. "To start with I want the church hall and the help offered."

"No!" cried Mother. "The hotel is already booked."

"Well, unbook it then," said Anna promptly. "We can't possibly afford it. Say your daughter has changed her mind."

"No," Mother almost screamed. "The church hall is no place for a reception."

"Well then," said Anna quietly, "Paul and I are cancelling the wedding. We shall go off to a quiet wedding elsewhere, probably in Oxford."

"You can't," said Mother anxiously.

"We can. We will," replied Anna quietly. She made a movement as if to get up from her chair.

Mother turned to her husband, sitting quietly.

"Say something, dear," she pleaded. "Help me, please."

"I can't, my dear," he said gently. "You know we really can't afford the hotel. Anna is right. She's saying the church hall to help us."

"Oh!" exploded Mother in exasperation. "I might have guessed you'd support your daughter! You always do!"

"It's not a question of support," said Dad. "It's a question of common sense. I'm retired. I haven't the money we had. And your guest list and the hotel would break the bank!"

Mother took to her other weapon. She began to cry.

Anna remained unmoved. Paul thought women had a better resistance to tears than men. But it may not be a true observation, he thought.

After a while Mother sniffed, and gingerly dabbed at her eyes with a tissue.

"I did so hope to give you a good wedding," she murmured.

"I realise that, Mother, and I am grateful," said Anna gently. "The trouble is, your ideas did not correspond with my ideas of a good wedding, nor with reality. Could I ask, please, for you to relax, and leave the decisions to Paul and me, and to Dad who alone knows about the costs and what we can afford."

Anna ended on a note of entreaty.

"Please, please, Mother dear. There's Christmas in just over three weeks. You concentrate on that festival, and we'll cope with the wedding."

Mother turned to Dad.

"And you agree with that?" she asked.

"Yes, dear," he said gently. "I feel it's only right. It's Anna's wedding. Let her plan it. She's more than capable, and you've been getting so worked up about everything, I'm sure it does you no good."

Mother got up, sniffed, nodded, and walked out saying she had a bit of a headache.

"Don't worry about her," said Dad gently. "She'll be all right, I promise you."

During the next few days Dad, Anna and Paul worked hard on wedding arrangements. After a few days they sat back with relief.

"You never finish with a wedding," Anna said with a sigh. "But I think we've broken the back of it."

Dad agreed.

"Do you mind, Dad, if Paul and I go off for a couple of days to visit his mother," continued Anna. "I've only met her once, and that was very brief. I've met his sister who's very sweet. We can fit it in a weekend if we can borrow the car."

Dad smiled and agreed.

And so matters settled down.

# Chapter 35

*The Treloar Visit*

Paul dreaded this visit to his mother. She had never seemed to forgive him for leaving Oxford, nor for his subsequent life.

"Your father would never have approved," was her constant cry.

In his heart Paul knew that it was true. Paul would send a prayer to heaven asking for his father's forgiveness. But he felt Dad would have tried to understand, just as Sis tried to understand herself, even if she was outspoken at times.

His mother had felt so aggrieved, especially when he became a Catholic, that she had never even invited him to her wedding when she remarried. Sis had gone, but not Paul! It was as if his mother was ashamed of her handicapped son, and his failure at Oxford. He had never met his stepfather until after the wedding, and that was only on an occasional visit home. Paul was glad his mother now had security, somebody to look after her, but he was not impressed by her choice of consort. He wondered what Anna would think of his family. She got on well with Sis, but would she get on with his mother?

Mother's new home was at Guildford, not too far from Bognor. They arrived in the afternoon, just in time for a cup of tea. Mother greeted them with distant grace, a peck on the cheek for him, a warmer kiss for Anna, who did him proud, looking lovely in a browny-green dress. She presented Mother with a bouquet of flowers.

"Oh, how kind!" Mother said all sweetness. "You shouldn't have, you really shouldn't!"

Paul was pleased to discover Sis was present, with her boyfriend. It made for a much more pleasant weekend.

They went into the house where they were greeted by the stepfather, a big man. His welcome was rather effusive, with a wide, toothy smile, especially for Anna. He seemed to regard himself as a lady charmer. But Paul saw Sis wink at Anna, as if to share feminine amusement.

"What do I call you?" Anna demurely asked the stepfather.

"Oh, Charles, my dear, as in Charles Dickens," the stepfather added. "I won't stand for anything else, especially from so pretty a lady."

He said this with another toothy smile, and held onto Anna's hand longer than necessary. Paul saw his mother looking rather cross, as if she knew about the over-attentiveness of her husband to lady visitors, and rather resented it. The handshake for Paul was much less attentive.

At tea, Mother went on the attack as Paul feared.

"Are you a Catholic, my dear?" she asked Anna.

"No, I'm afraid not," admitted Anna. "I'm traditional Church of England."

"Then, how are you going to get on with a Catholic?" she enquired. "Their rules for marriage are very strict."

"Oh, Mother, do you have to bring that up?" groaned Paul despairingly. "It's something between Anna and me."

"I must, dear," Mother insisted. "These problems need to be sorted out, need to be aired."

Paul sighed.

"The sorting out is for Anna and me, nobody else," he said abruptly.

But Mother looked unconvinced.

"We're family, dear," she said soothingly. "Surely Charles and I can help?"

Paul sighed. He didn't regard a stepfather he hardly knew to be family.

"Surely not, Mother, but if you must know, and many already do, I'm renouncing the Catholic faith, I meant to tell you, but you haven't given me much chance."

"Can you explain why, dear?" asked Mother. "I'd like to know."

It was as if Mother wanted a share in her son's life. But Paul sighed yet again. He was like many men hard of hearing all their life, he liked to keep thoughts to himself.

"No, Mother," Paul said firmly. "I don't wish to bare my soul on such an intimate subject. Anna knows my feelings, and that's all that matters."

Paul thought a moment. Then he added.

"And. Mother, if you try and wheedle it out of Anna through feminine wiles or companionship, I shall be furious."

"I never would, dear," Mother replied. "You know that."

But Paul did know. His mother had the habit of extracting every bit of gossip from the girls he had brought home, and then talking about the information with all and sundry. Fortunately he had known very few girls during his teenage years, and early Oxford time. But he quickly realised what had been happening. That was why he never talked to Mother of Marguerite, or even of Anna and Betty, and what happened in Cornwall.

Fortunately, Sis rescued him on the spot, realising the situation.

"Brian and I are going for a walk," she said cheerfully. "Would you and Anna like to join us?"

They both accepted at once, Paul breathing a grateful sigh of relief.

"Don't forget your coats," called out Mother unnecessarily. "It's cold outside, and it's getting dark."

"All right, Mother," said Sis. "Don't worry."

Paul was relieved that Sis, like him, used 'Mother' as a form of address.

They walked to the centre of the town to see the Christmas lights.

"Don't get too cross with Mother," Sis said. "Brian and I had the same grilling. But I think she means well."

Paul doubted it, but let it pass. There were other things to talk about with his sister.

When they got back, Mother was preparing supper. Both Anna and Sis went to help her. Paul and Brian were left with a very trying time with the stepfather, or Charles as they had to call him. He told a pointless story about his only child, a son, married and emigrated to Australia. It was long and rambling, and centred mostly on his own visit to Australia to see his son.

He hadn't liked the Australians, finding them rude and abrupt. He could never make out why women were called 'Sheilas'. He thought it a little uncomplimentary. He couldn't understand why there was so little class consciousness down under, rich and poor mixing openly together. Paul wanted to say that this was one of the attractions of Aussie land, but refrained from doing so.

It was after supper that Mother returned to the attack in her probing, wanting to know what Paul was doing at Oxford. It made Paul wonder about her. She was never like this when Dad was alive. It was as if widowhood, loneliness and middle age had brought it on. Mother was of a generation of women who had never worked, except on a voluntary level during the War. Her mind was devoid of reality. She would never in the past have considered a man like Charles as a husband. In character he was very much the opposite to Dad, so devoid of humour, personality, and positive feeling. In a way, both Charles and Mother were snobs, though they never realised, or accepted it.

"Anna tells me, dear," she said in her wheedling tone, "you are working on the railways as a porter on night duty. Is that wise, dear, when you are studying? You must get very tired."

"I have to work, Mother," Paul tried to explain. I've no money. Last time, I had a grant as you know, but not now."

"But why such demeaning work, and why at night?" Mother pleaded.

"Simple, really," said Paul. "I have to study during the day. It's the only time the libraries are open. That leaves only the night to earn money."

"But it's such a common job, with men not very well educated," Mother complained.

"I like the men I work with," said Paul. "Their language may be a bit rich at times, but they're hard-working and honest, much nicer blokes than the stewards on the cross-Channel boats."

"I don't care for it," said Mother, and again brought up the familiar argument. "Your father would never have approved."

"I don't believe that," said Paul firmly. "Dad loved the army because he worked with men of many backgrounds, and liked their company. It's money, Mother, money with a big M. I can't see any way round the lack of it. I have to pay my landlady, my food and personal bits. The money on the railways is helpful. You can't turn up your nose at it. I'm also getting married on very little savings."

But Mother shook her head.

For the moment she had nothing more to say. Peace reigned.

But it didn't last, sadly. Paul couldn't help feeling guilty. Did Mother really care about him, as mothers tended to do, or was she just an interfering, gossipy woman. In his heart he didn't know. He hoped it was because she cared. Certainly she was not like Sis, who would criticise, but seemed genuinely to care. The trouble was that Mother later brought up two issues which seemed to go to the very heart of his life and plans, and that of Anna as well.

"Do you think, dear, you ought to marry so quickly?" she asked. "Anna tells me you only met last August; that's only three or four months ago."

"Oh, Mother!" groaned Paul. He suddenly felt very tired, both physically and mentally. It had been a strain with Anna's mother, though Anna had borne the brunt of it. What was it that got into mothers? Was it the disappointment of their own marriage, a husband killed on active service, and a husband who was happy with life and sought little advancement? It was Sis who came to his rescue, bless her!

"Oh, Mother, Paul and Anna can make their own decisions," she pointed out. "Can we not give them our blessing and best wishes for the future, without interference from us?"

But Mother, as obstinate as Paul could be, shook her head.

"You marry in haste, regret at leisure," she said with conviction. "They have little money, Paul has no degree, and no career. He says he wants to be a teacher, but it's the last thing he should do with his hearing handicap. Moreover they hardly know each other in so short a time."

"Oh, I think they do," said Sis clearly. "The circumstances of their meeting brought them close together far more quickly than most couples."

"I know of no circumstances," complained Mother.

"And you won't," stated Paul. "That is entirely between Anna and me."

"Yet your sister knew," pointed out Mother. "Why shouldn't I know? It makes me feel something very wrong happened."

Paul's answer was to get up suddenly, take Anna's hand and move towards the door. He then stopped and stated clearly.

"Mother, if you persist in questioning our marriage, Anna and I will leave. We are going upstairs."

With that he walked out, still holding Anna's hand.

They left a silence which nobody knew how to break.

Up in Paul's room, Anna kissed him.

"We've both been from the frying pan into the fire," she said laughing. "I don't know which one is worse, your mother or mine."

She gave one of her delightful giggles, and Paul joined in.

"Well, we survived," said Paul. "Does it make you want to change your mind?"

But Anna shook her head.

"Let's keep things as we planned," she said. "We've discussed it enough by letters, phone calls, and when we meet. Unlike politicians we don't change our minds."

Paul hugged her and buried his head between her breasts.

"I pray God we are doing the right thing," he said. "Mother has the ability to undermine my confidence at times. It's why I don't go and see her as often as I should."

Anna ruffled his hair.

"Don't worry, Paul," she said gently. "We are doing the right thing, believe me. We've got somewhere to live. We've got each other. What more can we want? Life looks very rosy."

Paul gave a wry, but grateful grin. Anna had always been encouraging. He supposed it was one of the reasons he loved her. He felt at times she was stronger than him, mentally stronger, despite all that she had been through in Cornwall.

It was funny, a man admitting her strength, but Paul felt it was true, and it would always be so.

# Chapter 36

*Christmas, then the Wedding*

Mother gave no further disparaging lectures, which was a relief. Sis said she'd had words with her. Whatever it was, Mother remained uncharacteristically subdued. Paul never learnt what Sis had said, but he felt he could guess.

Christmas was surprisingly very enjoyable. Anna's brother, David, came to stay until after the wedding, bringing his wife, Lizzie, and their little boy, Peter, a four year-old. Somehow, Christmas is always better when a child is present. It has a sense of wonder for a child, a fascination that affects adults. David was a big man, hugely and outrageously extrovert. He worked in Scotland in the oil industry. His wife was Scottish, and put up with the extravagances of her husband easily.

"Ha, the knight who rescued my sister from the dreaded dragon," was his greeting to Paul in a voice which seemed to echo throughout the house.

"Sssh!" exclaimed Anna. "Keep your voice down, you goof!"

"Why?" asked David, bemused at the insistence in her voice. "The man deserves a medal."

"I agree," said Anna. "But I don't want Mother to know. It'll be all round the town, if she hears about it."

"Oh," said the brother, beginning to understand. "But you'll let me shake the hand of this handsome knight."

"Of course," agreed Anna, laughing, "but be careful. He's very strong. He'll crush that flabby hand of yours!"

"Hey," protested Paul at the exaggeration. They shook hands.

"You'll always be welcome in Scotland, you and Anna, won't they, Liz?" David said.

His wife nodded and smiled. For most of the time Paul had known her, she seemed to be her husband's echo. But there seemed to be a genuine love between them. Paul warmed to this big man. He brought a sudden open gaiety to the house, as did the little boy, Peter.

For the next few days, they almost forgot about the wedding. The girls helped Mother in the kitchen. Paul and David went out to buy a Christmas tree, pausing on the way home to visit the pub. They spent the afternoon putting up the tree, decorating it with lights, and putting a pile of presents at the bottom. Peter was given a rugby sock to put at the end of his bed for Father Christmas.

David and his family fitted into one room.

Mother and Dad had their own. Anna, hers when she was a child. And Paul was in the box room.

For most of the festivities, Dad looked on with a genuine smile. But he was also happy to read to Peter, or tell him stories. He seemed genuinely fond of his first grandchild. He took him for walks around Bognor and the neighbouring village of Felpham. They got on well, the very old and the very young. Lizzie was happy. Peter was thus kept occupied in a way he obviously enjoyed. Altogether the house settled down to a really good Christmas. Paul found himself slipping out to the pub with David who was an easy man to talk to, especially with his clear voice.

It was then that Paul learned of a possible career, other than teaching.

"What are you going to do when you've finished your degree?" David asked.

"I don't know," admitted Paul. "I had hoped to go into teaching, but everybody seems to think it would be unwise for somebody with a hearing handicap."

"It's not much of a handicap," commented David.

"I'm all right in a one-to-one situation," Paul remarked. "But in a crowded room, sometimes I'm floundering. It's this hearing aid. It picks up all sorts of extraneous noises, like the scraping of desks or feet."

David nodded in understanding.

"Have you thought of any other career?" he asked.

"Well, I thought of being a writer, or a reporter on a newspaper," Paul said. "For a writer you need money to have the leisure to write, which I certainly haven't. That's not the career for somebody planning to get married. As for a reporter I'd need good hearing. It's essential."

David thought a moment and then asked.

"What subjects did you enjoy at school?"

"Well, it was mostly on the humanities side, subjects I could read up in a library, like History, Geography, English, and Scripture. They were all subjects I could teach myself. I had no interest in Science and gave it up as soon as I could. Latin was all right, but it hardly leads to a career. The only other interest was working with my hands, woodwork and pottery. I really loved woodwork, but regarded it more as a hobby than a career."

What about Maths?" David asked.

"A good question," Paul remarked. "My Dad was adept at figures. He could add up a column of numbers in a few seconds. He worked for Barclays Bank. I seemed to have inherited much the same ability. I very nearly won the school Maths prize but was pipped at the post by a wretched boy called Howard. I've never forgotten him."

"Did you try Barclays Bank?" asked David.

"I did at one time, but they turned me down," admitted Paul. "I really don't know why. Perhaps because I left Oxford early, or because I went into the interview with entirely the wrong attitude.

"Why was that?" asked David in a kindly, enquiring voice. Paul found David a very easy man to talk to. There was something encouraging about his voice, as if he was really interested.

"I was silly, really," admitted Paul. "I knew somebody who was a really good short story writer. He was a bank manager in a small market town in Kent. Short story writing was really his hobby.

He seemed to be very contented. I went to the interview and said I would like to be like him, a man who wrote in his spare time from banking. They didn't take that at all well."

"They looked up some obscure bank rule which said that a man could not have a second money-earning occupation. I argued that it was a hobby like gardening, or playing the piano for some private function. But they wouldn't have that, as if they owned my soul. Anyway, they turned me down, and I wasn't sorry."

Paul thought a moment.

"It was funny," Paul said. "My Dad wrote film scripts. He didn't have much success. But the bank never seemed to know about it."

"Have you thought about becoming an accountant?" suggested David. "You could have your own independent business, and remain free for your other interests."

Paul liked the idea, and David said that he would look into it. He had a friend who was an accountant. Unfortunately this decision had unhappy consequences which neither David nor Paul foresaw.

David later happened to mention in the evening what they had discussed in the pub about the possibility of becoming an accountant.

Immediately Mother jumped up.

"I knew it!" she exclaimed. "In no way can I countenance this marriage until Paul has a settled career and can look after Anna."

"Mother!" cried Anna, rising in her turn. "You can't stop the wedding. Everything is arranged, invitations out and everything."

"Can't I?" muttered Mother.

"I can at least not go to the wedding, to voice my protest, my disapproval."

Anna turned to Paul, almost in desperation.

"Please, Paul, leave the room," she begged. "This is a family quarrel again, only we can settle. You've had enough trouble from your own family. I want you to avoid it here."

Paul shook his head.

"I'd really rather stay, Anna," he said quietly. "This argument concerns me more than anyone else. But your mother is right. I really am uncertain about a career. So many people tell me teaching is not an option because of my hearing."

It was then David entered the fray with a certain firmness.

"Mother, I really think you are behaving badly," he said. "I don't know what it is about mothers, but you tend to disparage the partners their children choose. You made the same mistake with me when I wanted to get married, and poor Lizzie suffered. You don't see Dad doing it. You were very unkind to Lizzie, and made her very unhappy. Yet she's been the most perfect wife, putting up with my extravagant moods. Now you are doing the same with Paul. Could I remind you of two factors?"

"One is that he is a guest in this house, and deserves every courtesy, which only Dad gives him. Secondly he is your daughter's choice, and he should be welcomed into the proverbial bosom of the family. But he's done more than that. He's saved Anna from a terrible fate, showing much courage."

"I don't know anything about saving Anna," said Mother querulously. "Nobody tells me anything."

"It must come out," stated David. "Anna didn't want me to say anything. She was afraid you, Mother, would gossip to everyone. It's not something one wants others to know."

"What is that something," Mother pleaded, still querulous.

"She was about to be raped," stated David, "by a man with a knife. Paul arrived just in time, took on the man, broke his arm and sent him packing. Eventually, after another uncomfortable incident, he, or someone, persuaded Anna to go to the police. The man's now in jail."

"Oh!" said Mother amazed. She turned to Dad. "Did you know this?"

He nodded.

"Anna swore me to secrecy. It's something we ought to keep in the family. I much admire Paul and realise why Anna regards him as a sort of knight."

Mother was reduced to silence. She left the room. Whether she was annoyed at not being told the facts, or was upset because she had been spoken to so firmly, it was hard to say. But she couldn't avoid the last word. At the door she turned and said,

"It doesn't alter the fact Paul has no career."

There was silence when she left. Then Anna rose and went to kiss her brother. Paul noticed there were tears in her eyes.

"Thank you," she murmured softly.

"It had to come out," David excused himself. "But I know Mother. She'll gossip. I can just imagine her saying – 'the children don't want me to mention it, but really Paul was so brave, I really must tell you' – and the whole story will come out. You can't stop her."

"Don't worry about Mother," Dad said loyally. "She'll come round. Just give her time. She gets very anxious about the children."

And there the matter ended.

Christmas was devoid of any acrimonious debate. Little Peter was a delight. He woke his parents first at 5.30, and subsequently the whole house. So Mother and Anna got up to make tea for everyone. It was going to be a long day. Peter emptied his sock of goodies from Father Christmas. They were mostly little things, including an orange in the toe.

The big presents under the tree were for later, much to Peter's chagrin. After a leisurely breakfast, they all went for a walk in the park. It was a cold, crisp day, but somehow they did not seem to mind. The only absentee was Mother, who had become much quieter since her outburst. She'd had a long talk with Anna about her ordeal in Cornwall. Mother came out of the talk with a greater appreciation of Paul, and relief that the marriage was not early because Anna might be pregnant.

"Mothers!" exclaimed Anna. "The things they think of!"

Paul nearly laughed.

"When you're a Mum, you'll be anxious about your children," he stated with a smile on his face.

Anna shook her head.

"No," she said firmly. "I hope I can trust them to behave properly, and I will not interfere too much."

When they got back from the walk they gathered round the Christmas tree for presents, munching warmed mince pies.

Peter once again was the centre of excitement. It made Paul sad that he had lost a father and had only for a while the kind of relationship Peter had with his grandfather.

They then listened to the Queen on the wireless. They had not yet indulged in a television set with its strange aerial clasped to the chimney.

Then came Christmas dinner, a superb, leisurely meal, starting after the royal speech, and lasting until nearly six o'clock. To Paul it was the only time he found in England a meal after the French tradition, namely no hurry to finish and plenty of spirited conversation, during which Peter fell asleep in his mother's arms. They all felt tired. Not only had Peter woken them early, but last night they had all gone to Midnight Mass, rudely interrupted by a couple of drunken revellers. They called the service 'Holy Shit' and the congregation 'a load of praying layabouts to a fucking God who didn't exist.' It wasn't pleasant. David, Paul and a number of other men managed to hustle them out. One of the two men collapsed in the street. The police were called from a nearby telephone. They were taken away.

Paul felt dismayed about such behaviour. It was sadness for the drunken men whose attitude would get them nowhere, except perhaps illness, isolation and self-misery. They were such a contrast to the quiet order in the church, the happy Christmas greetings, and the lights around the crib where Mary prayed.

What had gone wrong in England that such men existed? Paul could only pray and hold Anna's hand in the darkness of the pew.

After Christmas dinner the men washed up and the women put the food away, or the remains that were left. Then they sank into chairs, too tired but content. It had been a happy Christmas, and for once they were united as a family. David, the extrovert, raised the remains of his wine to Anna and Paul, Anna almost asleep on Paul's shoulder.

"Well, here's to you, kids," David said, raising his glass. "A long life together and lots of little babies."

"That's enough of babies," muttered Anna sleepily. "After seeing Peter's exhausting energy, I don't want any!"

She said it lightly, not wishing to offend Lizzie.

They all laughed. They raised their glasses to the sleepy couple, soon to be joined in wedlock.

Paul sighed.

"What's that about?" whispered Anna.

"I'll tell you later," replied Paul softly. "But you needn't worry, it was a happy sigh!"

That's good," whispered Anna, and promptly dozed off.

Paul sighed because at last in his short life he no longer felt lonely. Poor hearing and the loss of a father had made him feel isolated. Now he was no longer alone. And this was wonderful, so wonderful.

## Chapter 37

*The Wedding*

The memorable day soon came round, only a few days after the New Year. They had put the day slightly forward, mainly because some of the guests had expressed difficulty around Christmas and the New Year, which was understandable. Paul was on tenterhooks, anxious to be back at Oxford and his studies. Also the work on the railways preyed on his mind. They had given him extended, unpaid leave because of the wedding. It was difficult to find men who would work nights. They wanted to keep him, but hadn't expected such an extended absence. Paul talked it over with Anna. They came to the conclusion they would have to forgo any honeymoon. Their first night of marriage would be spent in the flat at Betty's house. Their honeymoon would be in the summer, hopefully in France.

The wedding itself was unforgettable. Paul's best memory was Anna winking mischievously at him under her skimpy veil as she joined him at the foot of the altar steps. She looked so radiantly happy. It did Paul a power of good. For once he wasn't thinking of his loneliness. He was spending, God willing, the rest of his life with this lovely creature.

Gone was lonely introspection, gone was his lack of friends. He had a loyal loving wife to have and to hold now and forever, to talk to, to support, to love. In his heart he thanked God!

Paul couldn't help reflecting on how things had worked out since leaving Oxford. It was as if events had come together perfectly - his life, his confidence, his well-being. It had started with his love for Marguerite, hopeless from the beginning. But the woman he had loved in France had been kindly, sympathetic, and they had talked for hours on the balcony in the summer warmth. Then there was the Catholic Church which had seemed so alive in France, so pious, almost saintly. It was as if God had guided him there, both Church and Marguerite, to watch over him and help put him back to normal life. He wondered if he would ever see Marguerite again, and how Anna would get on with her if he did. He was sure she would, the two women were so immediately likeable and sympathetic.

His thoughts were brought back to the present by a nudge from Brian, his best man, lent by Sis. Paul had very few friends he could call on as his best man.

Both Paul and Anna answered clearly and with conviction to the various parts of the service that concerned them.

Paul had asked that the word 'cherish' should be included as part of the service. He was reassured on that point. He thought it a lovely word, typical of his love for Anna.

It was a proud moment for Paul walking down the aisle with Anna on his arm. They smiled happily at everyone. The only disconcerting factor was the two mothers standing together, and not smiling.

'Well,' thought Paul, 'they couldn't do much harm now.'

His mother had her own prissy, disapproving look which Paul knew so well. He shrugged mentally. Perhaps his mother would come round once a grandchild was on the way. Perhaps Anna's mother might come round as well.

Afterwards, there were photographs outside the church. It was bitterly cold, and the heating inside was not working. Paul felt sorry for Anna and the two bridesmaids in their pale blue dresses, with no coat. Eventually David managed to persuade the photographer to up sticks and take his photos in the church hall where the reception was being held.

The lunch was a ribald affair, with many allusions by Brian to 'little blessings'. Paul and Anna didn't get away until after four.

When they arrived at Betty's house in Oxford, she greeted them warmly and offered them a light supper of mushroom omelettes. Neither Paul nor Anna felt like eating, but they didn't want to refuse Betty's kind offer. She had been so welcoming, so pleased to see them.

Betty gave Paul a bunch of letters which had accumulated while he had been away. It was then that Paul realised life had a funny way of hitting one unfeelingly when one was at the peak of happiness. Among the letters was one from the railways, saying they could not keep his employment open any longer. He had been away for over a month. They had been very busy over Christmas and the New Year and were now forced to take on another man to replace him. They expressed their regrets and hoped the wedding went well.

Paul groaned.

"What's up?" asked Anna.

For answer Paul passed her the letter.

"Oh, dear," exclaimed Anna. "But it isn't the end of the world. I'm sure I could soon find a job. Nurses are always wanted."

"But I hadn't wanted you to work so soon," Paul explained.

Anna went to him with a smile on her face.

"Better it happens sooner than later," she said. "You could settle down to your studies, without getting so tired."

"But I hadn't wanted you to work, or at least not immediately," Paul repeated anxiously. "What would your mother say, or mine for that matter?"

He began to look a little downcast. He groaned, shook his head sadly, and said.

"That this should happen the very day of our marriage."

He thought of the two mothers who were so uncertain that he could look after Anna. What they would say now he could not bear to think.

"Don't worry, don't worry," pleaded Anna. "I'm sure I can get a job soon."

But it didn't appease Paul. He didn't want Anna to be the breadwinner so early in their marriage. He looked so dispirited that Anna shook him gently.

"It's all right, Paul," she insisted. "The world's moved on since Victorian times. The War gave women a freedom such as they had never known before. We are now on an equal footing with our husbands. We can go out to work, share the burden of earning money, of life itself. I'll need support when the children come."

"Otherwise I'm free to go out to work, and I look forward to it. I can support you while you study, and I will be more than happy to do so."

Paul shook his head. It was not what he wanted, nor what he had envisaged. But reluctantly he came to accept the situation, with Anna's pleadings. In a way it was very good to have a partner to share problems, and not to have to worry on his own. Yes, it was a wonderful thought, this sharing of life's problems, known perhaps only to people with a hearing handicap, who had at times been so lonely.

But, though agreeing to Anna's suggestion, he still felt ashamed. What decent man would marry a girl, and not be able to support her on the first day of their marriage!

So, there began a life in which each morning Anna went to work, and Paul to study in the library. He did what he could to help Anna with the shopping and cleaning of the flat. To his great surprise, he started to learn how to cook. His life was a jumble, but it was full! He had no time for introverted thinking.

Anna took a job at the Radcliffe Hospital. They had rejected her before, but were happy to take her on now that she was qualified and experienced.

The only very important thing that happened that spring term was a visit from Marguerite. Paul had told her of his wedding, and she, generous as ever, was delighted. With Anna's permission he gave her an open invitation to stay with them in Oxford. She arrived in February intending only to stay for a few days. Anna couldn't arrange to get the weekend free. Like all nurses, her hours tended to be unsocial from time to time.

Marguerite arrived, looking more chirpy than he could remember.

"My husband took me to court," she told Paul in French. "He wanted to see the children from time to time. I had much problem. I no wanted the children to miss school. He could see them only at weekend. Then I want guarantee he return them. I no trust him."

"I hope it worked out," Paul said kindly. "Do the children accept the situation?"

"Well, no," admitted Marguerite, "that's part of the problem. Jean-Pierre refused to go. He's finding a firm voice of his own now. François is the only one happy to go. The rest resented a little leaving their home, even for such a short time. They had friends and possessions they hated to leave. The trouble is their father has become over the years a stranger. Curiosity persuaded them to go on the first occasion, but I realised that was all."

"Where is Jean-Pierre at the moment?" asked Paul. "He was the one his father really loved."

"He's with my sister," explained Marguerite. "Or, rather, he is with her husband, his uncle. They get on well."

Paul nodded. He felt Marguerite was having a complicated time, and had nobody to support her. She stood alone, no husband, no father. His heart went out to her, as it had done before.

The trouble was that Anna was a little isolated as she did not speak French. On the evening Paul talked to Marguerite, Anna had had a hard day at the hospital. She looked a little strained and went to bed early. Paul felt guilty, or worried, and wished she had been a closer part of the evening.

"You are lucky. Your wife is a lovely girl," remarked Marguerite, and added mischievously. "Are you glad now you never married me?"

Paul grinned weakly.

"I'm sorry you left the Catholic Church," continued Marguerite. "But I think I can understand. It's important that you, both you and Anna, are of one faith. But, well, I feel sad none the less."

Paul wanted to say that Catholicism did not really work in England, but he felt it difficult to explain.

When he went up to bed, Anna was asleep. He wanted to explain to her that he had found it difficult, meeting a former love, with his new love present. But it was just friendship with Marguerite now, nothing more.

The next day, Anna said nothing. Paul showed Marguerite around Oxford, and then she left for London, and went back to France. It seemed like that episode in Paul's life was over. He had a lingering sense of guilt but it made him sad. It had been a happy time with Marguerite at La Refaudio.

At home, Anna said simply.

"She's nice, Marguerite. I liked her. I'm sorry I was so tired and unsociable last night."

And then she smiled. It was all over, and Paul was relieved.

As Paul had predicted, the French part of his degree presented no difficulty.

But he nearly made a muck of it, such was his temper.

The written work went well, but when it came to the Viva, the situation was very different from the History Viva. During this, the examiner sat alone, while the examinees waited in a separate room.

They were called in one by one, into a private setting. But with the French Viva, they were in a large room, with three, not one, examiners sitting at a large table. One of the examiners was a woman. There were five nervous examinees sitting against the wall, opposite the table, waiting to be called up to a solitary chair. The examinees could listen to the interrogation, and the kind of questions asked.

One thing Paul hated about Oxford was the smug, intellectual superiority evinced by some of the tutors and lecturers. He found the genuinely helpful academic was quite the opposite, being, on the whole, a humble bloke, not showing superiority. But these three French examinees seemed to find the whole Viva occasion amusing, even laughable.

Paul could not understand why.

Two undergrads went up before Paul. With both of them the quality of their spoken French was not up to much. The examiners found it very funny, and were whispering and laughing openly. Paul thought it must have been very disconcerting for the poor examinees. Only the woman interrogator was trying to be professional. When Paul went up he was asked a question in English, and he replied in French which immediately caused a snigger. Paul suddenly felt very angry.

He got up, swore at them in French, and said bluntly, again in French, that he was not staying to be laughed at, and left the room. Outside he tore off his gown and went to have a coffee to calm down. His heart missed a beat. He thought by his action he would fail the French exam.

Back at college he went to see his history tutor, and told him what had happened. The latter had difficulty in believing what he was told, being a loyal man. But he told Paul not to worry; students rarely failed on the Viva. The important part was the written work.

Anyway, Paul passed. Examinees were not given grades for a Pass degree - they just passed or failed.

Nothing more was said on the matter, and Paul soon forgot what had happened.

Anna chided him, smiling.

"Your temper will be the end of you, if you're not careful. But you seem only to lose your temper in a good cause."

Paul started on the English set books and relevant background. Strangely for somebody who wanted to be a writer, he was less confident in this subject than the other two. The only writer he really liked was the poet Blake. He seemed to have a very realistic view on life. Milton and Shakespeare impressed him deeply, but it took him a long time to get into the swing of understanding them.

But in the exam at the end of term, he managed to pass, and the Viva went pleasantly, without incident or loss of temper.

Now was the crucial question. What career was he to choose?

They sat discussing it one early July evening, Anna and Paul, and Betty somehow was there. She had almost been accepted as a member of the family, a kind of honorary aunty. It was a situation Betty appreciated.

"Please, Paul," Anna pleaded, "teaching is out, I would say."

"Oh, why?" asked Paul, with a touch of disappointment.

"You need normal hearing for teaching," pointed out Anna. "Whatever you say, your hearing is not good. You're all right on a one-to-one basis, but in a crowded room you're lost. I also notice that on an individual basis you have to see who is talking to you. It's almost as if you lip-read or somehow sense what people are saying. I'm sorry, Paul, I've got to know you well over the last few months. There are still occasions when you don't catch what I am saying."

Paul looked rueful.

"Also, I've seen your hospital hearing tests," continued Anna. "There's a distinct falling off with the higher registers. You hear men's voices much better than women's. You mention also that, in music, you hear the lower register instruments better. Didn't you say you liked the oboe the best?"

They were silent for a moment, pondering the implications of Anna's words. Betty was touched by the fallen look on Paul's face.

"Poor Paul," Betty said. "I know you've set your heart on teaching, but I feel Anna is right. My own feeling is that you would be much better working with your hands. You've been so useful working around the house and garden. The other alternative is that you take some open air job like forestry or farming. You're strong and healthy."

Paul was silent for a moment. Then he smiled and said.

"I wanted to be a farmer at one time. I applied to an agricultural college, but they told me so many ex-servicemen were taking up places, I wouldn't have a chance."

He paused and then continued.

"The trouble with forestry and farming, is that they require a further three years of study. I don't want that. I don't like a situation where Anna is the breadwinner, as she has been since our marriage. It wouldn't be fair."

"Women are increasingly becoming breadwinners since the War," remarked Anna.

"Teaching would only require a further year of study for the Dip.Ed." remarked Paul reflectively. "That for me is one of the attractions of teaching, one more year of study rather than three."

Paul got up and stood looking down on the two women who had been so supportive, so kind to him.

"I'm slowly coming to the conclusion that your brother was right, Anna," he said gently. "A career open to somebody with a hearing problem is that of an accountant. I've been making some enquiries of accountancy firms in Oxford. Provided you have some ability in Maths, they will take you on, give you a salary while you study in the evenings for the various accountancy exams. Dad was good at figures, worked for Barclays before War broke out.

I don't like the idea of a desk job, but many do it quite happily. Would you mind if I applied to some accountancy firms in Oxford, and we stayed in the flat until we can afford a home of our own?" Paul asked Betty.

Both women nodded, and apart from a little discussion the matter was agreed.

Paul, with Anna lying in his arms, felt relieved. His life had gone through so many changes over the past few years, he now felt settled, or at least with some glimmer of realistic hope for the future.

FINIS